All about the
Cavalier King Charles Spaniel

Frontispiece – King
Charles Spaniels (also
called 'The Cavalier's
Pets') Landseer 1845.

All about the
Cavalier King Charles
Spaniel

EVELYN M. BOOTH

PELHAM BOOKS

PELHAM BOOKS

Published by the Penguin Group
27 Wrights Lane, London W8 5TZ, England
Viking Penguin, a division of Penguin Books USA Inc,
375 Hudson Street, New York, New York, 10014
Penguin Books Australia Ltd, Ringwood, Victoria, Australia
Penguin Books Canada Ltd, 2801 John Street, Markham, Ontario,
Canada L3R 1B4
Penguin Books (NZ) Ltd, 182-190 Wairau Road, Auckland 10,
New Zealand

Penguin Books Ltd, Registered Offices: Harmondsworth,
Middlesex, England

First published 1983
9 10 8
Copyright © 1983 Evelyn Booth

Printed and bound in Great Britain by
Butler & Tanner Ltd, Frome and London

A CIP catalogue record for this book is available from the British
Library.

ISBN 0 7207 1452 4

Contents

Illustrations

Photographs

Line Drawings

Photo credits

The author and publishers are grateful to the following for permission to reproduce illustrations in this book: Jeannie Bartram, 18; M.A. Booth, A.R.P.S., 10, 16, 19, 20, 22, 23, 24, 25, 26, 27, 28, 29, 30, 41, 42, 43, 44, 45, 49, 50, 51, 52, 53; K.M. Coaker, 33; C.M. Cooke, 48; Dalton, 38; Thos. Fall, 3, 5; Frank Garwood, 17, 47; G.L.C. Marble Hill House, Twickenham, 2; Leslie Studios, 40; J.H. Moore, 9; Diane Pearce, 34, 35, 46; Anne Roslin-Williams, 37; F.A. Scott, 36 (two pictures); Simms, 16; Trustees of the Tate Gallery, frontispiece; Michael M. Trafford, 39. (All numbers refer to photograph numbers.)

Acknowledgements

The author is grateful to the Kennel Club for permission to reproduce the Breed Standard.

1 History of the Cavalier

'ALL about the Cavalier King Charles Spaniel!' A pretentious title indeed for who can know all about this fascinating and beautiful breed? Surely no other breed has so much interesting history or about whom so many stories have been told. A Royal Dog indeed, as the name implies!

Although the Cavalier King Charles Spaniel has been an established breed since 1928 and on a separate Kennel Club register from the King Charles Spaniel since 1945, in the public eye they are the same breed, but of course to the enthusiasts in both breeds it seems inconceivable that they could be confused.

To understand how this came about it is necessary to delve into history. Some toy spaniels have been known since the fifteenth century and were found in most of the Royal Courts of Europe.

In 1486 Dame Juliana Berners produced a treatise on hunting *The Boke of St Albans*. It gave a list of recognised breeds including 'smalle ladyes puppees that beare away the flees and dyvers small fowles'. I wonder how the poor little dog rid itself of the fleas and lice it accumulated in this way!

Henry VIII decreed that no dogs should be kept at Court except 'Some small spanyells for the ladies'.

In 1570 Dr Johannes Caius, the physician in chief to Queen Elizabeth I, wrote a Latin treatise entitled *De Canibus Britannicus*. In this he divided all known breeds of dogs into five groups. The third group was devoted to 'Spaniell gentle or comforter – a delicate, neat and pretty kind of dog'. In the draughty houses and carriages of those times a little spaniel sitting on a lady's lap would certainly be a gentle comforter. Even in these days of central heating they are still a comfort! Dr Caius also called them 'Chamber companions, pleasant play fellows, and pretty wormes'.

The worthy doctor also wrote 'We find that these little dogs are good to assuage the sickness of the stomach'. He gave cases in which the disease and sickness of the owner 'changeth his place and entereth – though it be not precisely marked, into the dog, which to be no untruth. Experience can testify. For this kind of dog sometimes falls sick and sometimes die without any harm outwardly enforced, which is an argument that the disease of the gentleman or gentlewoman or owner whatsoever, entereth into the dog'.

There is a well known story that after the execution of Mary Queen of

Scots in 1587, her little black and white spaniel was found under her petticoats. Poor little thing!

Many tales are told of the Stuarts' love of the little spaniels. Charles I, when a fugitive in Carisbrooke Castle on the Isle of Wight in 1648, was accompanied by his little spaniel, Rogue. After the execution one of the Roundheads took the dog and exhibited him in the city.

However it is Charles II with which the breed is particularly associated and there are many contemporary pictures and writings to give us an insight into the place these spaniels had at the Royal Court after the Restoration in 1660.

Samuel Pepys records in his diary for 25 May 1660 (the day that Charles returned to England after his exile). 'The King was rowed ashore in the Admiral's barge, while I followed in a smaller boat with Mr Mansell, one of the footmen and a dog that the King loved'.

Henrietta d'Orleans. Favourite younger sister of Charles II with her toy spaniel. After P. Mignard, painted *c*.1665.

Henrietta d'Orleans, the youngest and favourite sister of Charles, was very fond of toy spaniels. A portrait by P. Mignard painted in 1665 shows a real toy Blenheim coloured spaniel, with a flat head and large dark eyes. Henrietta, called 'Minette', died suddenly, three weeks after visiting her brother. Charles had taken a great liking to Minette's lady-in-waiting Louise de Kéroüalle during their visit to England and after Minette's death she returned to Charles' court, possibly with Minette's dogs, and became Charles' mistress and the Duchess of Portsmouth.

His Majesty was seldom seen without his little dogs, a fact not always appreciated by some of the court.

'In all affairs of Church and State.
He very zealous is and able
Devout at prayers and sits up late
At the Cabal or Council Table
His very dog at Council Board
Sits grave and wise as any Lord.'
       Lord Rochester – an intellectual wit at Charles II's Court

Hugh Dalziel in his excellent book *British Dogs* writes in 1881 'The Merry Monarch did many more foolish things than take under his Royal Care and favour, and thereby raising to Court, the beautiful toy Spaniel which still bears his name'.

John Evelyn the diarist says of the King 'He took delight in having a number of little spaniels follow him and lie in his bed chamber, where he suffered the bitches to puppy, which rendered it very offensive and indeed the whole court nasty and stinking'.

Pepys complained bitterly that at a Privy Council the King apparently paid little attention to business but played with his little dogs.

On one occasion Charles was entering Salisbury in his coach, when a loyal subject came up and spoke to the King, keeping his hand on the coach door, in spite of the King's warning that he would be bitten by one of the spaniels within. This is exactly what happened, causing the honest citizen to cry out, 'God Bless your Majesty but God damn your dogs'.

A small blurred picture, unfortunately too unsharp to reproduce, shows King Charles II paying court to Nell Gwyn. With the King are two small black spaniels both wearing smart ribbon bows. Both are taking a keen interest in the proceedings while John Evelyn looks on dourly.

These little spaniels were frequently becoming lost, whether by carelessness or by unscrupulous people kidnapping them for the substantial rewards offered for the return of these much loved pets. Here are a few advertisements!

From the *London Gazette* October 1667.
'Lost in Dean's Yard Westminster on the 25 October – a young white

spaniel about 6 months old with a black head, red eyebrows and a black spot on his back belonging to his Highness Prince Rupert. If anyone can bring him back to the Royal Prince Rupert's lodging in the Stone Galliere in Whitehall, he will be rewarded for his pains.'

1675. 'A little white spaniel with some red spots on her back, sides and ears, with something sobish eyes lost on Sunday from Mr Fabian Phillips, Lincoln's Inn Fields.'
1677. 'From Sir Robert Howard's house at Mitcham January 4 1677, a black and white spaniel belonging to His Majesty with collar and chain. Return to the Exchequer.'

During Charles' last illness, a few days before his death, Bruce, the King's Lord in Waiting lay awake listening to the noises of 'the Scotch Coal Fire, the dozen dogs that came to our bed, and several pendulums that struck the half and quarter and all not going alike. It was a continual chiming'.

One of my favourite pictures of these times is by Thomas Dackerts, showing Mr Rose the Royal gardener presenting Charles with the first pineapple successfully raised in England at Ham House. In the foreground are two toy spaniels, one crouching on his front legs with his rear in the air, such a characteristic attitude even with today's Cavaliers!

A King Charles Spaniel painted 1665 by the Dutch artist Gysbert Vander Kuyl.

Legend has it that Charles II issued a Royal edict that no King Charles Spaniel can be denied entry to any public place and that they alone have the right to run loose in London's Royal Parks. Recently a newspaper reporter tried to prove that this was still the case. He took a ruby Cavalier bitch and tried to gain entry to the House of Commons and several leading hotels without success. However she was allowed to run loose in St James Park as long as she was under control – but so were other breeds!

After the death of Charles II, his brother James II carried on his brother's love of the little spaniels. It is reported that during an extremely rough storm at sea, orders were given to abandon ship. The King in most vehement voice called 'Save the dogs and the Duke of Monmouth!' One might think he had his priorities in the right order!

It can be seen from the quoted contemporary accounts that these dogs came in several colours, black, black and white, red and white and tricolours. They were small with very fine bone and fine muzzles.

With the coming of William and Mary the pug came into favour, although many portraits of the eighteenth century show ladies with their little spaniels.

The Hon. Mrs Neville Lytton (later Baroness Wentworth) wrote a monumental book *Toy Dogs and their Ancestors* in 1911. In this she traces her theory of the toy spaniel's evolution. The modern type King Charles, by which she means the domed noseless King Charles, as shown in picture 5, was not introduced before 1840.

Certainly Queen Victoria's tricolour Dash had a flat head and longer nose as depicted in the famous needlework picture of him. Sidney Lee wrote in 1838 of Queen Victoria on her Coronation Day, 'But despite her consciousness of the responsibilities of her station, the Queen still had much of the child's lightness and simplicity of heart. On returning to the Palace she hastily doffed her splendours in order to give her pet spaniel Dash its afternoon bath'.

The Blenheim or Marlborough Spaniel owes its name to the fact that this red and white variety of Toy Spaniel was bred for many years at Blenheim Palace the seat of the Dukes of Marlborough. Everyone knows the story of Sarah Duchess of Marlborough who is supposed to have pressed her thumb repeatedly on her spaniel's head while waiting for news of the Duke's Campaign at the Battle of Blenheim, thereby marking the 'Blenheim Thumbprint', or spot, which is so attractive and desirable in the Blenheim Cavalier.

These Blenheims were well known for their gaiety and sporting instincts. In the *Sports Mans Review* 1820, they are described as 'The very delicate small or carpet Spaniels, have exquisite noses and will hunt truly and pleasantly'.

Major Harding Cox describes the Blenheims at Blenheim Palace 'I once saw a small pack of these pretty little fellows perform prodigies of valour in covert and hedgerow, throwing their tongues for all they were worth, giving their quarry no peace, until they bustled him into the open'.

In an undated article written either in the late nineteenth or early twentieth century, the writer refers to 'The smallest spaniel passing under the denominantie of Cocker is that peculiar breed in the possession of the Duke of Marlborough and his friends. These are invariably red and white with very long ears, short noses and black eyes. They are excellent and indefatigable, being held in great estimation with Sportsmen who became possessed of the breed.' *Our Friend the Dog*, by Dr Gordon Stables R.N., published in 1885, says that 'The Palace of Blenheim was the home of the breed and still it was to be found in the villages of that vicinity at that time'. He continues that the original Blenheims were different from those in the show ring in 1885. The originals were larger and they were also longer in the nose. A delightful photograph taken in 1898, shows a bevy of ladies with the Blenheim spaniels at Blenheim Palace. The type of spaniel does vary almost as much as that of the ladies, but most of the dogs have longer noses and flat heads.

There is an account by G.R. Jesse (1866) which will horrify modern dog lovers of any breed, but does illustrate the Duke of Norfolk's misplaced pride in owning a toy spaniel.

'Our Marlborough and King James Spaniels are unrivalled in beauty. The latter breed that are Black and Tan with their coat almost approaching silk in fineness (such as Van Dyck liked to introduce in his portraits) were solely in the possession of the Duke of Norfolk. He never travelled without two of his pets in his carriage. When at Worksop he used to feed his eagles with the pups. A stranger to his exclusive pride in the race, seeing him one day employed in thus destroying a whole litter, told His Grace how much he should be delighted to have one of them. The Duke replied "Pray Sir which of my estates would you like to have?" The Duke certainly wanted the exclusive right to own the breed!'

The famous Landseer painting used in this book as a frontispiece is known nowadays as 'The Cavalier's Pets', but has been known as 'The King Charles and Blenheim Spaniel'. This was painted in 1845 and is now in the Tate Gallery. Enter any Cavalier enthusiast's home and you will surely see a reproduction. More of this picture later.

The Toy Spaniel Club was founded in 1886, and the name of Toy Spaniel was applied to the King Charles, each colour being known by a different name. The black and whites and black and tans were called King Charles – though Mrs Neville Lytton states in her book that Charles II never owned a black and tan! Tricolours were called Prince Charles or King Charles I Spaniels. Red and whites were Blenheims and the all red, rubies. 'King James Spaniels' seem to have been forgotten on the way!

With all this confusion the Kennel Club, in 1903, wished to classify them all under 'Toy Spaniels' and to drop the ancestral and Royal name.

The Toy Spaniel Club was appalled and made many efforts to have this proposition withdrawn. In the end King Edward VII intervened by intimating to the Kennel Club that it was his wish that the historical name 'King Charles Spaniel' should be retained. I am sure all lovers of the King Charles Spaniel and of the Cavalier King Charles are grateful to His Majesty for we must never forget that they are Royal dogs.

Col. R. Claude Cane writing in the *New Book of the Dog*, published in 1907, had some scathing remarks about the show King Charles Spaniel. Commenting on a sporting man's assessment of the Blenheim as being excellent and indefatigable in their work, and that a Mr Needham remarked 'The kind which attained the greatest distinction (for sporting purposes) is that denominated King Charles Spaniel,' Col. Cane then added: 'No one going around the toy dog benches at the Crystal Palace show nowadays (1907) could picture the goggle-eyed, pug nosed, pampered little peculiarities he would see there lolling on satin cushions and decked out with many ribbons, taking such violent exercise as would be entailed by even half an hour's hunting in the easiest of coverts, but there is no doubt that these effete little monsters have the same origins as most of our modern sporting spaniels. No longer ago than thirty years (that would be 1877) the writer had many a good day's sport shooting rabbits in gorse over a team of King Charles Spaniels, belonging to a cousin in Ireland, which were, however bigger and stronger than those which seem to catch the judge's eye nowadays (1907).'

These were beautiful show dogs with the most lovely eyes, gentle expressions and masses of soft silky coats, but a far cry from those depicted in the pictures of Van Dyck, Watteau, Gainsborough and many of the Dutch painters of the seventeenth century.

Ch. Dickon of Little Breach, Blenheim dog born 1.12.60 by Hillbarn Fabian ex Ch. Amanda of Little Breach. Owned and bred by Mrs L.R. Percival.

Up to 1859 there were no dog shows as such, and breeding was a very haphazard affair without any standard of points existing. It shows how strong the breed characteristics were for so many dogs over the centuries to be recognisable as Toy Spaniels.

With the beginning of dog shows, breed clubs and finally the Kennel Club in 1873, breed standards came into being. It was decreed that King Charles Spaniels and Blenheim Spaniels should have shorter faces, and breeders being what they are, bred for that characteristic until the King Charles standard stated 'The head should be well domed and in good specimens it is absolutely semi globular, sometimes even extending beyond the half circle and projecting over the eyes, so as nearly to meet the upturned nose. The nose must be short and well turned up between the eyes; the 'stop' or hollow between the eyes should be well marked; some good specimens exhibit a hollow deep enough to bury a small marble!'

Thus the King Charles Spaniel continued until 1926 when a new era began.

2 The Evolution of the Cavalier King Charles Spaniel

IN the Cruft's Catalogue for 1926 there appeared this announcement:

'Blenheim Spaniels of the Old Type, as shown in pictures of Charles II's time, long face, no stop, flat skull, not inclined to be domed with spot in centre of skull. The first prize of £25 in Class 947 and 948 are given by Roswell Eldridge Esq., of New York, USA. Prizes go to the nearest to type required.'

Cutting from *The Dog Owner* 13 May 1939.

Way back in 1898 handlers looked like this. Dogs are Blenheims belonging to the Duke of Marlborough.

Above the notice was a reproduction of the Landseer picture 'Cavalier's Pets' used in this book as a frontispiece.

Mr Roswell Eldridge had been very disappointed to find only the noseless type of King Charles in England and kindly offered £25 for three years, later extended to five years, for the best of the 'old type'. In spite of this very generous prize only two entries were received in the first year, but the seed was sown!

The winner of the first £25 class was Ferdie of Monham, born 19 November 1923, by Vital Spark ex Monham Reece.

The owner's husband wrote some time later 'This dog was a bit of a character and in the second year with the same dogs to beat, he tried to bite the judge when he opened his mouth, and he (the judge) refused to judge him. The same dog only won twice in the five years. The third year my dog was placed second, but in the opinion of the breeders, the winner was not a true Cavalier, it was suggested it was a miniature Welsh Spaniel. My wife appealed and was told by Mr Cruft himself "You can't expect the judges to know all the points of these old fashioned dogs".'

The majority of King Charles breeders were horrified by this Mr Roswell Eldridge's generous offer for it would have been quite useless to exhibit a King Charles with the slightest suspicion of a nose in the conventional classes. In the mid twenties £25 was an awful lot of money and to give it to dogs and bitches which they considered 'throw outs', and not fit for the show ring, was appalling. However it was a challenge to the enthusiasts to see what they could breed. Some King Charles breeders were quite glad to find an outlet for their below standard puppies. These would have good body conformation, but had, to the King Charles breeders, either the undesirable longer muzzle or the ability to breed it.

An interesting story is how one of these enthusiasts became involved in the campaign to produce the 'old type'. Mrs Hewitt Pitt was a well known Chow Chow breeder. She was a granddaughter of the artist Sir John Everett Millais, one of the founders of the pre-Raphaelite brotherhood and a president of the Royal Academy. Her father was Sir Everett Millais, a member of the Kennel Club and of the Pasteur Committee. He studied for his doctor's degree at St Thomas's Hospital so that he could further his work with blood hounds and bassett hounds. The latter breed he helped to establish in this country in 1880. Mrs Pitt attributed her appreciation of line breeding from her father, although he died while she was quite young.

In 1924 Mrs Hewitt Pitt bought a Blenheim King Charles bitch from Mrs Higgs of Carshalton as a pet for her mother. She called her 'Waif Julia' as it was some time before she had her full pedigree. Mrs Pitt took Julia to Miss Brunne, the extremely well known breeder of the Hentzan King Charles Spaniels, to be mated. Miss Brunne suggested that Mrs Pitt should show Waif Julia at Crufts in the class sponsored by Mr Roswell Eldridge. This Mrs Pitt did, and won the class, and to quote Mrs Pitt 'I got very interested in the possibilities of breeding this type of Spaniel, and the seed of the idea for the Cavalier Club was sown'.

A committee was formed of practical dog breeders with high ideals. They wanted an active, sporting, sound little dog free from any artificial trimming or colouring. The chairman was Miss Mostyn Walker who owned Ann's Son of whom more later. The secretary was Mrs Pitt who was a lady of great strength of character and determination. Her dedication to

Ch. Curtana Morgana born 26.3.76, top winning King Charles Spaniel of all time with 31 Challenge Certificates. Bred by Miss J. Pennington, owned by Mrs A. Pennington.

the breed has been largely responsible for the high standard of the best Cavaliers of today. Her prefix 'Ttiweh' (Hewitt reversed) will be found behind all Cavaliers the world over. It was a great pleasure for Cavalier lovers that she was able to be at the Golden Jubilee Show in 1978. Her last appearance at a Cavalier event was in July 1978 when she and her daughter, Mrs Bowdler, attended the Jubilee sanction show at Chacombe Priory, the beautiful home of Mr and Mrs Stephen Schilizzi. It was a perfect summer's day, in a lovely setting. I spent a very pleasant hour after lunch discussing early Cavalier photographs with Mrs Pitt. She died in December of that year, but her prefix Ttiweh will be remembered as long as there are Cavalier King Charles Spaniels.

The name 'Old type King Charles Spaniel' was rather confusing and with the founding of the Club at Crufts 1928 the name 'Cavalier King Charles Spaniel' was adopted. One personal plea – please do not call our beautiful breed 'Cavs' – such an ugly abbreviation! 'Cavalier' has such a Royal ring about it.

The Kennel Club would not allow a separate registration and early breeders would have to add 'Cavalier type' to the registration forms. The standard was drawn up by the committee with Miss Mostyn Walker's Ann's Son on the table before them. This dainty little Blenheim was certainly one of the founding fathers of the breed. His ruby son Peter of Ttiweh and his Blenheim daughter Daywell Nell are behind most present day Cavaliers many times over.

Here are some comments about Ann's Son by people who actually saw him. Mrs Pitt wrote in 1958 'In the early days the dogs were considered a joke. Some were, by modern standards, although the best at that time would still be the best in 1958'. (The dogs winning in 1958 were Ch. Aloysius of Sunninghill – still the breed's record holder with 19 c.c.s, Ch. Welland Valley Lively and Ch. Hillbarn Quixote.) Mrs Pitt continued, 'The two outstanding specimens were the Blenheim Ann's Son and the Tricolour Bridget of Ttiweh by Ann's Son's litter brother Wizbang Timothy, a black and white.' In 1962 Mrs Pitt wrote 'First of all we had Ann's Son, a small Blenheim dog, bred out of a short faced bitch. He was probably the best ever, as he really was a toy dog.'

A few months before Mrs Pitt's death I asked her what Ann's Son was really like. 'He was the ideal. We have had nothing ever to touch him' she replied. Showing her the picture of him I asked her if he wasn't long in the muzzle by present day standards. 'No,' she replied, 'this photograph makes him look longer than he was!'

Mrs Speedwell Massingham of the Loyalty Way Cavaliers who were to the fore in the early days wrote of him 'Ann's Son was a toy spaniel of 13lb (5.9kg), short in the back, entirely flat head, streaming ears to his legs, large dark eyes wide apart, nose long tipped with jet to match his dark eyes, a white blaze running right up the forehead, thick soft silky coat

Puppies born 24.8.29 by Wizbang Timothy ex Lucy of Ttiweh. One of these was Timon of Ttiweh, behind all modern Cavaliers and one was Bridget of Ttiweh considered outstanding in her day.

marked red and silver Blenheim and sound as a bell. He was supreme. I realise it is not only all the perfect points that gave him his glory. It was the overall quality which this exquisite little dog had and which shone out of his face, that made him Best Ever Born!'

Miss Phyllis Mayjew of the Mingshang Cavaliers wrote in 1961 'I have loved Cavaliers since I first saw Ann's Son at Crufts 1928, where I had been taken as a great treat to see the Pekingese. I was thrilled with the Pekingese, but it was the prettiest little dog of any breed that I had ever seen – Ann's Son – which remains in my memory.'

Drawn up by the Committee of Cavalier King Charles Spaniel Club.

STANDARD

Points of old type
Cavalier King Charles and Blenheim Spaniels.

	Points
General Appearance and Soundness Active, Sporting, Fearless	15
Head. Almost flat between ears no dome spot desired	15
Eyes. Dark, large and round, but not prominent	10
Nose. Slight stop about 1½ inches. Black.	10
Muzzle. Pointed	10
Texture of Coat. Long Silky	10
Colour. All recognised	5
Chest. Moderate.	
Ears. Long and feathered, high set	10
Tail. Longish, docked.	5
Legs and Feet. Moderate bone, feet well feathered	5
Weight. 10 to 18lbs	5
Faults. Under shot, light eyes.	
	100

Disqualifications.

Original Standard drawn up 1928.

This little dog was placed on the table and the breed standard was drawn up from his excellent points.

The King Charles Spaniel breed correspondent writing in *Dog World* 18 January 1929 said: 'I have been asked "What is a Cavalier King Charles Spaniel?" It is the name which has been given to the long faced King Charles in an effort to bring back and standardise the old type of Spaniel. I believe there have been several attempts in the past, but most of them have been doomed to failure, and the present phase dates from 1926 when the late Mr Roswell Eldridge of New York, offered two prizes of £25 each for the best Blenheim dog and bitch approximating to the old type. I shall never forget the storm that was raised about dogs that would not be eligible for a prize in a King Charles class on looks, being able to walk away with £25 for being a bad King Charles! In those days they were described as "Yiddisher King Charles", whilst another fancier, almost the grandfather of the breed (King Charles) informed us he had drowned all his eligibles as puppies! Because of all this bubble, my husband tried to get the King Charles Club to petition the Kennel Club to separate the "Nosey" from the "Noseless", but everyone was so certain it would fizzle out that nothing was done. They reckoned without Mrs Hewit Pitt, who has taken up the matter with such vigour that there is now a Cavalier King Charles Spaniel Club, with a separate standard recognised by the Kennel Club, and with nine classes at Crufts this year (1929) including the two twenty-five pounders.'

After Crufts for 1929 Mrs Budge wrote in *Dog World* 15 February 1929: 'At Crufts there was a good turnout of both recognised King Charles and the Cavaliers, the latter having a total entry of forty-six in seven classes, excluding brace and team.

'After what I have written recently about the Cavaliers I was naturally interested in them, so I took a walk around their benches as soon as I arrived at the show. I was rather intrigued at first by the diversity of type, but when I realised the judge had to pick out two of these dogs and make them a present of £25 each, I was struck by the job confronting the judge. I must say Mr Butler judged conscientiously according to the type he required, and although some of the classes looked like a variety class, it was always possible to follow the awards from the ring side.

'Miss Mostyn Walker won £25 for the dogs with a Blenheim called Ann's Son, a rather taking dog and not unlike a Welsh Cocker – (whatever could that be!). Mrs Raymond Mallock won the £25 for bitches for Ashtonmore Flora. I would like to say that Flora was, in my opinion, the best coated and conditioned King Charles of any type in the Show, and stood out in this class. Mrs Hewitt Pitt won both Brace and Team. The exhibitors turned up in good numbers. All the classes were well filled and they took the awards in a very sporting manner, a lesson that could be well learnt in other rings.'

A week later in *Dog World* for 22 February 1929, the breed correspondent reports that she had received a letter from Mrs Pitt enclosing the Breed standard. She quotes that Mrs Pitt and the Cavalier King Charles Spaniel Club's ultimate aim was to get them separated entirely, with a separate register and their own certificates.

Another paragraph of interest from the same letter shows the difficulty of the task. 'By breeding back for long noses, we have lost ground, naturally, and have had to sacrifice many points to obtain the one predominant difference, i.e. nose placement. I have all sorts of weirdly marked ones here, but I am getting the nose and ears to come nearer to the standard we require.'

The breed correspondent comments: 'There is a note of definite achievement here and the tenacity of purpose which it ill becomes any of us to scoff at. Although I have no intention at the moment of taking up the Cavalier myself I have never attempted to hinder their efforts in what must be a difficult task, and I do appeal to all King Charles lovers not to interfere if they cannot help. There is no doubt this club has come to stay and we must admire their efforts, even if some of us do not agree with them.'

How true this was! The Cavalier had come to stay, thank goodness!

A similar correspondence was being conducted in *Our Dogs* in February 1929.

A Mr Herbert Norcross had suggested that the Cavalier should be classified as 'Any other breed or variety'. Mrs Pitt, as secretary of the Cavalier King Charles Spaniel Club replied 'These Cavaliers have pedigrees as long and as pure blooded as many of the noseless Champions of to-day (1929). The difference does not lie in the pedigree, but in the type fancied by the individual. When the modern type (short faced King Charles) enthusiast has discarded all the specimens breeding too large a proportion of throw backs, i.e. long noses, we Cavalier breeders have fostered these persistent little spaniels and would try to get back to their "once-upon-a-time" type and have gradually evolved the small sporting little spaniel which now goes by the name of Cavalier.'

Mrs Pitt concluded 'It will be some time before these little spaniels are perfected for Show purposes and we ask for the patience of outside critics towards the second rate specimens which are seen and will be seen for some time when Cavaliers are on view. They are all interesting as they illustrate the progress of the breed.'

One cannot help feeling that those second rate specimens are still seen today, fifty years later, but when we compare them with the best the breed can offer we can really see how they have progressed.

Ann's Son continued his winning ways both in and out of the ring. The breed notes for February 1936 stated 'Miss Mostyn Walker of Costessey, must indeed be proud of the Cavalier King Charles Spaniel Ann's Son, who running through his classes at Crufts also won £15 special for the Best of Breed, and the £50 trophy – a bust of Mr Charles Cruft. Ann's Son, already a noted Cavalier, has won the £25 special offered at Crufts for this breed 1928, 1929 and 1930. He then retired, only to stage a "comeback" last Wednesday week having given all Cavalier King Charles Spaniel breeders six years start to compete with him again. He won all his victories under specialist Charlie judges and looked in perfect bloom and condition. Thus in his ninth year, he made his farewell to the public, finishing his record show career under such a noted judge as Mrs Raymond Mallock.'

AT

STUD

FEE
3 gns.
prepaid
return
carriage
extra

" Ann's Son "

The Noted King Charles Spaniel.

NEVER BEATEN.

Winner of the £50 Trophy and £15 Special at Cruft's 1936, also winner of the £25 Special offered for Old Type King Charles Spaniels at Cruft's 1928, 1929, and 1930.

A very beautiful little dog.

Sires small stock of unmistakable type and quality

Miss Mostyn Walker,

Clova Kennels   ::   Costessey,

Norwich.

TEL: COSTESSEY 76

Stud card for Ann's Son. The foundation sire of the breed.

Many attempts were made to breed another Ann's Son, but they were not successful. Ann's Son was unique. His influence on the breed both in the early days by endearing so many to the breed and by the importance of his progeny, cannot be over estimated.

His full brother was Wizbang Timothy! Mrs Pitt wrote of him in an old bulletin 'He was not so decorative as Ann's Son and very nearly a black and white. He had a lovely head and was a good stud dog. Unfortunately he was not lucky in his various homes and was often in poor condition and some time full of sarcoptic mange.' However he did play his part in the formation of the breed. Mated with a ruby, Lucy of Ttiweh (a daughter of Ann's Son), they produced a very interesting tricolour bitch Bridget of Ttiweh on 24 August 1929. Bridget played quite a role in bringing the breed before the dog showing fraternity in the 1930s. She was considered one of the outstanding specimens of the early days and indeed was only beaten once in seven years. From her photograph, by modern standards, we might think she was more like a blue roan cocker with a poor top line!

A chance business meeting had a marked influence on the breed. Mrs Jennings, later of Plantation fame, had always owned a King Charles Spaniel, even from childhood. After the 1914–1918 War she was dogless, but hankered after another King Charles Spaniel. Mr Jennings was at a business meeting in 1926, when the conversation turned to dogs. An unnamed business man told Mr Jennings that his wife had a Blenheim King Charles Spaniel which she wished to sell. Mr Jennings bought her for his wife. This bitch was Blenheim Palace Poppet bred at Blenheim Palace.

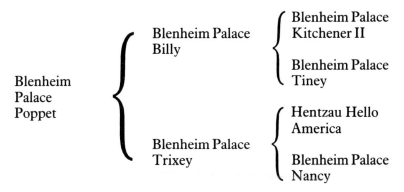

Poppet mated to Timon of Ttiweh (Bridget's full brother) produced Timonetta of Ttiweh, a key bitch behind all present day Cavaliers. When mated to Mark of Ttiweh, a Blenheim Grandson of Ann's Son, Poppet produced Plantation Pixie another important ancestor of present day Cavaliers.

Mrs Jennings thought Poppet's puppies were too big and after attending a Cavalier party, she could see Poppet was quite different from all the other Cavaliers present. However she decided to persevere and Poppet and all the ensuing Plantation dogs have had a marked influence on the breed.

Other useful stud dogs were Carlo of Ttiweh (Blenheim) and Duce of Braemore (tricolour). Both were short faced, but both sired long nosed puppies of note.

As late as 1935 Springvale Pharoah, a real short face, was used. His son

Top
Bridget of Ttiweh, second generation Cavalier, by Wizbang Timothy (almost black and white litter brother to Ann's Son) ex Lucy of Ttiweh, born 24.8.29. Only beaten once in seven years of showing. Considered to be one of the two outstanding specimens of the early days, the other being Ann's Son.

Bottom
Ch. Baridene Royal Serenade of Charlesworth born 23.9.78 by Kindrum Barnacle Bill ex Baridene Sweet Serenade bred by Mrs J.K. Gough, owned by Miss C.G. Greenall. Note the improvement in markings, quality of coat and top line.

Aristide of Ttiweh out of a short face bred Topsy of Ttiweh has played a big part in the modern Cavalier. Another influential sire was Kobba of

Kuranda, born 1927, a lovely black and tan, whose sweet head would be the envy of many present day breeders of black and tans! He was the only black and tan used in the very early days, because he was the only one of that colour which sired the correct heads. Others were tried, but they were not successful in producing flat tops and longer noses, and so they were discarded.

Kobba of Kuranda – first generation Cavalier born 1927 by Hentzau Bucks Hussar ex Hentzau Lady Babba, the only black and tan to be used as a foundation sire.

From these six stud dogs the breed was formed. It says a great deal about their stamina and genetic soundness for they were all inbred and line bred to time and time again in the early generations of Cavaliers.

In the second generation one of the influential sires was a ruby son of Peter of Ttiweh, by Ann's Son out of a short faced ruby bitch Ashtonmore Salome. A comment on him runs 'Peter was of excellent type, but much too big. A grand stud dog!' A show report in *Dog World* 1930 said 'A typical and wonderfully built ruby dog; and not withstanding the fact that he has been consistently shown for two years at all the Championship shows, he has not been beaten. He is outstanding in all points and an invaluable sire.' Remember there were no c.c.s for Cavaliers in those days.

Another second generation sire was Duke's Son, a Blenheim son of Ann's Son, and a short faced Blenheim – Nightie Nightie.

Mark and John of Ttiweh, Blenheim and Ruby sons of Peter also played their part. Mark was very important as the sire of Plantation Pixie, Judy of Ttiweh and Selena of Ancott, all bitches who played their part in the late 30s.

Breeders continued to strive for perfection as they are still doing today.

They were hampered by lack of interest from the public and so finding homes for puppies which did not fit in with breeding plans was difficult. There is a limit to the number you can give to your friends! Prices were very poor even by 1930s standards. Clarissa of Ttiweh, the winner of the Puppy Class at Olympia 1933, was sold for 4 guineas.

Breeders were hampered by having so few blood lines to use. Most dedicated breeders were against bringing in other breeds. One used to hear stories about Welsh Springers, Dachshunds and Papillons being introduced but these tales have never been proved and may well just be stories!

In 1931 Mrs Pitt wrote the following 'I must confess that our living specimens in the majority of cases fall very short of the standard, and are a great deal too big. Owing to the fact that for some unknown reason the greater proportion of our puppies have been dogs and not bitches, it has been very difficult to collect breeding stock in any quantity.'

She continues 'Another point to which I should like to draw attention is the fact that to continue breeding without intensive in-breeding, we Cavalier breeders have to continue to seek fresh blood from the only source open to us, i.e. the short faced dog which failed to throw noseless puppies. This is a slight handicap to continuity of type, but it is better than losing stamina!'

An interesting bitch of the 1930s was Rangers Nicky Picky. (She is so maddening to people doing a ten generation pedigree because she is down as 'registered but pedigree not given', so behind her there is an exasperating gap.) There are several stories about her from Mrs Laurensen who owned the Rangers Kennels of Clumbers, Springers and Cavaliers in the late 20s and 30s. 'Rangers Nicky Picky was known as Nicodemus because she was so odd!' According to Mrs Laurensen she was a black and tan with long legs, while Mrs Pitt wrote of her 'a very long faced black and tan, well bred but the owner would not give pedigree'. Nicky Picky certainly seems to be a character! One day she was lost and after a hue and cry she was found at 11 pm asleep with twenty little pigs! When due to whelp she disappeared and later was found in a large hole she had dug, with five puppies all dry and happily feeding!

Later she was owned by Mrs Jennings of Plantation Cavaliers who bred from her with good results. To the lovely black and tan Kobba of Korunda she produced the tricolour Plantation Twinkle, the mother of Plantation Banjo; while mated to the Blenheim, Plantation Robert, she produced the black and tan Plantation Dusky, the mother of Cannonhill Richey. Odd she may have been but to be grandmother and great-grandmother of Ch. Daywell Roger, the first Cavalier Champion was no mean feat!

Mme J. Harper Trois-Fontaines, a noted breeder of the de Fontenay Pyrenean Mountain dogs, turned her attention to Cavaliers in the late 30s. She founded her Kennel on four dogs.

Pippbrook Theobald (2 R.C.C.s) born 25.5.78, by Millstone Basil ex Matsy Duana, bred by Miss J. Burt, owned by Mr R. Dix. Theobald is 15 generations in direct line from Kobba who appears numerous times in Theobald's, and probably all Cavalier pedigrees through Ch. Daywell Roger – Kobba's great grandson. Note the almost identical profile.

1 Plantation Banjo a superb little black and tan bred by Mrs Jennings by Plantation Robert ex Plantation Twinkle.
2 Snow White of Ttiweh, an almost all white bodied Blenheim, with tan ears, by Peter of Ttiweh (a Ruby son of Ann's Son) ex Timonetta of Ttiweh (tricolour).
3 Freckles of Ttiweh by Peter of Ttiweh ex Clarissa of Ttiweh.
4 Judy of Ttiweh, a very mismarked ruby by Mark of Ttiweh ex Sally of Ttiweh.

Eight Ttiweh Champions. Photograph taken for Silver Jubilee of Cavalier Club 1954.

Left to right.
Ch. Comfort of Ttiweh.
Ch. Trilby of Ttiweh.
Ch. Jupiter of Ttiweh.
Ch. Amanda Loo of Ttiweh.
Ch. Little Dorritt of Ttiweh. Ch. Daywell Roger.
Ch. Harmony of Ttiweh.
Ch. Hillbarn Alexander of Ttiweh.

From these four dogs the de Fontenay Kennels bred many good Cavaliers who are found in the pedigrees of the forties, and are behind all modern strains. These include Princess Anita de Fontenay. She was the dam of the breed's first Champion Bitch – the black and tan Ch. Amanda Loo of Ttiweh. Emerald de Fontenay was the foundation bitch of Mr Vernon Green's Astondown line. Emerald's daughter Annabelle of Astondowns was the foundation bitch of Mrs H. Pilkington's famous line of Hillbarn Tricolours.

But back to Plantation Banjo. This delightful little black and tan mated to his half sister Plantation Dusky produced the ruby Cannonhill Richey. Richey and Banjo were used a great deal during the war so that in 1945, there was very little outcross from this line. However they had a great influence on the breed, as will be seen later.

Mrs Sawkins of the Grenewich King Charles Spaniels began taking an interest in Cavaliers in the late thirties and founded her own line away from Ann's Son. The most famous dog from that line was The Young Pretender of Grenewich, born in 1944. Miss Phyllis Mayhew bought him as an eight week old puppy when his breeder, Mrs Sawkins, gave him to be sold in aid of the R.A.F. Benevolent Fund. He was a good winner himself, but as a sire made his mark. To Mrs Helen Pilkington's Annabelle of Aston downs he sired two champions in the first litter Mrs Pilkington ever bred. When Miss Mayhew became ill after the war The Young Pretender went to live with Mrs I.J. Green, Miss Mayhew's sister, and became the founder of the Heatherside Cavaliers. He rewarded Mrs Green for adopting him by siring two champions, Ch. Heatherside Andrew and Ch. Heatherside Anthea in the same litter!

Ch. Daywell Roger (Blenheim Dog) the first Cavalier King Charles Spaniel Champion born 7.10.45 by Cannonhill Richey (ruby) ex Daywell Nell (Blenheim). A very influential stud dog siring eleven champions.

After the war the breed continued to gather strength. In 1945 the Kennel Club agreed to separate registration for the Cavalier King Charles Spaniels, and granted them Challenge Certificates.

The first Championship Show was held on 29 August 1946 at the School of Drama, Alverston, Stratford-upon-Avon. The judge was Mrs Jennings of the Plantation Cavaliers. There were twenty-eight Cavaliers entered making 109 entries. The entry fee was 10/6d (52½p) a class and prize money was £2, £1, 10/- (50p) – a better return for money than today!

Best in show was Mrs K. Eldred's Belinda of Saxham by Duke's Son ex Linooga. She was then seven years old. The war had kept her out of the ring and denied her her Champion status as she was compared very favourably with Ann's Son. However she made history by throwing Ch. Little Dorrit of Ttiweh another key bitch in present day pedigrees. The Best Dog was Daywell Roger, a Blenheim dog born 7 October 1945 and destined to become the breed's first Champion. He was by Cannonhill Richey (R) out of Daywell Nell a very pretty little Blenheim daughter of Ann's Son.

Daywell Nell
- Ann's Son
  - Lord Pindi
  - Ann
- Miss Ann's Son
  - Ann's Son
  - Nightie Nightie

Mrs Pitt bought Roger unseen because he was the nearest she could get to Ann's Son. Although he will be remembered as the breed's first champion it is as a sire he has his chief claim to fame. In all he was the father of eleven Champions, but his influence has continued.

Roger's full sister Daywell Amber was the bitch that produced the two Heatherside Champions Andrew and Anthea to The Young Pretender of Grenewich, so that close breeding to Ann's Son was very interesting. In the twenty years from the beginning of the Cavalier King Charles Spaniel, including six years of war when breeding was very curtailed and many valuable blood lines dispersed and were destroyed, to produce Champions who were grandchildren of Ann's Son the founder figure of the breed was really remarkable.

One important action taken in 1945 which shows how sensible Cavalier King Charles Spaniel people can be was the option to docking tails. There was a strong lobby for the abolition of all docking, but the commonsense action was taken that 'docking is optional'. Those who feel the need can still remove the last third of the puppy's tail, and those who wish the tail to remain entire are at liberty so to do without either being penalised in the ring.

The late 40s saw the emergence of the Pargeter Cavalier King Charles Spaniels owned by Mrs Keswick. These were a very important strain and Mrs Keswick's death in 1969 was a very sad loss to the breed. Not only did her generosity and clever breeding further the cause of Cavaliers in this country, but she was instrumental in their being established in the USA, in Australia and New Zealand. In all she owned or bred fourteen Champions, Ch. Pargeter Jollyean of Avoncliffe, Ch. Pargeter Bob-up and Ch. Pargeter McBounce being excellent stud dogs.

The Heathersides continued their winning ways while other important lines came to the fore. One, the Eyeworth strain was owned by Lady Forwood. Her first Champion was the pretty little Blenheim bitch Ch. Infantas Katherine of Eyeworth made up in 1958. The majority of the whole colour Cavaliers can claim the black and tan Ch. Cointreau of Eyeworth as an ancestor, while the tricolour Ch. Clarion of Eyeworth has also left his mark on the breed. In all there were nine Eyeworth Champions.

Ch. Aloysius of Sunninghill, tricolour dog born 27.11.55 by Amulet of Sunninghill ex Louisa of Sunninghill, bred by Mr G. Wilson, owned by Miss P. Turle. Breed record holder with nineteen C.C.s. Sire of eight champions.

Miss Pamela Turles' Ch. Aloysius of Sunninghill born 27 November 1955 was a great ambassador for the breed. He was shown fearlessly during the late 50s and won nineteen c.c.s – still a breed record. But it was as a sire that he made his mark. He had ten Champion children. Among these was the very beautiful Blenheim Ch. Amelia of Laguna, owned by Mrs F. Cryer and bred by Miss L. Mackay. Amelia made history by being the first Cavalier to win the toy group at Crufts 1963, which put Cavaliers really in the public eye!

I am sure Aloysius had a little of his great-great grandfather Ann's Son's exquisite charm which makes a good dog into something extra special. By modern standards he was heavily marked but it was his lovely head, expression and overall quality that made him outstanding and which won him so many admirers.

Ch. Vairire Charmaine of Crisdig (second from left) with her three Champion grandchildren, all from the same litter. Ch. Crisdig Candid, Ch. Crisdig Charm, Ch. Crisdig Celebration (by Crisdig Henry ex Vairire Venetia of Crisdig). Photograph taken October 1966.

1961 saw the first of the many Crisdig Champions, Ch. Vairire Charmaine of Crisdig owned by Brigadier and Mrs Burgess and bred by Mrs E. Burroughs. The Crisdigs were founded by line breeding to Mars of Ttiweh through Ch. Aloysius's son. In Ch. Sunninghill Perseus of Loch Fee and Vairire Candida, the Crisdig's have been very influential in many present day Cavaliers. One litter born on 20 February 1962 by Crisdig Henry ex Vairire Venetia of Crisdig contained three champions, Ch. Crisdig Celebration, Ch. Crisdig Candid and the lovely bitch Ch. Crisdig Charm. Up to the present time there have been twenty-one Crisdig Champions, eight of them sold as puppies and made up by their new owners. In 1970 Mrs S. Schilizzi made up the first Chacombe Champion, a black and tan dog Ch. Ivan the Terrible. He and the ruby Chacombe Champions were largely based on the Kormar breeding of Miss Marshall, while the tricolour Chacombe Champions are founded on the Little Breach line of Mrs Percival.

Many breeders with either a large number of dogs or with a few house pets continued to plan and work for the improvement of the breed. Certain lines 'click' and can be relied upon to produce winning stock in litter after litter. 1974 saw the first of a remarkably successful series of matings of Mrs M.M. Talbot's tricolour Minstrel Boy of Maxholt to Mrs Orde's Blenheim Dalginross Rosalind. This happy union produced four tricolour champions. In all Minstrel Boy sired seven champions.

Chandlers Cavaliers bred by Mrs Vera Preece have been instrumental in establishing Cavaliers of excellent quality in all parts of the world. Most present day whole colours can boast to having the black and tan Ch. Chandlers Phalaris and the ruby Ch. Chandlers Roberta in their pedigrees.

The west of England has always been a stronghold of Cavaliers. In 1969 Mrs Daphne Murray of Bath, who had been with Mrs Pitt in the 30s, made history by making Ch. Piccola of Crustadele the first ruby Champion. Mrs G. Biddle of Devon made up several Ottermouth Champions including Ch. Rosemullion of Ottermouth, a very prepotent sire in the late 70s. Mrs M. Coaker and her daughter, also of Devon, began the Homerbrent and Homaranne Cavaliers. Their first Champion, Ch. Homerbrent Lindy Lou, was made up in 1972. Since then nine Champions have been crowned. While Ch. Homaranne Caption has been top stud dog judged by the wins of his progeny for 1980, 1981, 1982, 1983, 1984, 1985, 1986. Amantra Cavaliers and incidently also King Charles Spaniels, owned by Mrs D. Fry and her daughter, have been very successful in recent years. During the early 70s the breed grew steadily with increased registrations and all General Championship Shows offering c.c.s for the breed.

1973 was a momentous year for the breed. Only forty-five years after the Cavalier Club had held its first meeting at Crufts 1928, Messrs. Hall & Evans' Alansmere Aquarius (not a Champion on the day, although he was to become one within the month) won the Best of Breed Cavalier, Best Toy and finally Best in Show at Crufts. He can trace his pedigree to all the great Cavaliers of the past. Mrs Pitt was quick to note he was a great-great grandson of Ch. Daywell Roger.

Sadly this great triumph had an unfortunate backlash. The general public saw on television this delightful little dog parading so fearlessly in that vast area of Olympia and the demand for puppies became phenomenal. The cost of feeding big dogs and the constant expense of clipping poodles and trimming terriers made people replacing lost pets think of the Cavalier.

Established breeders were inundated with requests for bitch puppies and young adult bitches. I had an enquiry for three bitches from one person. I was rather surprised and asked one or two searching questions. Finally I was told that she had been breeding apricot poodles, but 'the market had gone out of them' and she thought Cavaliers would be a 'profitable substitute'. Needless to say the person in question did not get any stock from me. If a large breed goes Best-in-Show at Crufts and the media makes capital out of the fact that that dog needs 2 to 3lb (.9 to 1.4kg) of meat a day, plus a daily five mile walk, that can be a deterrent to a would be buyer, but the Cavalier is ideal, of perfect size, and so beautiful and appealing.

There was a population explosion! Cavaliers appeared in pet shops, and multi-breed dealer kennels. They could be bought by credit cards and on 'the never-never'. They were even appearing in Club Row – the animal section of London's Sunday Street Market in Petticoat Lane!

Indiscriminate breeding for profit was taking place, not by the dedicated Cavalier lovers, but by the money making unacceptable type of breeder who could send a crate of puppies by train to a dealer, never to know or care where the puppies ended their days. Unsuitable dogs and bitches were used for breeding these puppies and so nowadays one sees so very many poor specimens as family pets.

Entries at shows became overwhelming. From the total entry of twenty-eight at the first Championship Show it is now commonplace to have more than that number in each class at most of the Championship Shows. These days entries are such that a separate judge for each sex is required, with Cavaliers often having the top or near top entry of all breeds.

However there is evidence that the peak has been reached and that several of the multi-breed dealer establishments have closed down. Perhaps the damage can be repaired if only the best is bred from, and people with sub-standard pets are dissuaded from breeding from them by stud dog owners.

1978 saw the Golden Jubilee Year of the Cavalier Club. The highlight being the Championship Show held at the Tate and Lyle Hall at the National Agriculture Centre, Stoneleigh, Warwickshire. The night before the show a most happy party was held, with Cavalier lovers from all parts of the world attending.

On the following day the Tate and Lyle Hall was not recognisable with gay bunting and floral decorations, and many stalls with exciting Cavalier souvenirs for sale.

What a task confronted the judges! Miss Pamela Turle of Sunninghill Cavaliers tackled the dogs and Mrs Vera Preece of the Chandlers Cavaliers, had an enormous task with the bitches. The total was 846 entries made by 617 dogs. Novice bitch was a class of sixty-one! The Best in Show was the beautiful Blenheim dog Ch. Leynsord Salutation, owned and bred by Mr and Mrs D.W. Reynolds, while the best bitch was Mrs

Cavalier King Charles Spaniel Club Golden Jubilee Show, March 1978. *Left to right*: Mrs V. Preece, judge of bitches, Mrs P. Thornhill with Ch. Kindrum Carousel, bitch c.c.; Mrs B. Reynolds with Ch. Leynsord Salutation, dog c.c. and Best in Show; Miss P. Turle, judge of dogs.

Thornhill's Ch. Kindrum Carousel. The referee for the show was Mrs Pitt and although she was rather scathing about the poorer specimens exhibited, I am sure it was with pride she watched the parade of forty champions of all four colours, all of them descendants of Ann's Son, Peter of Ttiweh and Ch. Daywell Roger. How glad we all were that she was with us on that memorable day!

It certainly was a case that from little acorns great oak trees grow! As if to prove the point 1981 saw another Cavalier King Charles Spaniel win the Toy group at Crufts. This was a Blenheim dog Ch. Jia Laertes of Tonnew by Breklaw Challenger ex Jia Lady Camilla, bred by Mrs D. Archer and owned by Mr and Mrs R. Newton. He was such a good ambassador for the breed and certainly was 'an active, graceful, well balanced dog, absolutely fearless and sporting in character, and very gay and free in action' as the standard demands. He really did take command of the vast ring at Earls Court and the more the crowds clapped the more his tail wagged!

For three Cavaliers to win the Toy group at Crufts in the last eighteen years speaks well for the high standard of our best dogs. Many breeds well established before 1928 when it all began have never had one group winner. Remember group judges are very experienced all rounders who would be looking for a winner with that extra quality.

Warned by the Cavalier population explosion after Aquarius's great Best in Show win in 1973, I am sure everyone will be on their guard to dissuade indiscriminate breeding.

3 The Breed Standard and Characteristics

ALL breeds have a standard of points drawn up by breed clubs and approved by the Kennel Club. The standard is there to be a useful guide to breeders and judges so that they can preserve the breed characteristics without damaging the individual dogs with extremes in shape and temperament. It is also a safeguard against any characteristic becoming detrimental to the health and well-being of the breed. It should be the aim of breeders to breed dogs that conform to the standard and so preserve balance and the essential points which set the Cavalier apart from all other dogs. The standard is perfection for which to aim. No dog has yet been born who has all the points which every judge would consider could not be surpassed. If that dog appeared he would never be beaten and that would make showing very dull!

The first Cavalier standard was drawn up by the original committee of the Cavalier King Charles Spaniel Club at Crufts 1928. Ann's Son and pictures of Toy Spaniels through the ages were discussed and from these the first standard was agreed. It was certainly brief and to the point. Breeders were very limited in the stock they could use. These had to be throw outs from the short faced King Charles. They were sound specimens, but would breed the required head with no dome and an 1½in (38mm) nose so loved by the Cavalier enthusiasts and abhorred by the King Charles lovers.

Because of this they had to accept many faults, especially markings. When the head type became established the elimination of other faults began. Although one often despairs of the ungainly, oversized light eyed Cavaliers seen in the ring today, one must rejoice that with such limited resources and a loosely worded standard from which to work, breeders have produced so many top class dogs in fifty-five years. Of course there is still room for improvement, both among the main stream and tail enders!!

A debating point in the early 30s was whether the Cavalier should resemble the type portrayed in pictures by Landseer or the earlier Van Dyck and Jan Steen. Some breeders thought that the Landseer 'King Charles and Blenheim Spaniels', also called 'The Cavalier's Pets', completed in 1845 was too late and that type was already showing a deep stop resulting from attempts to shorten the nose. Others thought that the pictures of the sixteenth and seventeenth century showed such skinny snipey faced creatures with disagreeable expressions. However the good old English compromise and common sense prevailed and the lovely gentle head of the true Cavalier, with such a pleasing expression, has evolved.

One can appreciate the importance given to the head. This was the chief

Delightful drawings by Jeannie Bartram which clearly show the difference in the head of the King Charles Spaniel and the Cavalier King Charles Spaniel, i.e. the length of nose and the shape of the top of the head.

difference between the conventional King Charles and the Cavalier. In any breed the head is the most distinctive characteristic. Compare the boxer, the whippet, the fox terrier or setter; all extremely different. Body characteristics differ but not to such a degree as those of the head. A well constructed body and a dog that moves well was and still is most desirable. In other breeds and even mongrels sound action and body conformation could comply with the Cavalier standard, but without the properties of the head could never be confused with a Cavalier. The first Committee placed so much importance on the head, eyes, muzzle, nose and ears on their point system that they allocated 55 per cent of the marks for these features. Later the point system was dropped – a very wise decision. With such a high percentage of marks for the head, breeders may have been tempted to concentrate on heads to the detriment of the rest of the dog.

It is the interpretation of the standard by breeders and judges that makes showing and breeding so interesting. If every one interpreted it in the same way, the same dogs would win every time and all the fun would disappear. As long as no point is exaggerated and no point ignored, well constructed and well balanced dogs will be bred.

Kennel Club Breed Standard
Reproduced by permission of the Kennel Club

GENERAL APPEARANCE: Active, graceful and well balanced, with gentle expression.

CHARACTERISTICS: Sporting, affectionate, absolutely fearless.

TEMPERAMENT: Gay, friendly, non-aggressive; no tendency to nervousness.

HEAD AND SKULL: Skull almost flat between ears. Stop shallow. Length from base of stop to tip of nose about $1\frac{1}{2}$ inches. Nostrils black and well developed without flesh marks, muzzle well tapered. Lips well developed but not pendulous. Face well filled below eyes. Any tendency to snipiness undesirable.

EYES: Large, dark, round but not prominent; spaced well apart.

EARS: Long, set high, with plenty of feather.

MOUTH: Jaws strong, with a perfect, regular and complete scissor bite, i.e. the upper teeth closely overlapping the lower teeth and set square to the jaws.

NECK: Moderate length, slightly arched.

FOREQUARTERS: Chest moderate, shoulders well laid back; straight legs moderately boned.

BODY: Short-coupled with good spring of rib. Level back.

HINDQUARTERS: Legs with moderate bone; well turned stifle – no tendency to cow or sickle hocks.

FEET: Compact, cushioned and well feathered.

TAIL: Length of tail in balance with body, well set on, carried happily but never much above the level of the back. Docking optional. If docked no more than one-third to be removed.

GAIT/MOVEMENT: Free moving and elegant in action, plenty of drive from behind. Fore and hind legs move parallel when viewed from in front and behind.

COAT: Long, silky, free from curl. Slight wave permissible. Plenty of feathering. Totally free from trimming.

COLOUR: Recognised colours are:

BLACK AND TAN: Raven black with tan markings above the eyes, on cheeks, inside ears, on chest and legs and underside of tail. Tan should be bright. White marks undesirable.

RUBY: Whole coloured rich red. White markings undesirable.

BLENHEIM: Rich chestnut markings well broken up, on pearly white ground. Markings evenly divided on head, leaving room between ears for much valued lozenge mark or spot (a unique characteristic of the breed).

TRICOLOUR: Black and white well spaced, broken up, with tan markings over eyes, cheeks, inside ears, inside legs, and on underside of tail.

Any other colour or combination of colours most undesirable.

SIZE: Weight – 12 to 18 lb (5.4 to 8.2 kg). A small well-balanced dog well within these weights desirable.

FAULTS: Any departure from the foregoing points should be considered a fault and the seriousness with which the fault should be regarded should be in exact proportion to its degree.

NOTE: Male animals should have two apparently normal testicles fully descended into the scrotum.

Now to analyse the standard in detail:

GENERAL APPEARANCE: This not only gives a word picture of the physical appearance of the breed but also defines the breed character. Though in the toy group, the Cavalier is not an inactive lap dog, but of course at the appropriate time, the lap is where he longs to be and is usually found! The standard states in its first sentence that the Cavalier should be active, graceful, and well balanced, absolutely fearless and sporting in character, very gay and free in action.

From time to time in recent years there have been suggestions in the canine press that Cavalier King Charles Spaniels are in the wrong group. Of course the heavy, clumsy, well over weight ones do look out of place beside the Chihuahua, but a small Cavalier within the weight limit is a toy dog, a sporting toy, a true King Charles Spaniel, whose pedigree can be traced back to when records began. They have always been classified as toys and long may they remain as such.

One hears of Cavaliers being good little gundogs, herding goats and cows, being alert and warning of intruders. This does not mean they should be in the gun dog or working group. It means they are being absolutely fearless and sporting in character as the standard demands. It must be remembered that the Cavalier is a *toy dog*. One cannot emphasise this point too often.

The essence of Cavalier is found in this part of the standard which states 'Active, fearless and very gay'. The true Cavalier temperament is the most important characteristic of the breed. If any point in the standard is to be exaggerated it is the preservation of this lovely temperament. Cavaliers should not be noisy, wild and bad tempered. Their ancestors have been bred for centuries to be comforters and this aim must be kept to the fore – never breed from a dog or bitch whose temperament you suspect, nor from a dog or bitch who has produced a bad tempered puppy. There is no excuse for a bad tempered Cavalier. You may be at a show two or three times a month in the busy show season to show off your specimen who is near perfect physically, but what misery to you and other exhibitors if he is noisy, yappy and snappy on his bench. I have groaned inwardly when I have found we were benched near this type. I once said to an owner 'What uncavalier-like language' when her dog was being unpleasant not only to other dogs, but to her. 'Yes', she replied 'He doesn't like getting his feet wet'. What utter nonsense! Imagine living with a dog like that at home! Yet he was used at stud!

Luckily this doesn't happen very often and the vast majority of breeders do try and usually succeed in breeding Cavaliers with the true temperament. After all, even the most successful show kennels have puppies to sell which are not suitable for show. Pet owners often do not mind mismarking or under shot teeth as long as their pet has the true Cavalier temperament, but they would be very upset if their Cavalier turned out to be a noisy, disagreeable specimen so untypical of the breed, however beautiful he might appear to the eye. Most reliable breeders sell their puppies by recommendation. Who is going to recommend a strain of dogs, whom to live with is utter misery!

Friends owning other breeds are often amazed at the way our family of dogs will welcome a visiting bitch into their midst, allowing the stranger to pile into the dog bed with them and to become one of the family straight away! One hears of breeds where stud dogs never meet for fear they fight and where there is a 'boss dog' who rules over the pack. This must not happen in Cavaliers. Of course owners must play their part by not breeding from dogs which show such tendencies and also by being scrupulously fair in the way you treat your pack. Do not give one extra tit-bits or cuddles in front of the others. If you make a fuss of one, make a fuss of them all. I must often look a funny sight with three or four Cavaliers on my lap wanting cuddling and a couple on the floor on their backs wanting their tummies rubbed with my foot! It is times like these I wish I was Siva with her many arms and legs!

The other important point under the heading of general appearance is 'Free of trimming and artifical colouring!' Regrettably now and again one or two exhibitors who should know better have been advocating trimming and have even been seen wielding scissors at Shows. This is most definitely against the standard.

Mrs Pitt, in a talk given in April 1974, produced a chart which she stated was drawn from probably the best existing standard, the perfect wired haired fox terrier. She continued: 'How I wish we could put forward a chart like this – well of course it is very difficult because in the wires they have this marvellously exact pattern and if your dog does not fit well, you trim it, pluck it, and shave it until it does approximately fit the pattern. We cannot do that under our rules which state that there must be no trimming nor cutting into shape. This was ruled at the first meeting when we drew up the standard for the Club because we did not want our dogs to become one of those breeds which are in decline because of excessive trimming.' It is still the rule and should not be broken.

Of course if your Cavalier grows mats under his feet or excessive hair in the ear which prevents a free passage of air into the ear channel these must be removed for the health and comfort of the dog. Retired show dogs and pets could have the excess feathering trimmed to prevent so much mud on the kitchen floor, but no dog should enter the show ring who has had his feet, neck, hocks, end of his ears or any external part of him trimmed. Judges should play their part to stamp out this nasty practice by penalising a dog who has been trimmed however good he may be in other points. It is against the standard of the breed just as much as light eyes and under shot mouths. However it often takes careful observation to distinguish between clever trimming and the perfect coat with the correct amount of feathering especially on his feet and hocks and around his neck. An experienced judge should know and penalise accordingly.

As for use of artificial colouring, it is not only against the Cavalier King Charles Spaniel Club's standard, but also against Kennel Club rules. Spot checks have been made at shows in certain breeds from time to time. A veterinary surgeon with Kennel Club officials have taken samples of coat from exhibits and sent them for laboratory analysis for artificial colouring which may be dye or coloured chalk. If proved positive the offending exhibitor can be penalised under Kennel Club Rule 17 subsection II which virtually means for them the end of breeding and showing pedigree dogs. Luckily this has never happened in the Cavalier ring and let us hope it never will.

HEAD AND SKULL: This is where the breed standard gives scope for interpretation for there are many different types of head. There can be no dispute that the top of the skull must be flat with high set ears and that the muzzle should be 1½in (38mm) long. However if the muzzle is snipey, that is with an exaggerated taper without any filling in under the eyes, it will look longer than 1½in (38mm). If the muzzle is too blunt without sufficient taper it will look shorter than 1½in (38mm). The ideal head should be balanced with a stop but not exaggerated as in the King Charles nor lacking as in the bull terrier.

Small brown, grey or even pink noses with small nostrils also add to an uncavalier expression. Remember artificial colouring of the nose by dyes or tatooing, is illegal under Kennel Club Rules. A whole book could be written on why noses 'go off colour' and what can be done to restore 'the jet' of Ann's Son. Various medications such as elderberry pills, iron tablets, seaweed, liquorice, the use of sun lamps, iron injections, even antibiotics have been given as a remedy for the condition! The use of antibiotics to attempt to produce a black nose for show purposes is to be highly condemned, because the dog will gradually become immune to it and if a serious infection occurs the antibiotic necessary for treatment would just not work. Any attempt to correct the condition by artificial means is to be condemned. Any one caught by the Kennel Club would risk disciplinary action. Besides it is fraud. A good dog who appears in the ring at all times, with a jet black nose would be a very popular stud dog. Breeders would use him to improve the pigment of their puppies. If it has been artificially coloured the resulting puppies might be pink nosed and the bitch's owner would have wasted time, money and nervous energy on a fraud. The cause of lack of black pigment is possibly hormonal, because bitches feeding puppies usually have lovely black noses even if they are normally pink. The answer is not pills and potions but by breeding for colour. This will be dealt with in that chapter.

The head should not be coarse with exaggerated cheek bones, but should be the frame for the eyes, supposedly the mirror of the soul. The ideal Cavalier head is unique with its own characteristics and could never be confused with any other breed, even if my first Cavalier, who had a really beautiful head even by today's standard, was once described, to my horror, as a cross between a cocker spaniel and a pekingese!

The Cavalier's head should not be domed as a cocker or King Charles, or snipey as in a whippet or dachshund. It should not have houndy lips as in a bloodhound. It takes time to establish in your mind the correct interpretation. You will know the type you like, but do check with the standard from time to time that the type you prefer does conform and is not exaggerated in any way.

The male dog should have a masculine head, but it should not be overdone so as to appear coarse or bullish. A bitch should have a feminine face without being snipey. She should be small and pretty in the head as well as in the rest of the body. Doggy heads on bitches and vice versa are undesirable. A line up of champions would all show their individual look! Some may appear coarse, some snipey and mean, but all have been considered good enough by at least three different judges to get their title of champion! It is the unexaggerated pretty head that is the ideal. Remember that is why we have a standard to prevent any exaggeration one way or the other creeping in.

EYES: These are what give the Cavaliers their loving, gentle, sentimental expression. The eyes should be large, dark and well spaced apart. A lot of nonsense has been written and spoken about eye colour. Some have said it should blend with the coat colour and need not be that dark. I have even read a judge's show report that said 'Eye too dark'. Utter nonsense!

If the eye is dark and gives a mean 'boot button' expression, it is not the eye colour that is wrong, it is the shape of the eye. One doesn't want bulbous eyes. They are just as ugly as the small or the almond-shaped eye. A gentle smiling eye full of generosity and fun without any mean expression is what is required. My grandfather used to say 'Don't trust light eyed men or light eyed horses' and I will add 'light eyed Cavaliers', because they are not what is required by the breed standard. An eye which shows a lot of white is ugly. Although it is not listed as a fault in the Cavalier King Charles Spaniel of Great Britain standard, when the C.K.C.S. Club of the USA drew up their standard, they stated, in the first draft, that no white should be seen. However they very thoughtfully had their standard scrutinised by a veterinary surgeon to make sure that no point could be interpreted in such a way as to be detrimental to the health of the dog. It was pointed out to them that breeding for no white at all could produce a 'tight eye' which could result in health problems. The directive of 'No white should show' was dropped in favour of listing a white surrounding ring to the eye as a fault, but not a disqualifying one. Although not listed as even a fault in the British standard, if a Cavalier has a lot of white showing it does not possess the true Cavalier expression.

EARS: Usually if the top of the head is flat, the dog has good high set of ears. The low set ear usually goes with the rounded skull. Feathering on the ears does vary. Black and tans and tricolours always have had plenty. At one time many Blenheims and rubies had little feathering on the ears which did detract, but nowadays one sees lovely specimens in all four colours with beautiful glamorous ears framing the face. Care of the ear will be dealt with under grooming.

MOUTH: The standard states 'level' – that is the top teeth resting on top of the bottom, scissor bite preferred. Scissor bite is when the back of the top teeth just fits over the front of the bottom row. Undershot, where the bottom teeth are in front of the top teeth is a fault. Considering all Cavaliers have been bred from the King Charles where the desired mouth is undershot, it is remarkable that today the majority of Cavaliers have good mouths. This has been achieved by selective breeding. However it seems to go in cycles. One hears little about undershot teeth for a year or two, then suddenly there seems to be a plague of them. Recently several cases of overshot or pig jaws have been reported in many different colours and strains. This is where the top jaw is so far over the bottom jaw so there is a gap between the two rows of teeth. It is hard to imagine this when as recently as 1936 the flat faced King Charles Springvale Pharoah was in the Cavalier breeding programme and is behind most of the winning Cavaliers today.

Fig. 1. Mouth correct – scissor bite

Fig. 2. Mouth incorrect – undershot jaw

Puppies with perfect mouths at eight weeks can go undershot later and can sometimes become perfect again by the time they are a year old.

Fig. 3. Mouth incorrect
– overshot jaw

Undershot puppies can cut a perfect set of permanent teeth. Sometimes when cutting the second teeth, the mouth looks a dreadful higgledy-piggledy mess and it is a nail biting time for the owner until the puppy has finished teething and the baby teeth have fallen out to find if the teeth are perfectly placed. Some puppies do not shed their baby canine teeth, and they may have the permanent eye teeth growing beside the first ones. Keep an eye on this situation, as the extra teeth could cause over-crowding and put the permanent teeth out of alignment. It is an easy operation for the veterinary surgeon to remove the baby canines before any permanent damage is done.

NECK: 'Moderate length, slightly arched.' All dogs have seven vertebrae in the neck, the same number as man and even the giraffe! It is the length of each vertebra and the thickness of each intervertebral disc which gives the length of neck. The angle of the shoulder blade also influences the appearance of the neck. An upright shoulder gives a short bull neck appearance. The shoulder blade that is well laid back, not only gives the impression of length, but also gives a more elegant line and influences the head carriage and front movement by the use of stronger neck muscles. By raising the head the dog's front legs can stride out more freely and so improve the drive and style of movement. On the other hand if neck muscles are overdone one sees the undesirable hackney style. Well toned muscles, ligaments with thick discs and moderate length vertebrae all combine to give a slight arch at the crest of the neck and the graceful elegant look required by the standard.

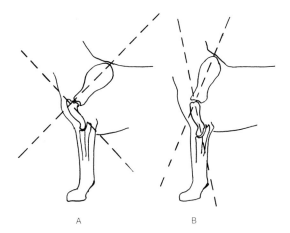

A   B

Fig. 4. (A) Correct well-laid shoulders and (B) incorrect upright shoulders

FOREQUARTERS: The standard states 'shoulders well laid back: leg moderate bone and straight'. We have dealt with shoulders under the heading of neck, as neck and shoulders are so interrelated! It is in the front end that Cavaliers have improved in the last few years. At one time there were many cowfronted specimens in the ring, particularly whole colours. They had very wide fronts, their elbows turned out and they even had bandy legs with feet turned out like P.C. 49! Selective breeding has almost eliminated these ugly faults. Nowadays most Cavaliers have straight fronts with neatly tucked in elbows, but occasionally one sees one of the old type. This should be enough to remind breeders to be vigilant and not allow this ugly fault to creep back.

If the width between the front legs is excessive the dog rotates his feet as he moves – a very ugly movement, but if there is insufficient width and both front legs seem to 'come out of the same hole', the dog will have a cramped front movement with a mincing gait.

A pin toed movement where the front feet point inwards is usually caused by excess weight on the shoulder and poorly developed hindquarters. However, the most perfectly constructed dog will turn his feet in if moving on a slippery surface. Hence a dog may move to perfection at an outdoor show, but when asked to walk on a slippery floor, or worse still a moving drugget, will turn his toes in to maintain his balance and grip.

Moderate bone means just that. Too fine bone gives a weedy spindly look, while too heavy bone gives a coarse inelegant appearance. The bones should be of good quality without any lumps and bumps and should be ricket free and straight. `

The lower part from the knee to the foot is known as the pastern. This needs to be straight. A dog who when standing has his feet ahead of his knees has a tired look. He is said to be 'down on his pasterns'. A dog with good straight strong pasterns gives the impression of being on his toes and is able to move with vigour. Weak pasterns can be anatomical weakness, but more often can be caused by insufficient exercise. A well exercised dog has good muscle tone which shows in his pasterns and feet. The feet should be well cushioned – that means thick pads! If the heart-shaped main pad of the foot is thin, the nails will not come in contact with the ground and will grow until they curl around and even grow into the front pads. If the main heart shaped pad is thick the nails will grow downwards and will be kept short by the filing action of striking the hard ground. Older dogs may gradually begin to grow long nails because their pads have lost their thickness and resilience. If young dogs, who are regularly exercised on hard surfaces, are continually needing their nails clipped, it is the shape of the main pad which is at fault. Long nails are very uncomfortable for the dog. They make the feet splay out and the dog walk with an awkward style, so see they are kept short – this is discussed under grooming.

BODY: The standard states 'Short coupled with plenty of spring of ribs, back level, chest moderate leaving ample heart room'. This makes breeding of Cavaliers so difficult as it is the length of each vertebra in the neck which determines the length of the neck, it would seem logical that the length of the vertebrae would determine the length of the body. So we need long vertebrae in the neck and short vertebrae in the body. This is true to a certain extent. If the shoulders are well laid back and the ribs well sprung the body will look compact. It is the length of the loin from the end of the ribs to the hindquarters which gives the length of the body. Coat markings on Blenheims and tricolours can give an optical illusion of length of neck and body. A white neck and shoulder with the colouring beginning well back and following the desired slope of the shoulder will give the impression of more neck. A small amount of white on the collar with colour following the undesirable line of an upright shoulder will spoil the general impression. This is where the table examination and the feeling of the bones is so important and 'ring side judging' often misleading. If the dog is carrying a heavy coat around the neck it can give a stuffy appearance. Unscrupulous exhibitors sometimes break the rules of the standard and use thinning scissors to thin out the neck hair. Once they cut that hair they will always be at it, because like a rose bush once pruned it will grow again thicker and curlier! No Cavalier should be trimmed. If this practice takes hold it won't be long before they are shaved down the neck like an American Cocker to give an exaggerated look!

Whole colours have neither the advantage of good markings nor the disadvantage of poor marking to give the illusion of a long (not over done) neck and short coupled body.

The dog has thirteen pairs of ribs. Nine pairs are attached to the sternum or breast bone. You can feel the ribs by running your hands over the dog's body. If the breast bone is short and the ribs cramped, it not only gives a longer loin, but less heart and lung room. The ribs should be slightly rounded. Again a happy medium is required. If the rounding is over done one gets a heavy barrel-shaped body, while if not enough rounding is present, one gets a thin slab-sided creature. Spring of rib must not be confused with excess weight. You should be able to move your fingers over the dog's ribs and feel each rib easily. If his coat appears tight and does not move easily as you feel, and if it is difficult to define each rib quickly your dog is too fat. However the vertebrae in the neck should be difficult to find because of the development of the neck muscles.

In an attempt to breed for longer necks some breeders have dogs with long rangey bodies. It should be remembered a Cavalier is a King Charles Spaniel – not a King Charles Setter! A good balance is obtained if the length of the body from the withers to the tail set is roughly equal to the height of withers from the ground.

The level back or top line is an important feature. Cavaliers are shown on a loose lead and not placed and held in positon as are cocker spaniels and setters. Those breeds can have their top lines held in place while standing propped up, but lose them when on the move. A Cavalier must show a level back both standing and when moving. If he dips at all times he is very likely long in the back or down on his pasterns. If he stands with a dip he is not 'standing tall' and really just standing slovenly. However if he tips his head right back to look at you, with his adoring eyes, this action could cause him to lose his top line. Hard exercise can improve this fault. If it is only a mannerism and not a structural fault, be on your guard not to allow your exhibit to make a habit of 'taking it easy' while standing, but to 'stand tall' with his pasterns straight, elbows tucked in and his back level! Not so easy!

Remember we require a dog which is balanced, neither stuffy in the neck nor long in the back. It is getting this balance correct which makes breeding good Cavaliers so difficult and so frustrating, but so rewarding when you do succeed.

HINDQUARTERS: Although a toy dog, the standard states that Cavaliers should be 'sporting, very gay and free in action', therefore they must have good strong well muscled hindquarters. The specific requirements for the hindquarters are 'legs with moderate bone, well turned stifle – no tendency to cow or sickle hocks'. The hindquarters are made up of several

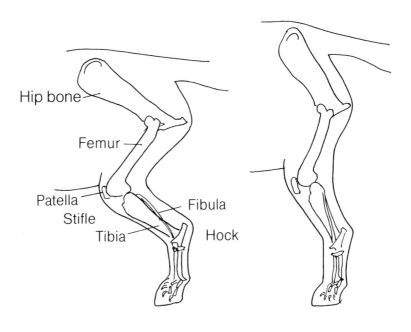

Hip bone

Femur

Patella
Stifle
Tibia

Fibula

Hock

Fig. 5. (A) Correct angles in hindquarters, giving a well bent stifle; (B) incorrect angles, giving a straight stifle

complicated joints namely the hip, the stifle or knee joint, the hock and all the joints in the feet. All play an important part in the movement. The look of the dog and indeed even the health and well-being of the dog are determined by sound hindquarters. Abnormalities of some of these joints appear in most breeds and how they could affect Cavaliers will be dealt with in a later chapter. A Cavalier with straight stifles looks unbalanced and unfinished. On the other hand an overdone stifle, so that the dog appears to crouch at the back end, is not desirable. A chubby rounded bottom with a well turned stifle and short hock is preferable to the spindly pinched hindquarters which lack drive. As with forequarters the angle of the bones of the hindquarters must be correct to give the dog a good stance and strong movement.

THE TAIL: The tail consists of the last few vertebrae of the spine. It can be docked with up to a third removed, but more and more breeders are leaving the tail entire. Some veterinary surgeons are refusing to dock tails. This is a doubtful policy until the docking of tails is made illegal or the showing of dogs with docked tails is prohibited by the Kennel Club. A veterinary surgeon uses his professional skill in docking and if he refuses, some breeders dock their own or their friends' puppies' tails with unfortunate results. Some even resort to the elastic band method where a rubber band is applied tightly to the end of the tail. It acts as a tourniquet, stops the blood supply and the end of the tail gradually withers and drops off – a very nasty procedure.

Although there is no mention in the standard how the tail should be carried, a Cavalier is certainly not well balanced if the tail is carried high or even curled over the back. The set of the tail is important. If the last few vertebrae before the tail (the sacrum) slope up, you will get a high tail carriage. No amount of tying weights, or hitting it with newspaper, or, horror of horrors, with a stick, will make a dog carry it level. It will only cow him and make him miserable. If the sacrum slopes away too quickly, you not only get a too low tail carriage, but usually a 'scuttly' rather restricted hind action which is contrary to the standard recommendation 'very gay and free in action'. The tail for which to aim, should be a continuation of the level top line of the back, well feathered and always wagging from side to side!

COATS: So far the standard has given us the framework. Now for the embroidery! A dog with the most perfect conformation does not appeal to me if the coat and markings are wrong. Equally a dog with perfect markings and the most perfect coat will be aesthetically wrong if it is badly constructed. Here, too, one must balance one point against the other. A breeder who goes all out to get perfect markings and loses the cobby, well balanced dog in the process is not improving the breed. In Cavaliers there are so many factors to get right to get the perfect dog. Long silky coats are a thing of beauty. The hair is fine and always has a sheen. Mud will drop out of it as soon as the coat is dry. If it is of the correct texture the coat is usually straight. The coarse coat tends to curl, does not have such a brilliant sheen and is usually more common in tricolours and whole colours rather than in Blenheims. The feathering on tricolours and black and tans is usually more prolific than on rubies or Blenheims, but in recent times one sees fewer featherless Blenheims or rubies.

A Cavalier should have the same perfect conformation whatever the colour. Whole colours should be able to stand the competition with broken colours. Although classifed as 'whole colour', the black and tan has, of course, two colours! The black should be a 'bluey black' and not a 'browny black'. It is surprising how many colour blacks there are! If you have several black and tans and tricolours living together, this will soon become evident. The tan on the black and tan should be rich, not yellowy. The tan eyebrows need to be well defined, while tan on the face should be evenly marked. Some have a tan bar at the end of the muzzle just before the nose, while on others the black hair goes right down to the nose. Legs, feet, ear linings, shirt fronts and feathering should be a rich tan, but often the tan in the tail and 'back petticoats' is less brilliant.

Ch. Millstone Beechking Tansy. Black and tan bitch born 17.6.70 by Millstone Eustace ex Highstead Renee owned by Mrs E.M. Booth. Bred by Mr & Mrs R. Clarke.

The ruby is the only true whole colour or self-colour. This should be a rich red, but not with a liver tinge. Although a dark colour this 'livery' tendency is not desirable nor is a light sandy orange colour. If a ruby is out of coat, he often looks pale and even speckled! When the new coat begins to grow it starts at the top of the body. One can assess the true colour as it gradually grows all over. A small amount of white on a shirt front should not, in my opinion, be a disqualifying fault in a whole colour, but taken into account when assessing the good and bad points of the dog. It will be noted that in the early standard 55 per cent of the marks were given for the head, ears, eyes, muzzle and nose, and only 5 per cent were given for marking and 5 per cent for coat! This is perhaps going too far the other way, but the perfect dog has yet to be born, so one must weigh up all the good points against the bad!

The aesthetic beauty of a Blenheim can be lost by unfortunate markings. The head colouring should be evenly divided. The pearly white should begin with the muzzle, continue between the eyes, and for perfection divide on the forehead to give the perfect spot or lozenge – or thumb mark. (Please do not call it a penny!) Lack of a blaze gives a rather sombre expression! The rich chestnut (not liver or even yellow tinted tan) should cover the eyes, the cheeks, and ears. White markings around the eyes are ugly and tan coming down further on one side of the face is equally unpleasant and in my opinion far more unattractive than white hairs on a whole colour's shirt front, because it gives an unbalanced look to the head.

The standard states rich chestnut markings, well broken up on a pearly white ground. Some Blenhiems could almost be mismarked rubies. They have white legs, tail, front, and possibly a thin white collar, but the main body is chestnut, rather like a horse blanket! Again when assessing the dog one must weigh up the points. Good markings can add to the general appearance by accentuating shoulder placement and length of couplings. The standard states that the white should be pearly white. That does not mean dazzling white like an advertisement for washing powder, but a subtle attractive soft shade of white. Dirty dingy coats, perhaps with yellow urine staining, should not be tolerated in any circumstances.

Tricolours are very attractive, but so difficult to breed with good markings. Think – three colours, all to be in that correct place in the correct amounts and with the correct intensity of colour! The tan must be

Ch. Barings Fortescue. Tricolour dog born 3.8.59 by Ch. Aloysius of Sunninghill ex Barings Angela. Owned and bred by Mrs M. Patten.

rich, again not livery or orangey, giving well defined eyebrows, ear linings, chests and under-the-tail markings. If a Cavalier has a white rump and the base of the tail is white, the tan markings are usually absent from this area. The body markings should be well broken with black and white. Many a tricolour has been condemned for being too heavily marked, but if the same markings were transferred to a Blenheim, he would get away with it! Some markings can emphasise points as with Blenheims. An owner once complained to a very experienced judge and breeder that the black markings of her dog which came down over the hock made it look as if her dog moved badly. The judge replied that if a judge could not tell the difference between markings and movement, they had no business to be judging and their opinion of the dog was worthless anyway!

A most unattractive feature of some broken colours is flecking or even roaning where the white hair is mingled with the coloured. One aims at clearly defined coloured and white patches with no hazy tweedy areas. Many pet owners love freckles on the muzzle. For exhibition a clear white muzzle is preferred with perhaps one or two at the most 'beauty spots'. How many breeders running on promising puppies have looked anxiously at the muzzles to see if any freckles are appearing and to count them frantically if they do appear. The relief when they stop at two or three and the frustration if they go on appearing! Luckily with selective breeding, one sees less really freckled faces on the present day Blenheims. However, recently tricolour body markings have improved, but the faces are often very smudgy and unattractive. Markings are after all the 'paint work' of dogs, and although I would not refuse an award to a dog out of hand for its markings, if they do detract from the all over attractiveness and the appeal of the dog, then I would.

In the original standard, black and whites were permitted but not desirable. These are marked like tricolours, but all the tan markings are missing. However in 1973 the standard was altered and after listing the four colours of all King Charles Spaniels, namely, black and tan, ruby, Blenheim and tricolour, the following was added: 'Any other colour or combination of colours is most undesirable'.

In the fifties and sixties one used occasionally to see most oddly coloured Cavaliers, black and whites and blacks were uncommon but could be easily be found. More odd were liver tricolours whereas the conventional tricolour is black, white and tan, these were liver, white and tan! They looked quite attractive until they turned and looked at you. Because they carry no gene for black, they had horrid yellow boiled gooseberry eyes and dreadful pink noses. Occasionally in the past, one could get a wall eyed Cavalier. The eye was blue. They usually had no tan or black around the eye. This gave them a very foreign expression.

WEIGHT: This is a problem. 12 to 18lbs (5.45 to 8.2kg) gives a lot of leeway. The majority of Cavaliers are in the 17 to 18lbs and over range, rather than in the 12 to 15lbs range. Fifteen pounds looks very small. The reduction of size should be the aim without losing stamina and the characteristics of the breed. No one wants weedy, unsound runty Cavaliers, but the well proportioned, gay, sporting little toy dogs should be the goal of all breeders.

MOVEMENT: The Cavalier has 319 bones in his contruction. If they are all in the correct places at the correct angles with the muscles and ligaments that go with them you are on the way to getting your perfect Cavalier. We are lucky that our standard does not allow any exaggerations such as long backs, over angulated hindquarters or short bowed front legs. Because the Cavalier body and limbs are in proportion, one should get a free flowing movement. The well laid-back shoulders and proud head carriage produce the light effortless action which gives the impression of spontaneous gaiety. The dog appears light on his feet, full of energy and raring to go. The dog with the upright shoulder holds his head badly and merely plods around the ring as if he has all the cares of the world on his shoulders. The majority fall between the two! For a really true movement the fore and hindquarters must work together.

If your Cavalier's conformation is poor he will not move 'like a dream', but even if his conformation is perfect, he will not necessarily do so either. Mannerisms creep in! An apprehensive dog scuttles along with his tail well down. Some dogs are just lazy and bored and will not move with any animation. Some are over exuberant and throw away their chances. The surface of the floor can also affect some. The clever owner is the one who studies his dog's movement and with the aid of a friend finds which is the best speed at which he must move so that the dog is not impeded by his owner's movement. How many times has one heard a disappointed exhibitor, after his young hopeful has thrown away his chances, complain 'He moves beautifully at home!' I expect he does because he is moving at his own pace and on a surface with which he is familiar.

The list of faults in the modern standard is self-explanatory, but when assessing Cavaliers one should weigh up all the good and bad points and find one that conforms most closely to the standard. The perfect dog has yet to be born. It is a long, often disappointing, task to improve, but compare the picture of the two tricolours, Bridget of Ttiweh and Ch. Baridene Royal Serenade of Charlesworth. Note the improvement in the markings, the quality of coat and outline – all in fifty years.

The only fault I would condemn out of hand would be bad temperament. Any dog which is snappy, noisy, nervous or bad tempered should be penalised, because that trait is so uncharacteristic of the Cavalier and must never become one.

In the thirties the following was added to the standard. Although it was intended as a postscript for novices, it should be taken to heart by all present day Cavalier owners, both novices and experienced breeders alike.

Breed standard: for novices only

In the Cavalier we have a little dog of ideal temperament for nearly all purposes. He is sporting – many of them have been successfully trained to the gun – he is an excellent child's companion; always ready to play – he is equally happy as the much loved and spoiled house pet. In breeding we want to remember this and to try never to lose this delightful happy nature. In so many show breeds that were immune from nerves one now sees nervousness amounting in many cases to panic and snappiness, and therefore we Cavalier breeders have been warned in time and must not let this happen to our breed. The Cavalier is also extremely hardy and must never be allowed to become anything else. Avoid all physical structural weaknesses, shelly bodies, cramped hindquarters with restricted action, pinched pelvises, narrow terrier heads with small mean eyes – all are hereditary faults, easier to breed in than out.

After reading all this, I hope you know what a perfect Cavalier should be. May I wish you luck in trying to produce one!

4 Choosing a Puppy and making him 'At Home'

IT is possible if you are reading this book that you have already purchased a Cavalier, but be patient if you have, while we consider the pitfalls for those contemplating acquiring a puppy for the first time. Besides if you have a Cavalier already, it is very likely you are wanting a second or even third!

Before buying any dog there should be a family conference to decide 'Do you really need a dog?' It is an important and serious matter to add a new member to a family and that is what one does when one takes on a dog. Every member of the family should be wanting him and should agree on the breed. How often the rescue services hear stories of the wife not wanting the puppy or that the husband cannot stand dogs, yet the other partner has gone ahead and purchased a puppy. Very soon there is another unhappy situation and another dog needs rehousing.

Have you the facilities to cope with a puppy? Remember the Cavalier is an active sporting dog and needs a garden so that he can run off his energy. Although classified as a Toy Dog, a town flat without a garden is not the place for any Cavalier. Puppies inadequately exercised become bored and soon find some mischief to perpetrate.

Is the garden securely fenced? Cavaliers are an inquisitive breed and will find any small hole to escape and explore the world.

One hears of people buying a puppy, leaving home at 8.30 am and not returning until 5.30 pm. It is just not fair to leave a puppy for that length of time. If you have to be out for more than two or three hours daily it would be better to buy two puppies so that they have companionship. They play together, exercise each other and it must be a happier situation to have one of your own species as a companion. Of course it has disadvantages as it is more difficult to house-train two puppies. Even with two puppies, do not leave them unattended for more than three or four hours.

One can often find an active pensioner, or a young mother tied to her home with young children who is trustworthy and fond of dogs. They will often be very willing to spare an hour at midday to pop in, feed the puppies and let them have a run in the garden. By this method, you can have the pleasure of owning the puppies and know they are being cared for while you are out.

If you cannot cope with two puppies, nor find a puppy minder for mid-

Puppies born mid thirties.

day, it would be unkind to go ahead and just buy a puppy. In fact most reputable breeders would not sell you one when they found out the circumstances in which you hoped to keep one of their precious puppies. If you are going to be out a lot arrange to have a few days at home when the puppies first arrive. They soon become accustomed to your routine and you can train your puppy minder to follow your pattern.

Remember there is a very vocal anti-dog lobby and it is up to every Cavalier owner to promote a good image for the breed and dogs in general. Puppies left to howl and cry do not reflect well.

Here is a simple dog owner's code which if obeyed will bring pleasure to you and enhance the image of Cavaliers in the eyes of the public. Remember your dog should at no time be a nuisance to any member of the public and it is up to you so see that he isn't. If by any chance your dog does transgress, don't be beligerent about it, but apologise and make reparations for his misdemeanours!

Dog owner's code

1 Do not allow your dog to foul buildings, pavements, lawns and gardens or open spaces where children play.

2 Never take your dog into a food shop.
3 Provide your dog with its own bed.
4 Feed your dog at regular times, and do not give titbits between meals.
5 Feed your dog from its own dishes, which must be kept apart from those of the family, and washed separately.
6 Keep your dog clean and regularly groomed.
7 Train your dog in elementary obedience so that he is under control at all times.
8 Do not allow your dog to be noisy to the disturbance of your neighbours.
9 Keep your dog on a lead anywhere near a road, or where there are farm animals.
10 If you do not wish your dog to have puppies, you should obtain advice from your veterinary surgeon.
11 Make proper arrangements for the care of your pet, when you are going on holiday.
12 Register your pet as a patient and yourself as a client with a veterinary surgeon of your choice. Do not wait for an emergency.

All is well! You can obey the Dog Owner's Code and all members of the family are willing to welcome a new member to the household. How do you go about acquiring this new addition? Always go to a specialist breeder where you can see the puppy's mother and possibly grandmother and various members of its family. You may not be able to see the father of the puppies because dedicated breeders will often travel hundreds of miles to use the dog which they think will fit in with their bitch.

You can find the names and addresses of specialist breeders in your area by asking the Kennel Club or by asking your local veterinary surgeon. If there is no Cavalier breeder locally, the local Canine Society would very likely help you by giving you the address of the nearest Cavalier Club in your region. Nowadays there are regional clubs in all parts of the British Isles. Even so, you may have to travel at least fifty or sixty miles to get the type of puppy you require. If this distance is too far, do you really want a Cavalier?

Most Cavalier breeders have puppies because they love the breed and rear them with love and care and often at considerable cost to themselves, both financial and physical. Those who rear the puppies in the house lavish much love on them. The puppies become socialised early by having people around them all the time and by hearing the household noises from their birth. Such breeders usually only have one litter at a time and so you may have very little choice.

A breeder with a larger kennel usually has pet puppies for sale, which have to be up to standard in health because the sale of these puppies is essential to finance the running cost of their kennels and the prospective show puppies. But do beware of establishments which smack of commercialism. The buying in of litters of both Cavaliers and other breeds from other breeders is to be viewed with suspicion.

Make up your mind what you are wanting to buy before you contact the breeder. We have all heard of cases of clients coming to buy a Blenheim bitch and going home with a black and tan dog! Telephone calls on these lines are quite common.

'Do you do King Charles Spaniels?'
'Well breed, Cavalier King Charles Spaniels.'

Then the poor breeder has to go into a long explanation on the difference! You of course know that you want a Cavalier! The next question will be what colour appeals to you. You can see from the standard that there are four colours, and colour is really personal preference.

The next question will be 'Do you want a male or female?' There are advantages and disadvantages in both. Luckily male Cavalier dogs are not usually aggressive sexy dogs and can be very loving and affectionate. If you really do not want to breed, a male dog can be a really excellent companion. When fully grown with a really well groomed coat, a male Cavalier can be very handsome indeed.

With a bitch one has to weigh up the inconvenience of the twice yearly season. I feel it is a pity to buy a bitch to have her spayed just because of the inconvenience of the season. A spayed bitch often becomes very greedy and easily puts on weight. Also she will grow an enormous coat which will need a lot of care. If there is a veterinary reason for a bitch to be spayed that is a different matter.

If you decide to buy a bitch search your heart very deeply. If you think there is the slightest possibility that you would want to breed from her do NOT buy a substandard puppy with a major fault or one whose litter mates have a major fault. If you think you may possibly breed even one litter, buy the best you can. Do tell the breeder what you want. If you are not going to show, but perhaps breed a litter or two, breeders often have extremely well bred bitches with a minor fault – unfortunately marked perhaps or a little too big for the show ring, who would make excellent brood bitches and sometimes produce better puppies than their more glamorous sisters who win well in the ring.

If you are wanting a show quality puppy you may have to go on a breeder's waiting list and even then be disappointed when the much hoped for litter arrives and the well marked tricolour bitch you ordered months ago is the only one in the litter to be undershot!

Study the breed standard which is discussed in Chapter 3 before committing yourself to a prospective show puppy. If you are not sure how to interpret 'shoulders well laid back', or any other point, ask at the shows.

Puppies born 1978.

Most exhibitors are only too pleased to show you the points of their dogs. Ask the owner whose dog has an 'air of importance' about him. Usually their dog will have good conformation. However, to make sure you understand the point do ask several exhibitors. Do pick a convenient time, not when the poor owner is changing dogs between classes and trying to get to the ring before the next class is judged. After judging is over is usually a convenient time.

Well the great day has come and you are going to see your puppy. Do not be surprised if the breeder puts you through the third degree! Someone who has lavished love on their bitches and the puppies is very concerned about the type of home you can offer. By that I mean they are not concerned if you live in a stately home or a 'semi', but whether it is going to be another member of the family and not just an animated teddy bear or just 'the dog'.

Puppies from reliable sources are often booked before they are born. The breeder may allow you to see the litter before they are ready to leave home. Sometimes you may be told you can have one of them, but the actual individual would not be decided until later. That is fair enough but do make sure when you collect your puppy you are not fobbed off with the runt – unless of course, that is the one you prefer.

Some breeders ask for a deposit as an act of good faith on both sides. Personally I do not. If the prospective owners come back for the puppy only because they have paid a deposit they are not suitable owners for one of my precious puppies. Of course I have been let down, but I often find if a sale falls through there is always an extra super home waiting around the corner.

You may pick a puppy at 4 to 5 weeks old, but unless it has some very distinctive markings you probably wouldn't know which one it was when you go back to collect it at eight weeks, especially with black and tans and rubies. Even with Blenheims the colour deepens. With tricolours the black hair encroaches over the white at an alarming speed so that often the markings look quite different from the puppy you saw a week or two earlier.

Gentian violet marks on the tummy, nail varnish on the nails, or cutting the curly hair of the end of the tail will mark a puppy with your code! It is not very satisfactory and you will have to trust the breeder that the puppy she said you could have when it was five weeks old is the one you have at eight weeks.

You may be going to a large kennels where the puppies and their mothers are not in the house. Note how tidy the premises are and how much attention is paid to hygiene. If you are asked to wipe your feet on a disinfectant pad or put your feet in polythene bags, do not be offended but commend the owner for their precautions against disease. More disease is carried on shoes than in any other way. I recently heard of a litter of Irish Setter puppies who developed parvo-virus and the source of infection was traced to prospective puppy buyers from many miles away, bringing the virus on their shoes.

If the puppies are house reared, again note the attention to hygiene. There should not be a nasty stale urine smell and cleanliness should be of the highest standard. Don't worry if today's dusting hadn't been done because puppy rearing is time consuming, but the general overall standard of cleanliness is important.

If the puppies are six weeks or older, their mother may not be living with them any more, but do ask to see her. After rearing a litter she will look bedraggled. Her coat will be coming out and she may look thin. However she should be lively and pleased to show you her family. Cavalier bitches are usually excellent mothers and love to play with their puppies long after they are fully weaned. Note any fault the mother may have, such as light eyes, and look for that fault in her puppies.

Whether you are wanting a pet, a brood bitch or a top show dog, the chief point is temperament. If the puppies disappear into their box screaming when you approach, do be very firm with yourself and don't buy one. If the mother and other near relations do not stop barking at you when told to by the owner, or if they run off and hide and eye you suspiciously from behind a bush, again do not buy a puppy from that source or strain. Cavaliers are friendly happy little dogs and should be pleased to see you in their charming welcoming manner. The puppies should be gay and come towards you with their tails wagging. If the Cavaliers you see give you an impression of a happy contented family that is fine.

Whatever type of puppy you are thinking of buying you will want it to be healthy. It should have bright, clear eyes, no discharges from the nose or mouth. Look inside the ear flaps. If there is a browny deposit or a cheesy smell, it is likely that the puppy has ear mites. The coat should be clean, but if the puppies have newspaper on the floor of their quarters, the printing ink does come off and give a grey appearance to the white on Blenheims and tricolours. Turn the coat back and make sure the puppy has a clean skin, with no tell-tale flea droppings or lice incrustations in the ear flaps. Look under the tail to make sure there is no dried-on diarrhoea to suggest it has had a bad tummy upset.

Many Cavalier puppies are born with hernias. If they are umbilical, i.e. a small amount of fat or tissue bulging through the umbilicial ring, and are small there is no need to worry. This will very likely disappear as the puppy grows and cause no problems. If they are excessively big or of the inguinal type beware! Puppies with this type of hernia should not be bred from and may well need a surgical operation later to correct the fault. Reliable breeders should point out any such fault to their client and reduce the price. Some will keep the puppy until he is old enough to have the operation before selling. Breeders should warn their clients that some veterinary surgeons unfamiliar with Cavaliers are very alarmist when confronted with a puppy with a hernia, even a small umbilical one. If it is small don't rush into an expensive operation, it will most likely disappear and give no trouble.

Puppies should be well covered, but not grossly fat. They most certainly shouldn't be pot bellied, but firm, active and really glowing with health and energy. Their legs should be well boned without being too heavy, but they should be straight and not bowed as if they were rickety.

If the temperament and health seem satisfactory, how are you to choose between all the engaging little creatures? You should have discussed your wants with the breeder. You should certainly be guided by her if you are wanting a prospective show puppy. However all the breeder can do is to tell you which puppy she considers the most promising at its present age. Puppies do change so much and when they are fully grown, the least promising puppy can overtake its litter mates! No reputable breeder will guarantee a puppy will be a show puppy, she can only say it is a promising specimen. So much can go wrong before the puppy is fully grown. It may go undershot, it may grow too big, it may not show and may lack that quality which makes all the difference. One can often see this quality in a young puppy. The way it moves, the way it holds its head with that extra confidence and elegance which makes a good dog a better one.

An obvious fault is marking. If you are buying a black and tan or ruby there should be no white, but often young puppies have white toe tips, a small star on the forehead or a white shirt front. Usually the white toe tips and small stars disappear. If the shirt front is a small spot or a thin white line, that will disappear. White covering all over the toes, a wide blaze between the eyes and wide shirt fronts will not completely disappear, although it will lessen considerably.

Tricolours and Blenheims should have a fairly wide blaze between the eyes because narrow white pencil lines disappear. The muzzle should be white without freckles or patches. Tricolours should have tan eyebrows, tan cheek markings and ear linings and tan under the tail. The black and white body markings should be half black and half white, but if the puppy has a lot of white do turn back the coat, and if you see black spots on the skin or black hairs coming in beware as that puppy may be developing ticking on the white – not very attractive and frowned on in the ring. Check that a tricolour has tan markings under the tail. A tricolour without black near the tail base often has no tan under the tail.

Blenheims should be well broken in colour approximately half tan and half white in attractive markings. The head markings should be even with tan patches over the eyes. As with the tricolour the muzzle should be white without freckles and patches. Blenheim puppies often look pale in colour and the tan deepens as they grow older.

The nose should be black. Puppies are born with pink noses and these gradually go black. By eight weeks they should be filled in, but it sometimes takes longer to go completely black. Often those slow to fill in do go jet black and keep their colour at all times. Those who go dark quickly but have a browny tinge to them often go off colour during seasons (bitches) and in cold weather, and then never regain the desired blackness.

The eye colour of puppies is difficult to assess. If they have a yellowy tinge they will probably be light eyed when grown up. Puppies with navy blue eyes usually have dark eyes when adult. They should be round and have a kind expression, not bulbous or staring. Small boot button eyes give a horrid mean expression.

Mouths are a problem even these days. If you remember the history and how all Cavaliers come from short faced King Charles, it is not surprising we still get undershot puppies. By breeding from good mouthed stock for generations it is less of a problem, but it is odd that it goes in cycles. We can have several years when mouths are all perfect and then suddenly a crop of bad mouths turn up. Do remember the term 'bad mouth' applies to the jaw and tooth placement not some infection (see the standard). It is no guarantee that a puppy with a perfect mouth at eight weeks will have a perfect mouth when adult or vice versa. An interesting article appeared in the C.K.C.S. Club *Bulletin* for Spring 1962 on how to choose a puppy.

Mrs Keswick of Pargeter Cavaliers wrote: 'Pick a puppy at six weeks with a broad head dark large eyes. If a Blenheim I shall pick a heavily marked one but with good and even markings on the face. Good bone, but not too much. Feet not too large and UNDERSHOT.'

Miss Marshall of Kormar wrote in the same article: 'Look at the jaws at three weeks; in general a puppy begins as he finishes. Right at three weeks usually ends up with a correct mouth by two years.' Mrs Patten, owner of the very successful Barings Cavaliers of the 1950s and 1960s wrote 'Look for one with a lovely sentimental expression, large dark eyes, and high set

Puppies born 1982.

ears. The mouth should NOT be undershot, I repeat not undershot.'

So you see, even the experts disagree! Of course they knew their own lines and knew which type stood a chance of being perfect when adult! Take the advice of the breeder as I have said before. They wouldn't want you to show a substandard puppy registered with their prefix. They would want your puppy to be a credit to them as well as to you.

Pick a medium sized dog with pretty head, not snipey but well filled in under the eyes. A good flat head is desirable (don't forget they are all descended from the domed headed King Charles and this fault does turn up). Above all choose a puppy with that heart-melting expression of the true Cavalier. You want a puppy with an elegant neck with a crest and not one whose head seems to grow out of its shoulders. You want a neat cobby body, good straight front legs which leave plenty of chest room and do not give the impression of both legs coming out of the same hole. Neither do you want a 'cow fronted' chest with legs wide apart to give a clumsy appearance. The puppy should have good strong hindquarters and really use his hind legs with drive when he is playing and running about.

Tail carriage is difficult to assess in puppies. To help balance while running and playing, young puppies often carry their tails higher than they would do when adults, but a tail curled right over the back should be viewed with suspicion. Many more breeders are leaving the tails undocked and this is the reason more curly tails are being seen in the ring.

If you are buying a male puppy for show and breeding you will want to make sure he is entire. That means that both his testicles are descended into the scrotum. At 6 to 8 weeks this is sometimes difficult to assess, but they feel like small peas between the thighs. Usually they are there by two months. There are many stories of breeders running on promising dog puppies. By the time they are seven or eight months old either one or both testicles have not appeared. After extensive vet examinations, these puppies have been sold as pets. On seeing the puppy two or three months later he is entire, and would have brought great glory to the Kennels. Usually his new owner is not interested in showing him or using him at stud – so very frustrating!

You have decided on your puppy. Conscientious breeders will give you a diet sheet and a list of 'do's and don'ts'. Read it through and make sure you understand it. Puppies should be having four meals a day, but the diet sheet should explain how gradually to reduce this to one meal by the time the puppy is adult. I recently heard of a nine-year old Old English Sheepdog still having four meals daily as he did when nine weeks old. I must say he looked well on it, but I would not recommend this for your Cavalier.

You should also receive a copy of the puppy's pedigree. Do ask for the colours of his ancestors to be put in. Even if of no interest to you, it may well be to anyone buying one of your puppies later on. Champions are usually written in red. It is not very likely that the breeder will have the Kennel Club Registration Card and transfer form to give you if the puppy is only eight weeks old. Breeders often wait until the puppies are four to five weeks old before registering them, and it takes the Kennel Club several weeks to check the details and issue the certificate. Make sure that the puppies will either be on the active register (that is registered with the breeder's affix and a name) or at the very least the litter has been registered. In that case you can register the puppy with your choice of name. Even in these days when registration is expensive, I feel if the breeders do not register their stock they are not proud enough of the puppies for them to carry their affix and this should be viewed with suspicion. If the breeder is selling a puppy with an obvious fault and it would be detrimental to the breed to breed from such an animal, that is a different matter. It would then be ethical for the breeder not to register the puppy or to register it 'Not for breeding purposes'. If a breeder offers you such a puppy, make sure that is what you want. Do not buy such a puppy just because it is cheaper. It may be more expensive in the long run if you have large veterinary bills, and distressing to you and your family if the puppy is not fully fit. Because a puppy is registered with the Kennel Club it is no guarantee that it is a good puppy because the Kennel Club does not inspect kennels. Registration really means that the parents were registered and so were their parents and so back to King Charles Spaniels, Rangers Nicky Picky and Ann's Son!

Progeny from unregistered stock cannot be registered and unregistered stock cannot be shown at any type of show held under the Kennel Club jurisdiction, except at Exemption Shows. They are called 'Exemption Shows' because exhibits need not be registered at the Kennel Club and such shows are exempt from the Kennel Club Rules. They are often held in the summer at fêtes and flower shows and are great fun. So you can see it is quite important to make sure your puppy is registered if you wish to breed, or show at Kennel Club licenced shows.

Vaccination and worming

Much research is being carried out into the best methods of vaccinating young puppies against parvo-virus, hard pad, distemper, leptospirosis and hepatitis, so your new puppy may or may not have had his preliminary vaccinations. If he has had some, but not the complete course, ask the breeder for the certificates from her veterinary surgeon so that you can take them to your veterinary surgeon. For satisfactory results your vet must know exactly what vaccine your puppy has had. Ideas are changing almost daily on the best methods needed to give puppies the maximum protection against these deadly diseases, so consult your veterinary surgeon to make sure your puppy has had all the necessary vaccinations before you let him meet other dogs.

We will deal with worms in greater detail in another chapter, but do ask if the puppy has been wormed and how many times. By the time he is eight weeks old, he should have had at least three doses. Don't be alarmed! Modern worming medicines are very safe and easy on the puppy, not like the dynamite compounds used in the past when worms were blasted out!

The puppy at home

With all these points settled you pay up and become the proud owner of a Cavalier King Charles Spaniel! The journey home could be quite horrific for the puppy. If possible do have a companion with you. Let her do the driving and you have the puppy on your lap to cuddle and reassure. I well remember buying a very confident puppy, but once in the car she hid her head under my arm, only lifting it up when the car stopped to see if it really was as bad as all that! Immediately the car started off again she hid her head again. Once we arrived home she became the self-possessed puppy we had chosen and then ruled over our household with a rod of iron and humour for the next twelve years.

If you have to collect the puppy on your own, do take a high sided box with a warm woolly in it. Place it on the floor by the passenger's seat. He is near enough for you to talk to him and reassure him and at the same time he cannot escape and wander around among the foot pedals – usually the motion of the car will send him to sleep. Once at home let the puppy settle in quietly before hordes of admiring friends and relations arrive. A trot in the garden, a drink of milk and a nap in his bed will soon restore his confidence. If he has been car sick, a teaspoonful of glucose added to the milk can be beneficial.

Do not spend a lot of money on expensive baskets or dog beds at this stage. A clean cardboard box, with one side cut down, and one of the family's old woolly jumpers makes an excellent bed. This can be renewed when necessary, usually when the sides have been well and truly chewed. When the puppy has stopped teething is the time to buy him a purpose-made bed. This could be for his first birthday present. There are many types on the market. If you are likely to take the Cavalier and his bed away for nights, the folding camp bed type is excellent. This can be folded flat, the frame is indestructable and the canvasses can be washed and renewed. They are expensive to buy but will out last several generations of Cavaliers. Wicker work baskets are traditional but are hard on owner's tights and very chewsome. Fibre glass beds and bean bags (a thick canvas type material filled with polystyrene pellets) are now popular. If you have room and the kitchen is draughty an enclosed travelling box type of bed is very useful. Modern ones are made of fibre glass. They are strong and light to move, and easy to clean. Cavaliers like to sleep in an enclosed area and do also love to sit up high. They can sleep in the box or sit on top to see what is going on! They are very inquisitive and love to watch the coming and going of their family. It is often useful to have a closed box that you can shut your puppy or adult in for a while. I am certainly not advocating that he should be confined to a box for long periods, but for a short time such as when he comes in wet and muddy. Rub him down with a towel, then pop him in the box until he is completely dry. Do remember to give him a clean dry blanket after he has dried out.

If you have one or even two Cavaliers, old woollies or pieces of blanket which friends bequeath make excellent bedding. There are now on the market many makes of synthetic fabric looking like sheepskin. These are first class bedding. All the moisture goes through, and so the animal is always on a dry bed. They also make excellent toys and have uses their manufacturers never dreamed of! They are indestructible and light and so make excellent tug of war ropes. The dog can dig in them, shake them and have hours of fun with them before collapsing tired out to sleep on them. They soon lose their pristine whiteness but can be easily washed in a washing machine and quickly dried. Above all they are extremely comfortable and warm. I was given one to lie on while in hospital and so can speak from personal experience!

The folding wire cage is also very useful for it can be folded away when not in use. The dog can see what is going on from all angles while he is confined, but they can be draughty!

If your new puppy is to sleep in the kitchen, make a small pen so that he doesn't wander and get lost. He will miss his family and be very lonely for the first few nights. Be patient with him if he does cry. Give him a soft cuddly toy or slipper and put an old clock in his bed. The regular tick of the clock could feel like his litter mates heart beats while a soft cuddly toy or sheepskin slipper would feel comforting.

Some people take the puppy to bed with them. Still confine him to a pen if you do. Remember he isn't house trained and the night is long! If he awakes you can comfort him, but unless you wish him always to sleep in your room, this is not a good policy to encourage. You will only have to break him into sleeping in the kitchen later. Habits once formed are hard to break. I really think it is easier to tuck him up in a warm bed in the kitchen, turn a deaf ear to his complaints, and you will find in two or three nights he has accepted his new way of life and will soon become used to the new routine.

House training

House training should begin straight away. Always put the puppy out in the garden immediately he awakes and immediately he has finished his meals. Once he performs in the desired place praise him lavishly. If he transgresses put him out at once, even if it does seem too late. Disinfect the spot well where he has made his mistake, so that he is not attracted to use that place again. A squirt from the soda syphon removes smell and reduces stains if used quickly after the misdeed. If the puppy repeatedly uses his, and not your chosen spot, I have heard it recommended that you give him his meals in that place. He is supposed to be keen to eat and certainly will not foul his dining area. I have not tried this, but if you do have a problem in encouraging your puppy away from an unsuitable place, it could be worth experimenting.

You will soon know the signs that he wants to go out. He will walk around in circles and look uncomfortable. Pick him up at once and put him out. You may have to wait a few minutes for any results, but do be patient. Time spent in the early stages of house training are well worthwhile.

Put newspaper in his play pen when you have to leave him for any length of time, and he will use that. Later when he has the run of the kitchen and if he has to be left, put down a sheet of newspaper and he will use that. Some puppies will spend time in the garden and then come indoors and use the newspaper. If he does this, put a piece of paper in the garden and they will often go to that. It should hardly be necessary to say that one should clear up the garden after your Cavalier has performed. A shovel and plastic bucket can be kept for this purpose and the debris flushed away. If you have several dogs, excrement can be put into a container with a chemical fluid used in caravan lavatories, and when the fluid exhausted, this can be washed down the main drains as one would with a caravan lavatory. There are purpose built dog loos available but one hears conflicting reports of the efficiency of them. Burning makes a nasty smell and certainly should not be undertaken unless your bonfire is a long way from any dwellings.

Nothing gives a worse image of a doggy household than a stale urine smell. A large shaggy mop, kept in a mop bucket to which either a disinfectant or household bleach has been added, can quickly and efficiently deal with puddles on patios and walls if the male dog has lifted his leg. It is more difficult to deal with lawns and bushes, but there are sprays available which discourage dogs from fouling such areas.

Remember a puppy can play only for short periods and then he will need a long period of sleep if he is to grow strong and healthy. After hectic games in the garden with either a human or doggy companion he should be allowed a quiet period in his pen and a good sound sleep. Cavalier puppies are so pretty and endearing that if you have children they *must* be taught from the beginning that the puppy is a living creature and must not be treated as an animated teddy bear.

Ensure that your puppy always has plenty of fresh clean drinking water available in a suitable container so that he will not knock it over. There are many purpose-made types of the market. The heavy based earthenware ones with high sloping sides are ideal. The puppy can neither carry it around nor paddle in it! The breeder should have given you a diet sheet. Stick to it for a few days however unsuitable you think it is, and gradually change over to your regime.

Early training

Soon a soft cat collar could be put on the puppy so that he becomes used to something around his neck from an early age. On no account should he ever be dragged along the pavement on a collar and lead, or even less in a 'harness'. Games in the garden to get him used to being on the lead cannot begin too soon. If you have another dog, he will often join in the fun and lead the puppy around. Never pull the puppy roughly as this will make him . hate the lead. Make lessons fun with plenty of love and encouragement. Never, never lose your temper with a puppy. Never take a dog out on to the roads or where he can come in contact with other dogs until he has been fully vaccinated. Once he is fully vaccinated take him to the local dog training classes. They are held in most areas. Find out about them several weeks ahead of going, because they often have waiting lists. Some run a course of six or eight weeks for puppies and you can only join at the beginning of such a course.

Clubs have different ways of introducing new puppies to formal lessons. It is important that he absorbs the atmosphere quietly so for a few meetings just let the puppy sit on your lap watching the proceedings. Cavaliers are very inquisitive and enjoy the activity going on around them. They are so appealing that many people will come and talk to them – all good confidence building. On the advice of the trainer gradually join in. Tell them if you want to show your dog and they will modify the 'sit'. Nothing is more annoying than a potential show dog who sits the moment his owner stands still. Even if you do not wish to take part in competitive obedience, a well trained dog will bring you great joy, but a badly behaved disobedient animal will be a trouble to you and others. Remember the dog code and see your Cavalier obeys it. Once when training gundogs I was startled when the trainer, a very famous gundog man in his day, declared there were no bad dogs only bad owners. This is rather thought provoking! Make sure your Cavalier doesn't make you a bad owner.

When your Cavalier is lead trained and you wish to take him out in public, make sure he behaves as a Royal dog should. Never allow him to foul the pavement. By this time you should know the signs that he is going to defecate. A Cavalier is small enough to pick up and put in the gutter to perform. Remember you are going to be a responsible owner. If the bye-laws decree that dogs should be kept on the lead or even barred in the public parks, do obey the rules. Do not allow him to run and chase in the flower beds and most certainly never allow him to foul the children's play areas. Even if the dangers of Toxicanae Canus have been greatly exaggerated, it is very unpleasant for children to find dog faeces where they play. There is no need to antagonise the anti-dog lobby and give dog opponents genuine fuel for their complaints.

Do not allow your puppy to get into bad habits in the house. Train him as you wish him to behave from the beginning. Never give him titbits from the table. It is annoying for family and guests to have a dog begging for food at the meal time. If he is not to be allowed on the furniture make it clear from the beginning. Let him have his own bed in the sitting room where he can feel at home. It is very hard on a dog who as a puppy is allowed to climb on furniture, sleep on his owner's bed, pester for food at mealtime, to find later he is forbidden to do these things.

I once sold a puppy to a very over indulgent home where she was given the run of the house, sat on the furniture, watched the television sitting on the best chair and shared her master's meals. I later saw her at ten years old shut in a kennel. The owner vowed she loved the bitch and would not let me have her back. That poor little old face looking out of bars has haunted me ever since, even though she has been dead many years now.

A short daily car ride will soon accustom your Cavalier to the car. They soon come to enjoy these trips and usually get over car sickness if the journeys are short and often. Dogs soon associate a car ride with the object of the journey! If he only goes in the car to the vet or to boarding kennels, he may view it with apprehension. If, however, there is a pleasant

Comfort loving Cavalier puppies relaxing in the 'best chair'. If you do not wish your puppy to sit on your furniture, firmly discourage it from the beginning.

happening such as a walk at the end of the journey, cars become things to enjoy.

Cavaliers usually come to love riding in cars whether because of the close proximity of their owners or because of the prospect of a walk at the end of the journey, or because they love to sit up higher on something, be it chair, cushion or even a sheet of paper! In a car they are up higher than the mere mortals on the pavement and so feel superior. Do make sure your puppy is not a danger in the car. Have him safely secured behind a dog screen – make sure he cannot climb through the appertures! It is surprising what a little space they can get through. Dogs sitting on owners' laps while they are driving are a menace, also those who paw the driver and jump about and distract the driver. It is no hardship for a dog to be restricted in some way and certainly safer for all road users!

Car sickness on a journey can be a problem and if your puppy really does not get over it quickly, consult your vet on the best travel sickness pills for your dog. He will take his age and size into account. Certainly do not give travel sickness pills intended for human beings without veterinary advice. Drugs entirely safe for human beings may have very bad effects on dogs especially puppies. Do give a trial dose, even with remedies supplied by your vet, to see what effects the pills have. One often hears of puppies being given a travel pill for the first time for the journey to its first show, and being so drowsy that he literally falls asleep in the ring!

Make sure your car is well ventilated if you leave your dog in it. One can buy window guards which allow the window to be open and air to circulate, yet keep your dog safe. Never leave your dog in a car on a hot day. The temperature rises rapidly into the hundreds and the dog will soon become very distressed and may even die of heat stroke.

The pet trade supplies a vast range of toys for dogs and puppies. Make sure the ones your puppy has are safe. Raw hide chews are fine and keep the puppy amused for hours. Beware of those with a squeaker in them. When the toy has been chewed sometimes the squeaker is exposed and could be swallowed. Be careful of cheap plastic toys. Even Cavalier puppies can quickly chew them up and plastic is not very good for the digestion! Very small balls can be swallowed, but a really hard large ball can last several generations. The inside cardboard tube of toilet and kitchen rolls are great fun for they roll and can be chewed without any ill effect. A really safe tin is also great fun and can be frequently washed! One of the best toys my puppies ever had was an old oven glove made from old fashioned knitting cotton. Cut in half they had a clean piece daily, the other half went into the washing machine. The traditional toy of a slipper is fine, but do examine the slipper carefully before giving it to your puppy. Do not give it to him if it is a man-made material or if there are any nasty little nails or rivets between the soles. The uppers from an old sheep skin or leather type are fine, but if you find the puppy is swallowing the pieces he has chewed off, do take care. Beware of any nylon material. Old stockings and tights were tied into a rope for our dogs to play with until a young adult fell ill and died before the vet could diagnose the cause and operate. She had eaten a piece of a nylon stocking! Now they are taboo in our household. Old woollen socks can be a great delight.

Begin grooming your puppy daily from the first day you own him. He will soon get used to a daily routine. A Spratts No 6 comb through the ears and feathering and then the body brushed with a Maison Pearson type pure bristle brush only takes a minute and accustoms the puppy to a daily routine.

Even if you obey all the rules, sometimes your puppy may have an upset tummy or be 'off colour', Don't take risks and leave it to luck but consult your vet. Puppies can dehydrate and and go down hill very quickly, but the vet's advice can nip 'nasties' in the bud and save the puppy suffering and you mental torment.

Having bought a good healthy puppy in the first place, do spend time on training him, and money on good food, which will all form a good basis on which your puppy will grow into a healthy well adjusted adult. Be consistent, do not laugh at his naughtiness one day and scold him for it the next. Dogs are great creatures of habit. Teach your dog *good* habits and I am sure you are in for years of happy, cheerful and sympathetic companionship with your Cavalier King Charles Spaniel.

5 Feeding

SINCE time began, dog has traditionally been fed on the leavings of his master's table. He made that bargain with early man when he became man's first friend and hunting partner. This delightful tale is told in Rudyard Kipling's Just-so-Story *The Cat that Walked*.

Before the war a few house dogs would be fed on household scraps with the addition of biscuit, stock and a meaty bone. Many kennel dogs survived on knacker's meat, greaves, which is a dehydrated fibrous meat by-product of tallow factories, biscuit meal and stale bread.

A few lucky pampered pets were fed extravagantly on the better cuts of meat, and even game or poultry – a real luxury before the war for both dog and man. Their indulgent owners also shared their sweet meats with them to the detriment of their pet's figures and teeth.

Commercially made dog biscuits and meal have been on the market since the 1860s. An advertisement published in *Our Friend the Dog* (1896) by Dr Gordon Stables R.N. offers '1st quality meal at 18/- per cwt.' – (90p), but as that was a working man's weekly wage and *Our Dogs* was 1d (2/5ths of 1p) a copy you can see that dog meal was expensive.

Feeding of dogs wasn't a very scientific affair and strange things occurred. Between the wars, to make flour appear white, agene was added. Although this seemed perfectly safe for human consumption, dogs fed on bread or biscuit made from this kind of flour developed a type of hysteria very unpleasant to behold. Agene was withdrawn and banned in 1946, and hysteria disappeared.

Maybe it was war-time shortages or the coming of refrigeration, but household scraps became rarer and after the war owners were glad to turn to commercially made food for their dogs.

Dog was traditionally thought of as a carnivore – a meat eater. He has the perfect mouth for this with teeth that can tear and chop. His saliva has no digestive powers, but just enables him to eat very quickly and swallow his food in quite large lumps. His digestive system can cope with a large amount of food at one filling. Dog has the ability to go without food for a few days such as a wild dog might have to between kills. Very occasionally some Cavaliers still eat normally for two or three days and although in perfect health prefer to go without for the next day or two. This may be a result of an ancient instinct or it may be attention seeking and wanting his owner to fuss, pet him and coax him to eat.

Researchers now classify dog as an omnivore – a creature that must have both meat and vegetable matter in its diet. A wild dog would eat the stomach with the vegetable contents of its prey before attacking the juicy rump. How many times have we seen our Cavaliers, so very far removed from wild dogs, eating grass when they have indigestion, although it may pass through the digestive system unchanged. They even offend our sensibilities by enjoying horse manure or sheep's droppings when on a country walk. Exhibitors know the frustration of trying to show a dog on grounds where sheep have grazed. The lovely smells and tasty snacks on the grass are far more attractive to the dog than the handler's endeavours to make the exhibit show his charms!

Basically all animals need food to create energy for growth, the replacement of tissues, the maintenance of body functions, reproduction, movement and for the fight against disease. Healthy active dogs need an adequate maintenance diet to keep in good form, while young puppies, growing youngsters, stud dogs, pregnant and lactating bitches and older dogs have special needs and requirements, which will be dealt with later.

This energy is supplied by carbohydrates, fats and proteins. Carbohydrates supply the largest portion of this energy. There are three kinds, sugar, starches and cellulose. If eaten in excess of the body's needs, they will be converted into fats and stored in the body making for obesity if this is carried too far.

Proteins are the body builders. It is thought that 20 per cent of a dog's diet should be of protein. This can be found in meat, offal, fish, eggs, milk, soya, peas and beans.

Dogs need some fat in their diet. If deprived of it, it shows in the poor condition of their coats and skin. Fat is a rich source of energy so during very cold weather extra fat will keep kennel dogs warm, but again if more is taken than can be used it is stored in the body as excess weight. Dogs love fat and can digest it well. One of my Cavaliers stole and ate ½lb (.22kg) of butter in one go without any ill effects. However, on another occasion she drank about a pint and a half of sunflower oil and was extremely sick!

Vitamins and minerals in the diet

Research has brought the correct need for vitamins and minerals in the canine diet into perspective. At one time conscientious breeders gave vast quantities of vitamin pills and cod liver oil, in the belief that if one was good, two were better. It has been found that excess of any vitamin is wasteful and in some cases harmful. Vitamins A and D are usually found in sufficient quantities in a wholesome balanced diet to maintain the normal bodily needs. Vitamin A keeps the dog healthy and helps fight infection. Vitamin D is essential for the correct utilisation of calcium and phosphorus. It is found in liver and dairy products and is essential for growing stock, pregnant and lactating bitches, although in giant breeds excess of vitamin D is thought to cause bone disorders.

Dogs do not need to take vitamin C in their diet for health, they have the ability to make and store it in their bodies. There is a very rare condition called bone scurvy in which the dog is unable to do this. Injections and pills of ascorbic acid – vitamin C – are useless. The giving of fresh orange juice seems to be the answer to this problem, but how to give a dog large doses of orange juice must be another one!

The complex vitamin B is essential. It is found in meat, liver, yeast, dairy products and cereals, but can be killed by cooking and by eating raw egg white.

Vitamin E is necessary for reproduction and muscle tone and is found in wholemeal products. Vitamin K is essential for the correct clotting powers of the blood. Indeed the antidotes to Warfarin (rat poison) which reduce the clotting power of blood, and snake bite are massive doses of vitamin K injected as quickly as possible after the poison has been taken.

All mammals need minerals for healthy living. Many are only needed in minute quantities and are called the trace elements. These include magnesium, copper, cobalt, zinc and iodine. Common salt is essential in small quantities. A good balanced diet would supply these in sufficient quantitites to preserve health, without adding extras except on veterinary advice.

Iron is necessary for the production of haemoglobin in the blood which is the pigment of the red blood cells and is essential for the transport of oxygen around the system. Without it any mammal will become anaemic. This leads to a lack lustre and generally run down state of health. Good sources of iron are found in liver and kidney, wholemeal and watercress.

Sulphur at one time had a lot of mystique attached to it. Sulphur tablets were given in the spring to 'purify the blood', while lumps of rock sulphur were put in the dog's drinking water to help with this process, and to 'keep the blood in good order'. As rock sulphur is insoluble no gain was forthcoming from this practice!

Calcium and phosphorus are very important minerals and must be present in the body in the correct proportion of two parts calcium to one part phosphorus and must be combined with vitamin D to be used fully. Breeders should make sure that young growing stock, pregnant and lactating bitches all receive adequate levels of these vital minerals, but again there is evidence that overdosing can cause harm. Youngsters need calcium and phosphorus to grow strong healthy ricket free bone, but of course Cavaliers are not at such risk from this disease as the giant breeds, where the growth rate is enormous.

Pregnant bitches need calcium and phosphorus with vitamin D for their own health. It seems the foetuses do not suffer except in very severe cases.

The developing puppies take their needs from the bitch's store. The bitch will suffer if drained of calcium. Her teeth and bone will deteriorate and she could even have eclampsia before whelping.

It is during lactation that calcium and phosphorus with vitamin D MUST be kept up or you could lose your bitch. Cavaliers are excellent mothers and produce vast quantities of milk in relation to their size, especially if they have five or more puppies who will each double their weight in the first week while just feeding on their mother's milk. This can drain her calcium supply. If the bitch is unable to maintain an adequate supply of calcium in her blood she can have an attack of eclampsia. This is very frightening and dangerous. Without warning the bitch will become very ill. She will begin to pant and shiver and become uncoordinated in her movements. She will then collapse, become unconscious and unless treated immediately, will die. As soon as you suspect the bitch is beginning an attack, get veterinary help immediately. An intravenous injection of calcium phosphorus and vitamin D, is like a miracle cure. The bitch will quickly respond, get to her feet, give a good shake, wag her tail and wonder what the fuss has all been about.

There are many proprietary brands of calcium on the market, but it is advisable to ask your vet for his advice on the type and dosage for your dog and its particular needs. Sterilised bone flour (make sure it is the sterilised variety and not the sort you use for the roses) is an excellent source of calcium but do consult your vet on dosage. Milk is a very good source of easily assimilated calcium. However, the milk sugar or lactose is very laxative and too much milk could result in a very upset tummy.

There are several excellent nutritional supplements made by reputable pharmaceutical firms which provide minerals and vitamins in the correct proportions. These need not be used daily for normal healthy dogs having a sensible well balanced diet, but adding during the growing periods, breeding times, periods of stress, and if the dog needs a 'pick-me-up'. Far better to use one of these proprietary brands in the correct dosage which has been very accurately balanced for the dog's needs, than a little of this and a little of that, which may overdose in one area and underdose in another.

Water

Two-thirds of the body is composed of water. This is continually being lost and has to be replaced by the fluids the dogs drink and by the moisture content of foods. It is essential that there is always an adequate supply of fresh drinking water available for your dog so that he can drink *ad lib*. If he or she seems to be drinking excessive amounts, do consult your vet as it may be the beginning of kidney trouble, or in the case of a bitch metritus. When refilling the water bowl, give it a good wash to rid it of the hairy dusty remains of the last filling, and the slimy alga which soon begins to adhere to the sides. The choice of water bowl is important. Choose a heavy based type that is not easily tipped over and one with sides sloping inward so that while lapping your Cavalier is not flooding the kitchen!

There are many ways in which you can give your Cavalier the balanced diet he needs. The canine nutritionalists advocate finding a diet that suits your convenience and your dog's tummy and sticking to it. They say dogs do not appreciate variety. Perhaps dogs don't but I would find it very dull, just preparing the same day after day. Whatever you decide to feed to your Cavalier make sure it is the best quality you can afford. By that I do not mean you to be extravagant and buy the better cuts of meat such as rump and fillet steak fit for human consumption! The dog's digestive system can quite easily cope with the tougher and cheaper cuts of meat. In fact if you cannot afford good quality food without extravagance, should you be keeping a Cavalier?

Meat

Beware of condemned meat – that is meat not fit for human consumption. If the poor animal has met with an accident, fair enough, but meat from an animal that has died of disease and may have been treated with massive doses of drugs can be dangerous. Condemned meat should be well cooked, kept in a kennel kitchen and not brought into the house. Cow beef from elderly cows is good, but expensive. If you are sure of your source this can be fed raw.

If you are buying mince from your butcher, be sure you know what you are buying. Cheap mince even if it is fit for human consumption sometimes contains a lot of fat, while a product often called 'Pet Mince' and considerably cheaper than beef mince may contain a high proportion of fat, lights (lungs) and melt (spleen). These are good sources of protein, but if dogs are not used to this type of feed, they can have upset tummies unless they are introduced to it gradually. If you are worried about the amount of fat in these raw minced meat products, cook it and allow to cool. The fat will come to the surface and you can skim it off. Of course you are losing some of your meat and having to pay for the fuel.

An old maxim states 'buy well – buy once, buy cheap – buy twice'. This certainly applies to buying meat!

Ewe mutton is an excellent source of protein but it is often too fat and really works out quite expensive if you cost out the bone and fat you have to waste. Emotionally, many people find feeding horse meat repugnant, but nutritionally it is a good source of protein. Several old wives' tales have become attached to its use, 'Feeding horse meat is over heating'. 'Feeding horse meat gives dogs light eyes' – I wish the last problem was as easy as that! Poultry meat has become a very useful addition to the diet in recent years. Before the war poultry was a luxury and only a few privileged dogs and humans enjoyed it except on special occasions. Of course there were the casualty birds and the tough old hens!

Chicken is excellent for convalescent dogs, bitches after whelping and for old age pensioners who find white meat easier to digest than red meat. I always have a couple of boiling hens in the dog section of the freezer. They are often available on special offers at very reasonable prices. They have more meat on them than the roasting variety and also a stronger flavour to tempt a jaded appetite. Cooked in a pressure cooker the flesh is easily taken from the bones and you have an appetising chicken broth as well. Do remember to remove the plastic from the giblets before you cook the bird or you will have a nasty sticky mess!

Two points of warning! As with preparing poultry for human use, do make sure it is completely thawed before you cook it. Do cook it thoroughly. Please do not tip the uncooked liquid which may have drained from the thawing bird on to the biscuit meal. Although salmonella is not a major problem with dogs, if it does occur it is very nasty and you certainly do not want it on your premises.

Every school child knows you do not give dogs poultry or chop bones. They do splinter when crunched up and can penetrate the stomach and intestines. Many well meaning people put poultry carcases out in their garden for the birds. The birds carry away portions of it and drop it in your garden! Your dog cannot believe his luck to find an unexpected titbit on the lawn! If you do see your Cavalier unexpectedly chewing something do investigate. Don't make the dog sick if he has swallowed the bones. They could cause as much damage coming up as going down. Give him a large chunk of dry bread or an extra meal of the porridge type of all-in-one foods as soon as possible. This will form a protective poultice around the bones to ease them through the digestive system.

Bones, even the marrow bone type, usually considered safe, can cause severe constipation. It sometimes needs a general anaesthetic and skilled veterinary help to remove the blockage. If you give your Cavalier bones, even only marrow bones, do keep a careful watch. If he is chewing off and swallowing quantities of bone, take the remains away before any harm is done.

A raw hide chew, manufactured in bone shape, can give hours of pleasure and has no harmful consequences.

Minced chicken and turkey is sold for pet food. This is a useful commodity for food value, but often the whole bird is minced and the resulting product contains a high percentage of minced bone. This is far too small to be dangerous from splintering, and is probably a good source of calcium, but I find such mince can cause constipation, especially in older dogs. A good way to deal with this type of mince is to thaw it out thoroughly, place in a baking dish with a little water and cook it in the bottom of the oven. Stir it occasionally and make sure it is thoroughly cooked. When feeding it, use half poultry mince and half other meat.

Tripe is a very popular food with Cavaliers, if not with their owners. Dogs do very well on it as it is a good form of protein. By tripe I do not mean the dirty white dish cloth substance sold at butchers for human consumption, but the fresh untreated stomach of the cow. I can remember seeing working gundogs returning to the keeper's kennels at night after a gruelling day in the shooting field, wet and tired. They were given a bowl of hound meal which had previously been soaked in water and on top was placed a large piece of tripe or paunch, just as it had come from the animal. These dogs did very well on this diet, often working four or five days a week in the season. I do not advocate this type of feeding for your Cavalier. In fact I am sure you would have difficulty in finding a supplier as most of the small country slaughter houses which supplied such kennels have closed down. The meat and offal not used for human consumption is now sold in bulk to the animal food dealers. However many of these dealers do supply cleaned mince tripe in frozen blocks which makes a useful change. If you haven't used this type of food, do be prepared for a strong, and to some, unpleasant smell.

Liver and kidney are rich sources of minerals, but if fed too liberally can cause tummy upsets. Do be careful of the supply. Ox liver is usually available from the butcher at a reasonable price and I would use this and not that sold 'not for human consumption'. A small amount as part of the meat ration once or twice a month can be beneficial and thoroughly enjoyed by most Cavaliers, although I have one who really dislikes liver. Even if I have put a piece in her dish by mistake and removed it before giving her the dish, she wrinkles up her face and turns away although normally she has a healthy appetite and never refuses any other food.

Fish

Fish is a good food for dogs. White fish is a good convalescent food, as it is with humans. Fresh herrings, pilchards and sprats are good food value. They can be fed raw if finely minced to break down the bones or cooked so that the bones are soft. They are rich in calcium and so good for pregnant and nursing bitches. The oil in this type of fish does help coats but if fed for long, dogs do put on weight.

Preparation of foods

If you decide to feed your Cavalier on cooked meat, poultry or fish which you prepare yourself, it is an excellent plan to invest in a pressure cooker and keep it for the dog food. Not only does it cook the food quicker and so save fuel, but all the goodness and flavour is sealed in. Tough joints of meat such as oxcheek and shin of beef can be cooked very quickly and then they are not so tough to cut up. The seal of the pressure cooker also cuts out some of the cooking smells and because the food is cooked at 122°C or 252°F in this type of cooker, meat not fit for human consumption will be sterilised at a higher temperature. When buying a pressure cooker do buy one that is high enough to cope with a boiling hen. You soon recover the extra cost by being able to cook fairly large amounts in one operation and save the annoyance of just not being able to get the bird into the pot!

A very valuable old fashioned food is sheeps' heads. Cooked in a pressure cooker they provide a lot of meat and gravy. It is time consuming to take the meat off the bones, but if you can get them from the butcher they are very cheap. Rabbit used to be an extremely cheap food – 6d or about 2½p for the whole rabbit – skin and all! Of course they were bought from the keeper or butcher down the road and not imported from China as they are today!

Healthy adult Cavaliers do not need all their food minced. Their stomachs can cope with quite large pieces of meat, at least the size of the top joint of your thumb. Dogs do not chew their food, but bolt fairly large pieces without any ill effect. Their saliva does not contain any digestive enzyme and so chewing into small pieces is of no advantage.

The feeding of dogs entirely on fish, meat and poultry is a very bad plan. It is very expensive and certainly not balanced. Meat contains no calcium and little roughage. Roughage is essential to ensure good bowel action.

Milk

Milk is an excellent food. It is very rich in calcium and phosphorus, fat, protein and carbohydrate in the form of lactose or milk sugar. Too much lactose can cause loose motions. The easiest type of milk to obtain is cow's milk from the milkman. Unfortunately this is the least suitable for dogs and puppies. The protein and fat content of cow's milk is much lower than in bitches' milk, while the lactose is much higher in cow's milk than in bitches' milk!

The nearest to bitches' milk is sow's milk and that is impossible to obtain! However goat's milk is an excellent substitute. It has many advantages over cow's mik for dogs and puppies. They love it. It is excellent food value. The fat content is higher than in cow's milk, and in a form which can easily be digested, even by young puppies. The lactose content is lower, while calcium and phosphorus are higher compared with cow's milk.

Goat's milk can be deep frozen so it is useful to find someone with a herd of goats who will sell in bulk when their animals are milking well, in readiness for the time when the yield decreases. By finding a producer and buying in bulk, I pay the same price as I would the milkman for cow's milk. The local deep freeze shop sells it 50 per cent higher than the fixed price for cow's milk, while a food hall in a large department store was selling it at 125 per cent higher than I could get it from the producer.

Many pharmaceutical firms produce excellent milk powders which are manufactured to the formulae of bitches' milk. It is worthwhile buying the best quality product because they are the nearest approximation to the real article.

Cheap milk powders are sometimes made from outdated milk powders originally formulated for human babies and are not satisfactory. Feeding puppies on reconstituted milk made from milk powder intended for human babies is also undesirable. Human milk is very high in lactose. The protein content is lower while calcium and phosphorus are dramatically low.

If feeding dried milk powders, do follow the manufacturer's instructions. Do not add a little extra powder to make it richer or a little less to make it 'go' further. These products are very carefully formulated and to get the best value it is essential to use them as they were intended.

If puppies have consistently loose tummies after having a meal containing milk reconstituted from the powder, change the powder. Sometimes one hears of owners diluting cow's milk with water to make it more digestible. This is not a very sensible practice as it reduces the food value and should only be done if advised by a vet in severe digestive cases.

Biscuits

If you wish to feed your Cavalier with fresh protein you will need to add a meal for the carbohydrates and roughage. Buy the best wholemeal biscuit meal you can. For puppies, young stock and the oldies use the puppy grade, while adults can cope with the terrier grade. Prepare it as instructed by the manufacturers. Some makes are slimy when moistened and my Cavaliers do not find that type as palatable as the crumblier type. When moistening the meal do not make it too wet or sloppy like porridge but more like bread crumbs. Milk, gravy or just water can be used for this purpose.

Dog biscuits come in many shapes, colour and sizes. They also have various ingredients added to the wholemeal or flour base to add flavour or colour. There is just plain wholemeal, cheese, charcoal and even chocolate. Meat fibres such as beef, chicken or rabbit are also used. A hard biscuit at bed time is very good for teeth and jaws, and Cavaliers do enjoy them!

The balanced diet

One can only give the average amounts of food a Cavalier would need.

Each dog is an individual. Some, like their owners, keep lovely figures and can eat 8oz (227g) of meat and 4oz (114g) of meal and biscuit daily. Others get fat on half that amount. Some people suggest feeding ½oz (14g) of food to 1lb (454g) body weight. On that scale a St Bernard would be very much overfed and a Cavalier rather underfed. If your dog has a good figure, is lively and healthy, you have found the correct amount for him. If he is overweight or too thin, do study his diet! How often owners, visiting the breeder with the puppy they bought some time ago, are distressed when the breeder complains the puppy is too fat. The owner vows and declares he has one meal a day. On investigation he may have *one* meal, but it begins at breakfast and continues throughout the day until supper time – no wonder the poor creature is fat!

Try your adult sedentary Cavalier, who has no special needs, on 4oz (114g) meat, fish or poultry, plus 2oz (57g) wholemeal terrier meal, prepared in gravy for the main meal with 1oz (28g) hard biscuit at night. If he keeps his figure, his coat is in good condition and he is healthy and full of beans, you have found the ideal amount. Some dogs are greedy and will eat everything given, and also steal food if given the opportunity. Others have a well regulated appetite control and will only eat what they need. Sometimes they will go without for a day or two to the exasperation of the owner. If this becomes a regular pattern and the dog is not losing condition accept it as his way of life. Do not spend time coaxing him unless he is ill, as he could quite well be attention seeking. Take up the food after a while and offer it to him again later. If your dog is not eating, is listless and losing condition, do consult your veterinary surgeon as soon as possible. If he is thin, always looking for food, and gobbles his meals down ravenously, you are probably underfeeding him. Gradually increase the amount at each meal. Beware of those 'fatties' with their great big eyes and sentimental expressions telling you they are starving. You will have to harden your heart and remember 'a fat dog is not a fit dog'.

If your dog is becoming overweight, take a look at his meals. Are you feeding too much fat or carbohyrate? Or are you just giving him too much, too many titbits. Is a member of the family undoing your good work by giving secret snacks? One sometimes doesn't notice that the dogs have put on weight until a friend points it out. This happened to our dogs. After years of always weighing out their rations, I became lazy and thought 'after all this time I can guess 4oz (114g) meat and 2oz (57g) meal and it will save washing up the scales!' Imagine my horror to find I had gradually increased their meals to 6oz (171g) meat and 5oz (142g) of meal. No wonder they were fat. This was a case of just too much of everything.

Remember too much fat and carbohydrate cause excess weight so give less of these, but do not cut them out altogether as even an obese Cavalier needs a balanced diet. Do not try the kill or cure method of drastically cutting the food down in one go unless advised by your vet, but gradually reduce the amount fed until your dog is the correct weight. Watch carefully he doesn't get too thin. Slimming your Cavalier is not as hard as slimming his owner. He cannot cheat by helping himself to a snack, but his misguided owner can ruin the dog's chance of losing weight by feeding titbits. Make sure all the family are co-operating. If you are trying to put on or take weight off your dog, be scientific about it. Weigh him on the same scales at the same time of day every few days. Keep records of any change both in his weight and the amount of food he has eaten. This way you can make adjustments that are necessary.

Commercially prepared dog foods come in several forms and certainly have their place in modern society. Again buy the best quality you can afford and make sure you know what you are buying.

Tinned dog food comes in two main forms. One type is protein with added cereal. This can be fed straight to the dog without any additional biscuit meal. This is cheaper than the all meat variety. Do read the label for guide lines on the amount necessary. Reputable firms offer diet sheets and advise on caring for your puppy. These are obtained by writing to their public relation departments. The other type of tinned meat consists of all meat products, possibly with the addition of soya, but no cereal. The meat products are left-overs from slaughter houses after the carcases have been dressed for human consumption. Most tinned meat manufacturers add vitamins and minerals in the correct proportions. Check the contents list on the label before adding any extra supplements of your own. With this type of tinned food you will need to add wholemeal biscuit or the manufacturer's recommended meal to get a balanced diet.

Although I would not feed my dogs wholly on tinned food, many people do, quite satisfactorily and there are many advantages. The major firms employ highly qualified scientists who study the dietary needs of dogs and cats. On their findings the firms base their products.

Some tinned cat foods appeal to Cavaliers. Again make sure what you are buying. Some have added cereal, some not. One chain of supermarkets sell an all-fish cat food – which my Cavaliers love as a change!

Most deep freeze shops and pet food dealers sell frozen blocks of cooked and uncooked meats of various types, such as beef mince – often the 'meat dust' from band saws in the butchery departments, chicken and turkey mince, tripe mince, minced fish, and mixtures of several meats. They also offer meat or fish in a thick plastic bag in which the contents can be cooked. These are a useful source of protein but make sure the food is thoroughly defrosted before feeding, and that once thawed it is used up quickly. If you only have one or two Cavaliers, it is better to buy this type of food in 1lb (454g) packages rather than in larger quantities, even if it is more expensive that way. Of course if you have a handyman who can break up the bigger blocks into convenient sizes with a cold chisel and club hammer, this is the economical way to buy this type of food. Incidentally the dogs love the meaty crumbs left after that operation!

There is also a type of fat sausage on the market sold as pet food. This is treated with a preservative and wrapped in a thick plastic cover so that it keeps for some time without refrigeration. I cannot comment on this type of food as I have never used it.

Two-thirds of your dog, and incidentally of you, is water. So also is the fresh or tinned meat you buy. It would seem sensible to buy food without all the water and add what is needed from the tap. Manufacturers have been producing specially formulated dry foods for domesticated farm animals for many decades. In the last few years they have turned their scientific knowledge to making carefully balanced foods especially for dogs. The ingredients are blended to give the correct balance of all the nutritional requirements, including mineral and vitamins. Do read the maker's instructions if feeding this type of food. By adding extras to it you are upsetting the balance.

Some makers have devised slightly different formulae for dogs with special needs. Puppy foods have a higher protein content, special diets are made for breeding stock, working dogs and racing greyhounds, while a maintenance diet for pet adults is available at a slightly lower price. It is worth comparing price and quality as these dry meals do vary in content and the cheapest may work out more expensive if you have to feed more to satisfy your dog's needs.

These complete feeds come in several forms. One is a dry meal, looking rather like a Swiss breakfast cereal. There may be pellets of soya in the mix which need careful soaking. Again, do follow the maker's directions as the preparation needed for this type of food varies. They contain meat, bone and fishmeal and cereals such as wheat, barley and flaked maize. Some animal feeds are now containing tapioca and maize gluten, while in one make potato crisps have been found! The majority of the compounds are more palatable and easier to digest if the cereal is cooked. Some still leave it raw. There has been some evidence, but not proved conclusively that the raw cereal can cause skin disorders in hot weather.

These dry foods are usually soaked for varying times before feeding. Most advocate using boiling water for this purpose. By using milk, gravy or other additives, you may be upsetting the balance of the food, but it does seem to make it more palatable.

The second kind of complete food is in pellet form. The ingredients are compressed into small sausage shapes about 1in (25.4mm) long. They may be moistened or served dry. The third kind is the expanded type which is cooked in steam and when exposed to normal atmospheric pressure they expand forming a crunchy product which different firms mould into various shapes.

Another form of complete food is the semi-moist type. These products come packed in sealed sachets and have the consistency of malleable putty.

At a quick glance it looks rather like mince or meat chunks, but it is a complete food correctly balanced, made from vegetable protein, meat products, cereals, minerals and vitamins. Semi-moist foods can be a useful aid to firm up loose bowel motions, but only give on veterinary advice if using this type of food for that purpose. If on holiday, you will find this type of food very useful. It can be used quickly without any preparation – no tins to dispose of, no time to wait while the food is soaking! Remember, once the sealed sachet is open, use the contents up quickly as they will quickly deteriorate when exposed to the air.

All these foods have a place in our modern society. The advantages are many – they keep well without needing freezer or fridge. They are readily available and most manufacturers give discount for large quantities. Friends often share the advantages of bulk buying. Some dog clubs have a 'bulk' buy and share the savings among members.

Although the compound of complete feeds does produce a balanced product, the individual ingredients may differ and give different flavours, so try one or two different makes before deciding on your final choice. In fact it is often recommended to change the make occasionally in case one brand has some essential ingredient in a form your dog finds hard to assimilate. It is essential that dogs have an adequate supply of fresh drinking water at all times. If feeding these dry foods, even if moisture has been added, one must keep an eye on the water bowl as the dog will need greater amounts to make up the balance they would get from fresh or tinned products.

The stools from dogs fed on this type of food are usually firm, but if your dog is passing large amounts, out of proportion to his size, you may be feeding a complete food which has excess of roughage. It may be as well to change the brand. If at any time his motions change drastically in colour or consistency, or smell, check the reason. I was really alarmed when one of my Cavaliers passed a dark red motion. Ghastly thoughts went through my mind about what horrifying disease she had developed until I discovered it was chewed-up raw beetroot! If, however, there is no simple explanation for such changes, do consult your vet.

Often foods intended for human consumption can be bought cheaply. Watch out for special offers such as boiling hens, gluts of fish, trays of cracked eggs, packets of baby cereals near their expiry date. These are good food value and if your dog is used to a varied diet you can take advantage of these. Stale wholemeal bread cut into fingers and dried on the bottom of the oven or even on top of the boiler make lovely crunchy rusks which Cavaliers love. Egg custards are excellent for puppies and elderly dogs. They too can be baked in the bottom of the oven while the Sunday joint is roasting!

Although it has been stressed that a dog needs a balanced diet, owners need not be fanatical over food and think their pet will fall to pieces if he has 1 per cent over or under of protein. During the war dogs in the Channel Islands were kept alive with a diet of seaweed and limpets! Common sense seems to be a very essential ingredient to feeding your dog. If he is healthy, energetic and in good bloom then his diet is suiting him. If it is convenient for you to purchase, prepare and is easy on your pocket then it should be suiting you.

Basic hygiene is essential when preparing dogs' meals. Apply the same rules you would when dealing with your own food. Keep all utensils clean. Have chopping boards and knives just for the dog meat. Keep a special tin opener for them and don't forget to wash that!

There are dozens of dog dishes on the market in every conceivable colour and shape. Choose one of the unbreakable sort. These come in plastic, enamel, aluminium or stainless steel. Make sure your Cavalier does not include the plastic dish as part of the meal! After eating his dinner young dogs will often take the dish away into a quiet corner and chew it! If you have a dog on a special diet, allocate him his own special coloured or shaped bowl. If you prepare the food in advance this colour or shape coding will quickly tell you which to give him. Dishes of a uniform shape are stackable and easy to store while those of different shape and sizes can be a nuisance to keep tidy.

It should hardly be necessary to say each dog should have his dinner in his own bowl and not have to share. The only exception being young puppies having milky meals. Even then they should be very closely supervised or else the greedy ones will have more than their fair share. If you have several dogs to feed at the same time, always feed them in their own place. Put down the dish and clearly say the dog's name. They soon learn to wait until they are called. Give the slow eaters their meal first. The greedies can be fed last or even put outside. Please don't feed extra meals to some in front of others! Those needing supplementary dinners should be fed out of sight of those who are restricted to one meal a day. I had a puppy once who I used to pop into the larder to have her extra puppy meals. She was still being fed there many years later, when she was a dignified retired champion! Make sure the gluttons do not gobble their own meal and then try to help themselves to the others. As soon as they have finished take up the dishes and wash them up. Some Cavaliers go through a fussy stage and won't eat. It is most annoying. Often these nuisances will eat if their dinner is put on a flat plate rather than a bowl, or if the meat is 'accidentally' dropped on the floor or put on a piece of kitchen paper. It is difficult to know what causes this peculiar behaviour pattern.

Dogs have very well regulated appetite clocks, and always know when it is near meal time. There is no optimum time of the day when to feed the main meal. One theory is if you feed early in the day the dog uses up the excess calories by being active after the meal. If you feed later, they rest after the meal and so store the extra! By that theory, if you wish to slim your Cavalier, feed in the morning, if you wish to fatten him, feed in the evening. The only way to find if this works is to try it!

I suggest you feed him at a time convenient to you. Do not be slavish to the clock and always feed him exactly at a certain hour, but do vary the time an hour or two either way so that if it is convenient for you to feed him a little earlier or later, he is not worrying where his dinner has gone.

Storing of dog food is important. If you are buying in small quantities, that is usually no problem. If you are buying in bulk to save money and time, it is no saving if the food deteriorates by bad storing. If you are buying fresh meat already frozen, apply the same rules as you would to your own food. Get it to your freezer as soon as possible. If it has unfortunately thawed at the edges cut these parts off and use first. Allocate one part of the freezer just for dog food and see that the meat is well wrapped in thick plastic bags. If you have a large amount to deal with, secondhand freezers can be bought quite cheaply from the deep freeze shop. Their motors are in good condition, but the cabinets are too shabby for shop display.

Tins need a dry store because if kept for long periods they will rust!

Complete dry food and the various form of biscuits are usually supplied in strong multi-layered paper sacks. If you are going to use the food up quickly it is fine to keep it in these bags, but if kept for any length of time in them, the contents can get damp and mice can nibble their way in! Plastic dustbins with firm lids are very useful and come in several sizes, although I have recently heard that during an exceptionally cold spell mice found their way into a garage and gnawed through several such bins, no doubt trying each diet to see which suited them the best! If you are likely to be troubled with rats or mice use the galvanised iron dustbins.

Special requirements

Old dogs need special care with their diet. While still needing all the essential ingredients they need less protein as this is a strain on their kidneys. If you are feeding a complete dog food choose the type with a lower protein content. Oldies also find fats more difficult to digest. If you are feeding your own mixture give the oldies the better quality protein such as eggs, chicken, rabbit and fish. I find they love cheese as well. Cottage cheese is particulary good for them and they quite enjoy it. The cooked chicken giblets from your own chicken meal will be appreciated by your old ones. Old dogs can often cope better with two small meals rather than the one main meal a day. If a dog seems to want his food but is slow eating, do have his teeth checked. Unfortunately teeth in the older Cavalier do loosen and it must be very uncomfortable trying to eat with loose, or even worse, aching teeth.

Sick and convalescent dogs often need their jaded appetites stimulated. Feed little and often but on veterinary advice. Usually if they make a start, they will quickly take an interest in food. Useful tempters are chicken skins, chicken livers, honey, cheese, sausages, fresh tripe and even kippers! The type of baby rusk which becomes mush in milk mixed with honey can be a useful standby. If the invalid refuses to eat from the dish, hand and spoon feeding can be resorted to, but unless it is vital for the patient to eat, do not make a regular habit of this practice as Cavaliers love the attention and do play on their owner's sympathy. A tasty morsel casually tossed into an invalid's bed often tempts and is eaten.

Honey and Virol are very useful for a sick dog. Offer it to him on a spoon and if he refuses it smear it on to his whiskers. He will lick them clean involuntarily and so get some easily assimilated nutrition. Brand's Essence is also good, while powdered protein and Complan are a valuable source of good quality nourishment.

It would hardly be necessary to say do not change a diet abruptly. If you decide to change from one type of feeding to another, do it gradually.

Finally, you should always remember each dog is an individual. Treat him as such when it comes to feeding and you should have a healthy, active dog for many years, but if things do go wrong get expert help.

6 Coats and Coat Care

No dog, Cavalier or any other breed of dog can look at its best unless its coat is in good condition. Luckily with Cavaliers this is an easy matter. Most breeders breed for the long silky coats as stated in the standard. The harsh curly coats seen in the past, particularly in the tricolours and black and tans seem to have almost vanished. The texture and quality of the hair is genetic and if several generations behind your dog have had good coats, the chances are that he will have inherited a potentially glamorous jacket. However, the owner must play a part in making the most of what the dog has.

Feeding is important. If the coat lacks lustre and the skin is dry, add a little sunflower oil or polyunsaturated margarine plus vitamin B12 to his diet. If feeding a complete feed, several manufacturers make a type with added vegetable oils which would help. Beware of magic powders and potions which promise too much. Simple remedies are often as efficacious and much cheaper. 'Powdered margarine at inflated price', my veterinary surgeon remarked about a wonder powder which was supposed to work miracles with the most difficult coat! If your dog has the genetic requirement, is in good health and is well fed, it is up to your management to see that he has a good glamorous coat.

In nature all dogs moult twice a year, male dogs in the spring and in the autumn. Bitches moult three to four months after their season. If she has had a litter, the bitch usually has a more thorough moult. With modern central heating and artificial light, both dogs and bitches tend to shed hair all the year around. The moult can be speeded up by giving a really good bath, massaging the skin thoroughly, combing and brushing out the dead hair. It is surprising what vast amounts can be got out of a moulting dog!

Caring for the coat of a pet Cavalier only takes a minute when he is a puppy and only five minutes when he is an adult in full coat *if* it is done daily. It is not the time that the actual grooming takes, it is the effort of actually getting down to it daily that is the difficulty. If it becomes routine to groom him either first thing in the morning, or after he has had his meal, this helps. It is getting into the routine and keeping to it which takes the effort. Once it becomes a pattern it really takes little time and very little effort. A moulting adult coat will knot up in a few days if neglected. The grooming can then be a misery for both you and the dog. It is not necessary to bath your pet Cavalier very often unless he rolls in something smelly. The white shirt fronts of Blenheims and tricolours can be smartened up with a dog dry shampoo. A Cavalier can return from a walk muddy and wet, but if he has the correct textured coat he will soon dry out and the mud disappear. It should hardly be necessary to say you must not trim your Cavalier. If you read the standard before buying him, you should have noticed 'free from trimming'.

If one visits a general championship show one will see stalls groaning under a cornucopia of grooming equipment. The Cavalier's needs are simple. Buy the best quality you can afford and it will last for several generations of Cavaliers. Gone are the days when ladies groomed their King Charles Spaniels with silver backed pure bristle brushes. The modern equivalent is a brush with pure bristles set in a pneumatic base and made for the human race. They are expensive, but well worth the money. Beware of whale bone and nylon bristles, and above all wire brushes. They are too un-yielding for the silky coat of the Cavalier and could well damage the hair.

A useful luxury is a hound glove with bristle one side and either velvet or chamois on the other.

Two combs are necessary. Again buy the best you can afford. A fine No 6 comb and a coarser tooth variety with a handle are ideal. Wooden and plastic handles made to look like horn are not as good as the all metal type.

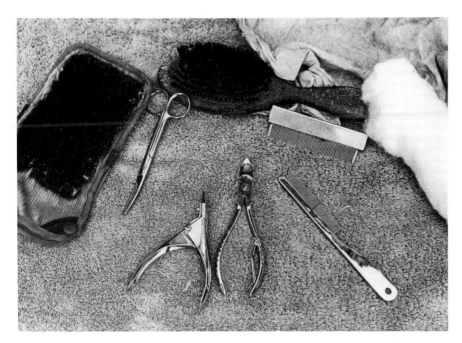

Grooming equipment needed for Cavaliers. Bristle brush, two types of comb, nail clippers, hound glove, round-nosed scissors for matts under feet and keeping ear passages clear, chamois, cotton wool and towel.

If you have need to sterilise the comb by boiling, the plastic and wooden handles will distort and will often loosen and come away from the head of the comb. The metal types in which the handles are 'all in one' with the head are ideal. Make sure the metal is well plated so that it will not rust.

There are two main types of nail cutters. There is the guillotine type where the nail is placed in the aperture. With a quick movement the tip is sheared off. The second type is the more conventional clipper type. Which type you use is really personal choice.

To remove mats of hair from between the pads, a pair of round nosed scissors with turned up ends are excellent and if not used by the family for general use, they will last for years.

To put the finishing touches, a piece of supple chamois or real silk is ideal to put on extra sheen, especially with tricolours and black and tans. Keep all this grooming equipment clean. Regularly wash the brushes and combs. It is useful to have a bag or box in which to keep the tools with a roll of cotton wool.

If knots in feathering are combed roughly it can cause the dog pain. Knots should be teased out with finger and thumb – not cut away. Knot-free feathering can be easily combed. Of course, with conscientious grooming, knots should not occur. However, we all get one now and again!

Suggestions for grooming

DAILY ROUTINE:

1   Place the dog on a steady table with a non slippery surface. A wobbly slippery-surfaced table can frighten a puppy and may well adversely affect him being shown on a table later on.
2   Talk to him so that he associates grooming with a pleasant experience.
3   Comb out the ears with the coarser comb followed by the finer comb. Groom inside his ears and take particular care behind them; knots are often found here. If they are dealt with daily they do not become a problem. Give him a firm vigorous brush with bristle brush or hound glove.
4   Do the same for the rest of him, taking care with mats or knots which may appear in the 'armpits', his back feathering and tail.
5   Wipe his eyes and the corner of his mouth with damp cotton wool.
6   Finally polish him with the chamois or silk.

This really *does* take only five minutes.

WEEKLY ROUTINE:

1   The same daily routine should be followed, but spend a little longer on brushing and teasing out any mats. There should be very few if the daily routine has been followed.
2   Inspect feet and take out any mats between the pads and toes.

This would take ten minutes.

MONTHLY ROUTINE:

1   Follow daily routine.
2   Inspect feet and nails. Clip nails if necessary. On Blenheim and tricolours it is easy because one can see the quick through the transparent nail and can cut just short of that. Black and tans and rubies are more difficult. The nails are black and one has to guess where the quick is. Incidentally if a whole colour has a transparent nail, it had a white foot, before the colour grew in! If you find it difficult to assess where to cut and if you have made the nail bleed on previous occasions, it might be as well to file the nails with a fine wood worker's file. If your dog still has his dew claws, make sure they are kept short as they can grow around and penetrate the leg, causing nasty sores.

A grossly overgrown nail about to be cut with the guillotine-type nail clippers.

3   Ears benefit from monthly attention. It is advisable, each month, to put in a few ear drops obtainable from the vet. This keeps the ears free from ear mites and fungi which can cause trouble if allowed to become chronic. With the pendulous ears of the Cavalier air cannot circulate freely in the ear channel. The moist warm ear is the ideal environment for these mites. If the ear channel is blocked or even partially blocked by excess hair, this is a case where trimming should be used for the health of the dog. Do not prod and poke into the ear. If there is a dark, cheese smelling discharge, consult the vet.

4   Some Cavaliers form heavy deposits of tartar on their teeth. Some will allow their owner to keep these scaled. A monthly inspection will reveal the condition of the teeth. If the tartar is building up, and the dog does object when you remove it with your finger nail, consult the vet. If neglected the teeth can loosen and then fall out.

5   Anal glands. Unfortunately many Cavaliers suffer from anal gland trouble. Some need these glands to be emptied regularly. Do not try to do this yourself unless you have been trained by an expert how to do it. Neglected and half emptied anal glands can become infected and very painful abscesses can form.

Bathing

Unless you are showing your Cavalier, regular bathing is not necessary if you keep up your daily, weekly and monthly grooming. If he rolls in something smelly that is a different matter. Apply tomato puree paste to the offending area, leave for a few minutes, and then wash it off. This takes the nasty smell out of the coat. Follow this with a good bath, and your Cavalier will be fit to met his friends again. Cavaliers are usually very good and enjoy baths. Show dogs soon associate having a bath with going to a show the next day. It is sad for the retired oldies who get excited when they see the younger ones being bathed and they vainly hope it will soon be their turn and they will be going to a show again.

It is essential that your Cavalier isn't frightened, especially with his first baths, so for the first few have some help. Some like to bath the dogs in the bath. I prefer the kitchen sink as it is the right size for the Cavalier and is at the right height so it isn't back breaking. If you have the type of mixer tap where the arm can be swung to one side, that is a great help. If you are worried about the hygiene when the bath is over and the dog removed, give the sink an extra good wash and then rinse it with household bleach. This will kill any nasties! A tap fitted with a spray attachment is extremely helpful. Failing that a large bucket and a jug should be used. The water should be very slightly above human blood heat, i.e. it will feel pleasantly warm to your touch. However, dogs do have their preferences and if he shows he is uncomfortable, cool the water.

SHAMPOOS: The types are legion! Hundreds have been made for specialist dog use with added unguents to perform special tasks. Medicated and insecticidal shampoos are extremely useful if the dog is itchy or has parasites. If using this type of shampoo it is advisable to purchase it from the vet. He will prescribe the correct type for the skin condition. What type of shampoo you use for ordinary use is really a personal choice. Find a type that suits your dog's coat and keep to that brand. Some people use shampoos for human use and even washing up liquid. It is preferable to use shampoos made especially for the dog. It should hardly be necessary to say that shampoos and rinses to improve coat colour are illegal by Kennel Club rules. Persons using a blue rinse to whiten the white on Blenheims and tricolours should be reminded of the standard which states 'pearly white' not 'Persil White'. It isn't the shampoo that improves the coat, but the removal of the dirt and the general massage of the skin.

Before wetting the dog have all your needs ready: shampoo, vaseline, hair dryer or fan heater, towels, cotton wool, comb, scissors, brush, chamois, old nylon tights and aprons for owner and the helper.

Let us explain the tights. If your Cavalier has a coat which tends to curl, the tights can be used as a hair net to straighten out the coat. Cut off the feet and the elastic waistband, and separate the two legs. When the dog is practically dry, put on the stocking! Make sure his coat is as smooth as possible or you may set in his unwanted curls.

Put his tail through the tail hole, his front legs through their appropriate hole, and tie the dangly piece under his chin. Leave the stocking on until he is completely dry, but never for a long time unattended. I did years ago. A youngster removed the stocking from her companion during the night, swallowed it and died from the consequences.

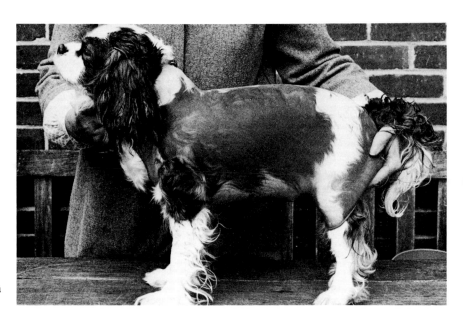

Dizzie in a nylon tight 'hair net' to straighten a coat after bathing.

BATH ROUTINE:

1 Put your dog out to relieve himself.
2 Give him a quick brush and comb to remove as much debris as possible.
3 Smear his eyes with the merest trace of vaseline, and plug his ear channel with cotton wool.
4 Adjust the temperature of the water so that it is comfortable without being too cold.
5 Gently put him in the sink. If he is inclined to slip, stand him on a rubber mat or failing that a thick wodge of damp newspaper. Your assistant can be at his head to re-assure him, if he becomes apprehensive. Wet all but his head and ears very thoroughly, apply the first application of shampoo and massage it well into the coat so that it does reach the skin. It is surprising how waterproof a good Cavalier coat can be and one has to be very thorough to get the skin really wet and clean.
6 The ears are next. Make sure you clean the inside of the ear flaps as

well as the outside. Thick hair grows behind the ears and knots often appear here so extra care is needed.

7 Last of all the face. No dog is going to enjoy future baths if he gets soap in his eyes during the current one. Be careful! Your assistant could hold the dog's eyes closed or even hold a face cloth over them while you wash him. Take care to clean lips and the little folds around the mouth.

8 Thoroughly rinse out all the shampoo.

9 Repeat the whole process with the second application of shampoo.

10 Rinse very thoroughly making sure no shampoo whatsoever is left behind.

11 If you want to use a coat conditioner do so at this stage. Follow the manufacturer's instructions. If it is the type that has to be left in the coat for several minutes, make sure the dog does not get chilled and begin to shiver.

12 Finally wash out the conditioner as thoroughly as the shampoo. Any deposits of either shampoo or conditioner left in the coat will give a dull lack-lustre appearance.

The final appearance of the dog after a bath will depend on how you dry him.

1 Squeeze out as much water as possible, especially from his ears and feathering.

2 Put him in the garden and encourage him to shake. It is surprising how much will come out as you will soon find out if you stand too close! Keep an eye on him as he may well decide to roll!

3 Put him on a table with a non slippery surface.

4 Gently dry his face and then give him a good towelling with a thick warm towel. Household 'cast offs' are often handed down for the dog. These may be satisfactory for wiping feet and feathering when he comes in from a walk, but they are often too thin and worn to be of much use after a bath.

5 Run a comb through all the coat and feathering. This will reveal any knots which had gone undetected, especially under the forelegs, and behind the ears. These can be teased out easily when the coat is damp.

6 Take particular care in drying the ears. Remove the cotton wool plugs if they are still there after the good shake. Dry the inside of the flap as well as the outside. This is where a little gentle heat can help. Some dogs hate hair dryers, but will sit quite happily in front of a fan heater. Do not have the heat too fierce.

7 If you do not require that extra glamorous finish on your dog which is required of show dogs entering the ring shortly, and if the weather is

warm and sunny – allow him to finish off drying by running in the garden, but again beware of rolling!

If you want that glamorous finish – brush the coat dry in the sun if it is warm enough, or with the aid of a fan heater or hair dryer. If your dog is being shown the next day, brush the body coat down with the contours of the body and brush the feathers out. If you lift the coat away from the body it can give an illusion that your dog is fat. With whole colours and some tricolours one can bath them several days before the show. Dry the dog by lifting the coat with a brush away from the body. This gives it an excellent finish and it will have a few days to settle to the body shape before the show.

8 If you wish to eliminate the curl, this is the time to apply the tights as previously described.

9 If you have dried your dog off with heat, do allow him to cool off gradually so he does not get a chill. Never put a dog to bed damp, and make sure his bed is dry before you say goodnight.

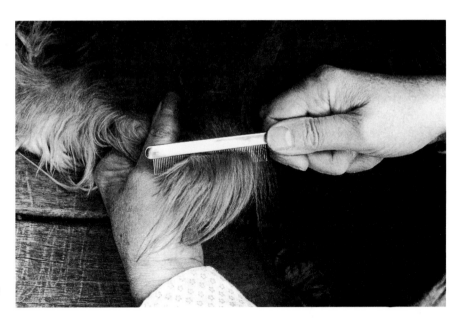

Feathering free of knots can be combed easily .

Skin parasites

Even royal dogs such as Cavalier King Charles Spaniels fall prey to parasites, both internal and external. A dog who is not used to such external company becomes very uncomfortable when bitten, and his vigorous scratchings should alert the owner that all is not well.

FLEAS: Fleas are very difficult to see in a coat. Even if the dog is combed with a fine tooth comb the fleas may run ahead of the comb and escape detection. The presence of flea excretion is the real evidence. These are tiny brownish-black specks which if dropped into water give off a reddish dye. Once you suspect your dog has fleas take immediate action. Fleas can multiply very rapidly and lay eggs in carpets and furniture. These can wait for up to a year for the right conditions of warmth and moisture to hatch. Many pet shops and veterinary counters at chemists sell anti-parasitical compounds suitable for dogs, but I prefer to get preparations from the vet who can prescribe the suitable shampoo or wash for the condition.

Bathing a dog in a veterinary wash which one does not rinse out of the coat is good. The dog must be dried by heat and not towelled dry. On a warm sunny day this is no problem. Do not delay the treatment until the weather is suitable because the fleas would have a field day and the condition will be more difficult to treat. An insecticidal deposit is left in the coat and deals with hatching eggs. It is usually recommended to repeat the treatment in 10 days time so that the second generation of fleas is killed off. Surprisingly the powder left in the coat does not leave it dusty nor dull, and must be very soothing to an itchy skin as my hands always feel pleasant after using it. Although manufacturers recommend these washes as a dressing, it is well worth bathing the dog thoroughly first and then use the wash as a rinse. This ensures that the coat is thoroughly wet and the wash does penetrate to all parts of the skin.

Make sure bedding and sleeping areas are treated. An aerosol insecticide is useful for this especially with furniture and around the edges of fitted carpets. Don't aerosol the dog and bath him at the same time. Use one treatment or the other. Using both together could cause dermatitis. Late summer and early autumn are the danger time for fleas. Some years are described as 'bad years for fleas', which really means it is a good year for fleas, but a bad year for dogs and their owners. This is usually when the weather is damp and warm and so the ideal condition for flea eggs to hatch.

Owners are often puzzled as to where their Cavaliers caught fleas. They can be caught from other dogs, cats, hedgehogs and rabbits, from long grass and even from carpets and furniture where the eggs can remain unhatched for a considerable time. It is very important to deal with fleas as soon as they are suspected or you may have a problem for years. Besides making the dog uncomfortable with flea bites and possibly a secondary skin infection, fleas are dangerous because they are an intermediate host in the life of the tape worm.

LICE: Lice are easier to detect than fleas because they are less mobile. They are usually found in the ear flaps especially in that little pocket in the ear known as 'Harry's pocket'. The whitish eggs which adhere to the hair and known as nits are quite easily seen. Immediate action should be taken to eliminate lice. Follow the same procedure as for fleas, but repeat the treatment three times to insure lice which have hatched between dressings are killed. Although somewhat easier than fleas to treat, lice are very dangerous not only by causing skin irritation, but by causing anaemia. In severe cases the dog can become very debilitated and young puppies could die. Lice also act as an intermediate host for the tape worm.

SHEEP TICKS: This is an unpleasant parasite which can be seen with the naked eye. It embeds its head into the skin and feeds on the blood of the dog. Its body remains on the surface of the skin and looks rather like a bluish grey wart. Do not try to pick off the tick, because its mouth pieces will remain in the dog's skin and these will turn septic and make unpleasant sores. There are several old fashioned remedies to remove this horrid creature intact:

1   Burn the blister-like body with a lighted cigarette.
2   Paint the creature with surgical spirit or brandy!
3   Use a modern canine insecticide aerosol spray.

Although known as 'sheep' ticks dogs can pick up these pests from long grass in which hedgehogs or rabbits have left them, perhaps miles away from any sheep.

HARVEST MITES: If a dog is seen vigorously biting between his toes, examine carefully. If clusters of very tiny orange parasites are seen, these are harvest mites and should be treated with a veterinary approved wash. Since farmers have taken to burning stubble less of these mites have been seen.

MANGE MITES: These are a family of unpleasant skin parasites which cannot be seen with the naked eye. If a dog is persistently scratching for no visible cause, he should be examined by the vet. A skin scrape is taken and examined under the microscope. This will determine the type of mange and the vet can prescribe the appropriate treatment. Mites come in four main forms:

1   Ear mites. This was dealt with in the section on the monthly grooming routine (see page 86).
2   Sarcoptic mange. This is an extremely uncomfortable condition and can cause severe irritation to both dog, and in many cases, his owner. It is quickly cleared up by the use of veterinary recommended baths. They should be repeated at least three times at seven day intervals to break the life cycle of the mite. Again all bedding used by infected dogs should be treated or better still destroyed. It is essential that the

treatment is carried out thoroughly and that all parts of the skin are thoroughly wetted with the wash for these mange mites are very persistent.

3   Demodectic or follicular mange. This is a very serious condition and is passed from bitch to puppy while the puppy is feeding from the bitch, although the bitch shows no sign of the mite herself. This mange mite destroys the hair follicules and causes disfiguring baldness, and is very debilitating. Secondary infections often set in, causing dreadful sores. Veterinary help should be sought immediately for it is a difficult condition to treat. Luckily research continues and recently there have been hopeful results with modern treatments. Dogs suffering from this condition often have a musty mousey smell.

4   Cheyletiella. Often the first sign that puppies have this condition is when owners have a very irritating rash on their hands and tummies if they have been cuddling puppies with only thin clothing on. On turning back the puppy's coat a thick dandruff type scurf will be seen. Again a veterinary wash repeated two or three times at seven to ten day intervals will clear up this condition.

RINGWORM: Another unpleasant skin condition which effects both man and dog is ringworm. This is not a worm but a fungical infection. It begins with a reddening of the skin, followed by a yellowish discharge and then a crusty scab. It is very irritating so help should be sought quickly. If the lesions are scratched, secondary infections can follow.

It cannot be emphasised too strongly that all treatments for parasites must be extremely thoroughly carried out both on the animal and his living quarters. Slovenly half-hearted treatments will only prolong the condition and could cause the parasite to persist for a considerable length of time.

Grooming tools which have been used on dogs with any skin problems should be sterilised between each dog. Good quality plated combs can be boiled in water for three minutes, and brushes washed in a good quality disinfectant. Ideally each dog should have his own equipment.

A dog which suddenly begins to scratch and bite his skin should be thoroughly examined for parasites. They can cause a lot of trouble and if secondary infections set in these conditions are difficult to clear even with modern medication.

Some dogs scratch because they are bored. This is a nuisance because they can damage the coat and there is really no cure, except to make life more interesting!

Owners who suddenly find their Cavaliers infested with parasites are naturally alarmed, but with modern preparations and very thorough treatments, most of these conditions can be quickly cleared up. The key word is THOROUGH.

7 Breeding

IF you have a well-bred bitch there is the temptation to have a litter from her. Before you embark on this venture do stop and contemplate. Why do you wish to breed Cavaliers? If you think it would be lovely to have a litter of five or six cuddly Cavalier puppies do remember the work. There is the cleaning up, the food preparation, the nursing if anything should go wrong, the tie to the house and the parting with them at eight weeks, and above all making sure they go to the right homes. Experienced breeders have made mistakes when selling puppies. They think the buyers are genuine but are horrified to find two or three years later that the puppy they sold as a pet was now producing sub-standard puppies at every season for a multibreed dealer kennels, or was on a rescue service book as wanting a new home.

If you think breeding and selling a litter would be a useful addition to the housekeeping money, think again. Even before the litter arrives, you will incur a lot of expense.

1   Stud fee and travelling expenses.
2   Vet's fee if you wish him to examine your bitch to make sure she is fit to have a litter, and perhaps to provide a certificate that she is free from any vaginal infection.
3   Extra feeding.
4   A whelping box and the modern synthetic fibre bedding.

After the puppies are born the expenses go on, extra heating, extra feeding for the mother and the puppies, more veterinary bills for the removal of the dew claws. No amateur should attempt this operation. I once visited a litter by one of my stud dogs. The owner also had an accidental litter of Cavalier Cross Poodle puppies. I remarked that she hadn't had the dew claws removed. 'Oh yes, I did them myself', she replied. On closer examination both litters still had their dew claws, but the breeder had removed the stopper or carpular pad at the back of the 'leg'. Ten poor little puppies had to suffer her amateur bunglings and still had their dew claws.

Continued expense would be advertising the puppies, and registering them with the Kennel Club. This is assuming that all goes well, but bitches do miss and some do have expensive caesarian operations. So you can see that rearing a litter is not all monetary profit.

Sometimes owners think that having a litter will cure a bitch of false pregnancies. This is a condition when two months after her season, although not mated, a bitch thinks she is having puppies. She will dig nests in the garden under shrubs or sheds. She will produce milk, and cuddle toys as if they were puppies. Sometimes the bitches are really ill and miserable. If a foster mother is ever needed, a bitch with a false pregnancy will produce milk and care and feed orphan puppies as if they were her own. Bitches recover from this condition often without veterinary aid, but in very severe cases they need treating by the vet. Having a litter will not cure this condition. In fact bitches who have had several litters, can have false pregnancies every time after they have been in season for the rest of their lives. The only permanent cure is to have the bitch spayed.

Another old wives' tale is that a litter is good for the bitch and prevents pyometra. This is an infection in the uterus of middle aged and elderly bitches. This can occur in any bitch even if she has had several litters. Antibiotic treatment is very successful in mild cases, but acute cases can be very dramatic. Quick action and an emergency hysterectomy is then necessary to save the bitch's life.

Some parents think allowing their pet bitch to have a litter is an easy way to give the children their sex education. So it will be, but it is an expensive way. Only good dogs should be bred from. A sub-standard bitch mated to any Cavalier dog may teach the children the facts of life, but will also produce sub-standard puppies. Then there is the problem of finding homes for these without resorting to pet shops and dealers.

Is your bitch the type of Cavalier from which you should breed? She may have a beautiful pedigree with lots of Champions in it, but when you bought her did you buy her as a pet bitch or as a brood or show quality specimen? Why did her breeder consider her as 'pet quality' as opposed to 'show or breeding quality'? If it was just marking, or teeth out of alignment, or some minor fault, this should not matter too much, but if it was for some major structural fault such as slipping patellas or inguinal hernias, or that a litter mate had some ghastly hereditary fault, then it would be very foolish and irresponsible to breed from her. This may seem hard, especially if she had a lovely temperament and you love her dearly. Recessive faults can lie dormant for many generations before they appear again. Say your bitch seemed sound, but her full brother had patella luxation. Your bitch could carry the recessive gene for this deformity. She could well produce puppies showing no sign of the fault. Suppose one of the puppies became a Champion and was widely used at stud. In time people would line breed to him and be very disappointed when puppies appeared with patella luxation passed down from their great-grandmother through recessive genes.

The stud dog

If after all that gloom and doom you decide to go ahead and breed a litter, how do you set about it? The first thing you need to do is to find a stud dog. Get expert advice. Contact the breeder of your bitch and see if she has any helpful suggestions. If she has the 'ideal' stud dog, do not commit yourself to using him until you have made further enquiries. Go to a breed show, preferably a championship show, meet the people and look at the dogs.

Choosing a husband for your bitch is a very difficult task. Don't necessarily choose the top winning dog of that day. Because he has won the highest award as a show dog and is very handsome, he may not have the ability to pass on his virtues to his progeny. Some pedigrees 'click', and dogs and bitches of certain lines when mated together produce winner after winner, while two champions bred together may only produce mediocre stock. Ask several exhibitors who have Cavaliers from the same line as your bitch, which lines would suit. Look at the progeny of any dog you are thinking of using. Do they please you? Is the mother from the same line as your bitch? Do the puppies from that stud dog have the same faults as your bitch, even though the dog himself has not?

You are not breeding on a whim and so effort must go into the task. The aim is to breed puppies who have all the good points of their parents and who have improved on their weak points. Each generation should be an improvement on the last, but we do not live in an ideal world and that is a forlorn hope. However, with patience and many disappointments, it can

Cavalier puppies, one of each colour!

be done. Consider Mrs Jennings in the 30s and her Blenheim bitch Blenheim Palace Poppet. Mrs Jennings said she was quite different from the rest of the Cavaliers at that time, but by picking the right stud dog, going for correct type and temperament and with an eye to know which to keep, she produced stock which helped to standardise the breed from a very limited number of stud dogs.

Later on the section on colour will give you some indication of what to expect. With your first few litters it would be wisest to keep to the conventional colour combinations, i.e. Blenheim to tricolours, Blenheim to Blenheim, or tricolour to tricolour. If your bitch is a whole colour, stick to a whole coloured stud dog for your first few litters, and even then proceed with great caution before you mix broken colours with whole colours.

A popular stud dog may produce three champions from the three hundred puppies he has sired, which will give him 1 per cent success rate. A less popular dog may sire one champion from his litter of four which would give him a success rate of 25 per cent!! It is important to find out why a stud dog is so popular and also to look at the overall quality of his puppies, not necessarily his Champion progeny. His grandchildren are also an indication as to whether his good points are being passed on and his faults are being eliminated.

There are several schemes run jointly by the British Veterinary Association and the Kennel Club which screen dogs and bitches for certain hereditary abnormalities. Animals passing the schemes are issued with certificates stating that they are clinically free from that disease. These schemes are a great help, especially when several generations can be certified free. However, it is as well to realise that the animal with such a certificate is only clinically free from the abnormality, and he may well carry a recessive gene for the undesirable characteristic. This means he is not genetically clear and could pass on the unwanted recessive to his progeny.

The ability of a good show dog to produce good show puppies is curious. Some top winning Champions with impeccable pedigrees fail to produce any memorable stock even to equally well bred bitches, while a dog who has a very modest show record sometimes produces winning progeny to mediocre bitches of all lines. The true worth of a stud dog, is not how many top awards he has won, not the number of puppies he has had, but the overall quality of his progeny in health, looks and temperament.

The first few matings are very important and should be made as easy as possible for the dog. Ten months to a year is the best time to begin. Some dogs are mature enough to perform at that age, while others are just not interested. It is a good idea to let him have two or three litters at the beginning of his stud career, then to wait to see how the puppies develop before allowing him any more. An older bitch who is flirtatious, and who

Swedish Ch. King Maker of Ttiweh. Born 18.11.59. Bred by Mrs A. Hewitt Pitt and exported to Sweden where he had a successful show and stud career.

encourages him, is ideal for a young dog to begin with. If at his first encounter he is presented with a maiden bitch or even an experienced bitch who snaps, snarls and tries to bite him because she is frightened, or because it isn't her correct day, he could well be put off bitches for a considerable time and perhaps always be a reluctant stud dog. If he is presented with a friendly bitch who is at the height of her season, and who encourages him from the beginning, there will be no traumatic experience and he will be willing to perform another day. I will always remember the look of absolute surprise and bewilderment when a young stud dog of mine mated his first bitch. It must have been a pleasant surprise because he has always been a keen stud dog after that!

If after two or three bitches your potential stud dog seems reluctant and even refuses to mate a bitch, it is only fair to tell any client who seeks his services. It is very disappointing after putting much thought into who is the best dog to use, to travel miles only to find the dog will not co-operate. Some bitch owners will take risks, especially if the stud dog owner has another dog who could be suitable.

From the beginning of his stud career it is as well for the dog to get used to being handled during the mating and also to allow the bitch to be held. Some young stud dogs show reluctance if the bitch is held or if he is guided. Of course if the bitch handler has gripped the bitch firmly around the waist and there is no room for the dog to mount, one must expect him to be reluctant. However, with encouragement and patience, these difficulties can be overcome, providing the dog has enough sexual drive.

When using a young dog, do allow plenty of time. Don't try to rush things. A quiet calm atmosphere is very important. It is very nerve racking if either owner is looking at her watch every few minutes and trying to rush things because she has to pick the children up from school or it is time to be preparing dinner. This nervous tension can be transmitted to the dogs, and often makes matters worse.

Some owners are tackless with young adolescent dogs who often mount bitches not in season and even dogs while playing. They scold them for these antics and then later expect them to mount bitches in earnest. A very keen dog would not be deterred by this, but a sensitive dog may well be confused, so until a young dog knows his job – don't discourage him!

A young reluctant dog can be encouraged by making him jealous. The stud dog owner can pick up the bitch and make an extravagant fuss of her, dangle her hindquarters just above his nose, and pretend to take her away. Also another male can be brought on the scene to stimulate him and make him keener. Putting a reluctant male just out of reach, but within sight of the bitch, then making a great fuss of her can make him jealous and rouse his curiosity. Usually with an experienced bitch to lead him on, and owners making encouraging noises it isn't very difficult to get a young dog to mate his first bitch.

A young dog who is used too frequently, and at too early an age, can quite easily become disinterested. If he is given a long rest, maybe of several months, and then introduced to a very flirtatious bitch, he may well overcome his difficulties and become a useful stud dog.

If after mating two or three bitches satisfactorily, no puppies or very small litters result, the dog should be given a veterinary examination. Seminal fluid should be examined under the microscope for the presence and condition of live sperm. A low sperm count or weak non-vigorous sperm could account for the infertility. There has been talk that dogs who have had parvo-virus, or who have been in contact with it, without showing any clinical symptoms, can have a low or even a negative sperm count. If a dog who has a lot to offer, but fails the sperm test, it may be well worthwhile after a period of several months to have him re-examined to see if there is any improvement.

Some infertile dogs respond to hormone treatment, and even surgery to correct kinks in sperm carrying ducts. However, if such treatments are necessary, the owner must think very carefully before placing such a dog at public stud. Both high and low fertility can be inherited by both sexes and to keep the vigour of a strain, only dogs and bitches with high fertility should be used. In the 50s and 60s litters of eight, nine and ten were quite common in Cavaliers, but now the average seems to be three or four. There may be many reasons for this which will be dealt with in the chapter on bitches.

As bitches tend to come into season as the light intensifies, there are peak demands for the popular stud services. Research has shown that in theory a dog can be used every two days for several weeks without his fertility being impaired. After a very active few weeks, it is as well to give him a rest. In practice some veterinary researchers advise leaving five days between the mating of two different bitches. This is to prevent any vaginal infection being carried from one bitch to another via the dog. Such infections only live for forty-eight hours on the dog, but bitches can harbour them from season to season if not treated.

If a young dog is over-used in his first year, he may well lose his sexual vigour by the time he is seven, but if he has been well managed, kept fit with regular exercise, good feeding and not allowed to get fat, he may continue his stud work with discretion until he is eleven or twelve years. I often think it is sad to visit a kennel and see Champions and even those who never quite made it, but who brought great credit to the line, in an unkempt, uncared for condition. The owner would never have shown them in that state and it hardly seems fair that now they are no longer on view they are neglected. A client who comes to use him at stud, will be disappointed to see a fat ungroomed 'hay bag' instead of the elegant, not-a-hair-out-of-place dog whose picture she had seen in the *Year Book*. I remember with what pride the late Miss Beryl Sadler of Dendy fame, looked after Ch. Abelard of Ttiweh, and Mrs Lena White of Lenharra Ch. Raoul of Ttiweh. Even if they were retired old gentlemen, they were groomed to perfection and kept in tip top condition. The bloom on their coats and their trim figures testified that it wasn't a last minute job, but they had been cared for throughout the year.

Feeding the stud dog is only a matter of common sense. A good balanced diet with all the essential ingredients is what he needs. Perhaps a little extra good quality protein such as a raw egg or extra good quality meat could be added if he is having a busy time. Giving extra vitamins is not necessary if he is receiving the true balanced diet. The stud dog should be kept in tip top condition. If he is living on the same premises as bitches in season, he could well fret and refuse to eat and quickly lose condition. Extra food is then needed to put back the weight he has lost. Keep a careful eye on his weight because he could quite quickly regain that which he lost *and* put on extra. An overweight stud dog will not perform so efficiently and trying to could put extra strain on his heart. Beware of hand feeding if he is off his food, because he will love the extra attention and expect the same treatment when all the bitches are well over their season.

Keep a careful watch. Although it is most likely that it is the bitch in season which is causing the weight loss, if he is lethargic and generally out of sorts don't take chances but consult the vet.

Regular exercise to keep him in good hard condition is desirable. A word of warning! If you take him out for a free run, do take care. A keen dog is very persistent. He will remember the bitch in season at home and could run off to get back to her. With the state of the traffic these days it doesn't need much imagination to realise what a sad end that could be.

If you have more than one stud dog, often a little tact is needed in management. Usually and ideally several dogs can and should live together without any problems. However, stud dogs do, unfortunately, sometimes become jealous of each other when in-season bitches are around. If there is any tendency for this, do not return a dog straight from a mating into the company of the other dogs, as this could lead to a fight. Allow him to rest away from them, sponge him off with a deodorant, or disinfect or spray him with a deodorant spray made for dogs.

To be a successful show dog a male must have two testicles fully descended into the scrotum. It is unwise to use a monorchid at stud without knowing the reason why he has that condition. Monorchids are fertile, but if the condition is a hereditary one, it is not advisable to use one at stud, as they can breed the non fertile cryptorchid who have no descended testicles.

Occasionally a dog is a monorchid because injury has caused one of his testicles to atrophy. That dog could be used quite happily because he will not pass on his defect. Make sure the testicle wasn't removed by the vet when the dog was having an operation to correct an inguinal hernia. Such hernias are hereditary and dogs and bitches with that condition should not be bred from. If a monorchid sires puppies with the same condition, he should be withdrawn from stud. Although fertile, unless there is some very special reason, it is better not to use him.

One of the most difficult duties of the stud dog owner is to say 'No'. If you have the good of the breed at heart, times come when you must refuse a bitch to your dog. The line may not mix. You may know that the bitch has had litters every season. You may know the bitch owner sells puppies to multi-breed kennels or pet shops. Unfortunately if you are high minded and refuse the bitch, such breeders usually find any other stud dog whose owner does not have such scruples. Even worse, they buy their own stud dog who may be totally unsuitable for their bitches. However you must stick to your principles.

The ideal stud dog should be dominant for his virtues, virile and masculine in his behaviour. If you have such a dog you are lucky and you will find it satisfying when his progeny are successful in the ring and in their homes. What delight it is to see his name in the top ten stud dogs named in the Club's *Year Book*, for that means he has many progeny who have been winning points during the year.

In-breeding

All ills, real and imaginary, which assail the dog of any breed are blamed on 'in-breeding' by the lay person. 'In-breeding' is when two close relatives are mated together, eg father to daughter, mother to son, brother to sister, niece or nephew to uncle or aunt. The good visible or dominant points are brought out and strengthened, but also any hidden recessive points in both parents are brought to light. It does not introduce any good or bad points, but concentrates what is in the genetic make up of the dog. This can happen in any breeding programme, but by in-breeding the process is quickened.

In the early days all Cavaliers were in-bred. They had very little stock to choose out-cross lines. If this practice had not been used the process of evolving the Cavalier would have taken much longer.

In-breeding should not be practised by the novice and only very occasionally by an experienced breeder who by very selective breeding wishes to establish a characteristic as a pure dominant and to eliminate an undesirable recessive. In-breeding without careful selection and without knowledge of the faults the common ancestor had, or carried as a recessive, could be courting disaster.

Colour inheritance

Genetics, or the science of heredity, is a very complicated matter and I do not propose to delve into it in any great detail. For those who wish to pursue the subject in greater depth there are many comprehensive books with mind boggling diagrams, Punnett squares and a vocabulary of their own, written by geneticists especially for dog breeders.

There are simple laws of heredity which should be understood. The basis is Mendel's law. Mendel was a Czechoslavakian monk living between 1822 and 1884. While trying to breed better plants for the monastery's garden he discovered that if two plants with contrasting characteristics were bred together the first generation cross (F.1) were all like one parent and that parent was called dominant. On breeding two F.1s or first crosses together for a second generation (F.2) the result was a ratio of three plants like the dominant grandparent and one like the other grandparent which is called a recessive.

Whether a creature or a plant is like its dominant grandparent or its recessive grandparent depends on the genes given to it by its parents, who in turn inherited them from their parents and so back *ad infinitum*. Chance does play a part and all the F.2 could be dominant or all could be recessive if the genes united that way.

Any creature is a product of its genes. We all receive one gene from each parent for all our characteristics from the colour of our eyes to the length of our big toe, although sometimes several genes are involved for one characteristic. The same applies to Cavaliers. Colour inheritance can illustrate hereditary in the simplest form, but that can become very complicated if you pursue the matter beyond the simplest practical application.

Each parent gives to its progeny a gene for colour. These genes are usually either dominant which means their characteristics can be seen or they are recessive which means they are masked or hidden if a dominant is present, and can only show when associated with another recessive.

In our first example we will deal with broken colour Cavaliers – that is Blenheim and tricolours. In Cavaliers tricolour is dominant and Blenheim is recessive. That means if a dominant gene is present it will show and the dog must be a tricolour. A recessive is always hidden by the dominant.

Dominant Tricolour	X	Recessive Blenheim

Produce F1, all looking like dominant parent but carrying recessive genes

F1 Dominant Tricolour carrying Blenheim recessive

Two F1 mated together:

F1 Dominant carrying recessive	X	F1 Dominant carrying recessive

could produce by Mendel's 3 to 1 ratio:

F2 Dominant	F2 Dominant carrying recessive	F2 Dominant carrying recessive	F2 Recessive
Tricolour dominant like grandparent	Tricolour carrying Blenheim like parent	Tricolour carrying Blenheim like parent	Blenheim recessive like grandparent

Minstrel Boy of Maxholt tricolour dog born 2.69, by Chandlers Selwyn of Maxholt ex Barings Carlotta owned and bred by Mrs M. Talbot. Minstrel Boy has sired seven champions.

Diagram: key

	Tricolour gene – dominant
	Blenheim gene – recessive
	Black and tan – dominant
	Ruby – recessive

We will begin with a tricolour from two tricolour parents.
Tricolour gene from each parent makes a genetic pattern like this:

This dog has received a tricolour gene from both parents and is therefore a dominant tricolour without any recessive Blenheim genes. He is mated to a Blenheim bitch. He gives a tricolour gene because that is all he has to give. The bitch gives a Blenheim gene because that is all she has to give.

The resulting puppies will be tricolour because

tricolour is dominant and shows but they will carry the recessive or hidden Blenheim gene.

Two tricolours carrying Blenheim genes

mated together can produce dominant tricolour if both parents contribute tricolour genes.

Tricolour carrying recessive Blenheim gene, if one parent contributes a tricolour gene and the other a Blenheim gene.

Blenheim as both parents contribute only the recessive Blenheim gene.

Whether a dog is dominant tricolour or carries the recessive Blenheim gene cannot be seen by looking at him. One can only prove which he is by mating him to Blenheim bitches. If any Blenheim puppies result he must carry the recessive gene. One litter of all tricolours won't prove he is a dominant tricolour. If after three or four litters no Blenheim has appeared, it is fairly safe to assume he is dominant. Scientifically he should have had thirty-two puppies before he could be declared free from carrying the recessive Blenheim gene. It can be seen from this that it is possible for two tricolours carrying Blenheim genes to produce Blenheim puppies. These puppies are not capable of producing a tricolour unless mated to a tricolour. Broken coloured Blenheim to broken coloured Blenheim can only produce Blenheim puppies, because neither parent has any other colour gene to give.

The same principles apply to whole colours. Although black and tan is strictly two colours they are classified as whole colour with the self-coloured red known as ruby. Here black and tan is dominant and ruby recessive.

This dog has received a black and tan gene from each parent so he is dominant black and tan.

If he is mated to a ruby, he will give a black and tan gene because that is all he has to give. The bitch can only give a ruby gene because that is all she has to give. The resulting puppies will be black and tan because black and tan is dominant and shows. The puppies will be carrying the recessive ruby gene.

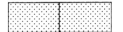

If two black and tans carrying recessive ruby genes are bred together the resulting puppies could be:

 Dominant black and tan receiving only black and tan genes from each parent.

Black and tan carrying recessive ruby gene, receiving black and tan gene from one parent and ruby from the other.

Ruby, each parent contributing the recessive ruby gene.

Ch. Homaranne Caption Blenheim dog born 6.76 by Australian Ch. Homerbrent Henry ex Ch. Homerbrent Captivation, bred by Miss Ann Coaker owned by Mrs K.M. Coaker. Top winning stud dog judged by the wins of his progeny 1980, 1981, 1982, 1983, 1984, 1985, 1986.

Champion Salador Celtic Prince, tricolour dog born 12.5.81, by Salador Chelsea of Loranka ex Salador Cherrybird, owned and bred by Miss S.E. Smith. The youngest Cavalier to win Champion status.

It can be seen that black and tan carrying the recessive ruby gene can produce black and tans or rubies, but two whole colour bred rubies will always produce rubies and never a black and tan when mated together.

Complications occur when whole colours, that is black and tans and rubies, are bred with the broken coloured tricolours and Blenheims. Whole colour is dominant to broken colour. In Cavaliers each parent not only gives a gene for the colour but also a gene to determine whether the colour is whole colour or broken. Black and tan is dominant to all colours. Thus if a dominant black and tan carrying only whole colour genes is mated to a Blenheim, all the litter will be black and tan, but the puppies will carry a recessive for broken colour (tricolour, Blenheim), and ruby. If two black and tans carrying all those recessives are mated, a litter of all four colours could result!

A black and tan dog with a recessive ruby factor but dominant for whole colour will only produce black and tan and rubies if mated to any conventional colour whether whole or broken colour. Often puppies resulting from whole colour and broken colour matings are mismarked. That means white appears on the whole colours, usually on the chest and feet. It is worthwhile introducing broken colour into a whole colour strain to improve necks, shoulders, coat texture and a recent problem, light eyes. In fact many of the whole colour champions can boast a broken colour parent or grandparent.

Within the Mendel's law chance does play a part. One knows one will not get tricolour puppies from two Blenheims nor black and tans from Blenheim and ruby. However, because fertilisation is a random procedure one can get a litter of six Blenheims from two tricolours because both parents gave only recessive Blenheim genes. The litter could equally have consisted of six tricolours if the parents had only given dominant tricolour genes, but chance took a hand.

Cases have been reported of black and tans mated to tricolour producing all rubies, although the black and tan who carried the ruby recessive gene never did that to a ruby. Always he had black and tan to that colour! Two black and tans both carrying recessive red and broken colour genes have produced a litter of five Blenheims!

It is certainly nerve racking waiting for a litter if you have whole colours carrying recessive factors for broken colour. You can have a real assortment. If it is too traumatic stick to recessive Blenheim to recessive Blenheim and you get only Blenheims!

If you use a Blenheim who has come from either black and tan or tricolour parents, do remember that dog is genetically a Blenheim and will have only broken coloured Blenheim genes to pass on. He cannot give his progeny any black and tan or tricolour genes because he has none to give. If you want a black and tan from that dog you must mate him to a black and tan, preferably a dominant whole colour black and tan because if you use a black and tan bitch carrying recessive gene for broken colour and red, you could have a whole litter of Blenheims!

Ch. Steller's Eider of Pantisa. Ruby dog born 31.8.68 by TTiweh Black Prince O'Cockpen ex Cuckoo of Pantisa, bred by Mrs S. Halsall, owned by Mr & Mrs D. Gillies. A great influence on whole colours since the early seventies.

A case was brought to my notice of a dominant for whole colour ruby, from two black and tan parents, being mated to a Blenheim from two black and tans. They were hoping for a black and tan because all four grandparents were black and tan. They were very disappointed to get a litter of five mismarked rubies! Simple genetics show that no other colours were possible.

Basically colour is inherited by the Mendel theory of recessive and dominants, but modifying genes do complicate matters! Whether a ruby or Blenheim has the desired rich chestnut colour or the not so attractive lemony colour or the red almost verging on liver, depends on the action of modifying genes. It has always been the accepted practice not to breed too many generations of Blenheim to Blenheim, ruby to ruby, tricolour to tricolour or black and tan to black and tan, but to mix the colours every few generations to keep the richness of the tan. I am of the opinion that if a rich Blenheim is mated to a rich Blenheim carrying only factors for the rich colour that the tan will remain rich and become established because modifying genes can be eliminated. Breeds which have no choice for colour seem to have established rich colouring, for example the Irish Setter – for a rich red, and the Gordon Setter for rich black and tan. If the colour becomes weak they have no other colours to which they can resort, but must use dogs with the desired colour to correct the fault in the next generation.

When mating a wishy washy Blenheim to tricolour to improve coat colour, do make sure all the Blenheims in the tricolour's pedigree are a good colour or you may make matters worse. The same applies to the mating of a pale ruby to a black and tan. Make sure the black and tan ancestors had good tan whether they were black and tan or ruby.

Modifying genes also determine the amount of white on a tricolour or Blenheim. In genetic language this is known as 'piebald spotting'. Little, a Canadian geneticist whose book *The Inheritance of Coat Colour in Dogs* published by Cornell University Press goes into this in great detail. A very heavily marked tricolour would carry 'plus modifiers' going through a ten point scale to a very lightly marked animal with 'minus modifiers'. The appearance of white on the feet, chest and chin of whole colours is known as 'Irish spotting' and again is caused by a modifier. These modifiers or variants often occur by chance. If desirable the breeder will encourage them by using them in their breeding programme. If they are undesirable they should be discarded for breeding purposes.

Extremely rarely a gene does not reproduce itself exactly. This causes a variation in the progeny and is called a mutation. From time to time in the 60s chocolate coloured tricolours were born. Technically these were tricolours because they had three colours and were marked like a tricolour. Chocolate or liver coloured hair replaced the black; the tan and white markings were the same as in the conventional black haired tricolour.

Because the mutating gene had lost the ability to reproduce the black, the eyes were very light, like boiled gooseberries, and the nose brown to dirty pink.

One could speculate as to whether each case was a mutation or with time the ability to produce chocolate coloured tricolours could remain as a very rare recessive and only appear when such illusive genes meet. Because chocolate is not a recognised Cavalier colour, the breeding of such animals was not pursued. Anyway light eyes and pink noses are alien to the standard and gave them a very ugly expression.

If a chocolate coloured Cavalier was mated back to its parent, grandparent or siblings it could be possible to establish a chocolate strain, but please don't try. It is not a recognised colour and getting perfect markings on the conventional colours is difficult enough without adding further problems. Tricolours are sometimes born without any noticeable tan under the tail, or perhaps only one tan eyebrow. This usually occurs where very little or no black is present in those areas. On very close examination one can usually find just one or two tan hairs. These Cavaliers are still tricolours because they carry the tan gene, but tan hairs are only present in small or uneven quantities.

Occasionally puppies are born who are black and white, the gene for tan having been lost. By selective breeding it is possible to establish a strain who constantly produced black and white. Attempts were made in the late

Highcurley Phyzz at 10 weeks by Paper Tiger of Tanmerack ex Highcurley Athena.

The same dog a year later, showing he has fulfilled his early promise.

60s to produce all black Cavaliers. This was done with black and whites and whole colours. In fact a stud dog appeared who had the ability to sire six colours – black and white, black, tricolour, Blenheim, black and tans and rubies! However in 1972 the breed standard was amended. After listing the four recognised colours as black and tan, ruby, tricolour and Blenheim, the following sentence was added "Any other colour or combination of colours is most undesirable". So the project to produce black Cavaliers was not pursued.

Extremely rarely one hears of litters who do not obey the laws of hereditary. For example it has been reported that a tricolour to Blenheim mating produced a litter of black and tans and rubies; impossible by the rules of colour inheritance we have come to accept. As all the puppies had white on them in varying degrees from a few white hairs to quite wide shirt fronts and white feet, could they have been broken colours with the maximum plus modifying gene making them very heavily marked?

If strange irregularities happen in your Cavalier litters, before you are convinced you have made Cavalier history by producing a litter which defies the accepted rules, check your security. A bitch can be mated unknown to her owner. I once saw a cross between an Old English Sheepdog and a Corgi. The Old English and the Corgi were in adjacent runs and the mating took place with a chain link fence between! It makes one realise if the dog is really keen and the bitch at the peak of her season one should have no difficulties at mating with dogs of equal size and with no artificial barriers between them.

Ch. Crisdig Ted. Blenheim dog born 12.78 by Ch. Crisdig Leading Seaman ex Ranee of Jann-Graye of Crustadele. Owned and bred by Mrs J.R. Burgess.

Do not try to fit the colour inheritance in other breeds to that of the Cavalier. In the Cocker Spaniel black and tan is very recessive and very hard to establish. Occasionally Irish Setters can produce black puppies, while two red Dachshunds can produce black and tans. To sum up:

In Cavaliers black and tan is dominant to all colours.
Tricolour is dominant to Blenheim and ruby.
Ruby is dominant to Blenheim.
Blenheim is recessive to all colours.

Remember colours do not mix. By mating a tricolour and a Blenheim all the puppies will be either tricolour or Blenheim according to the genetic make up of the tricolour. You will not get a tricolour with a chestnut patch in the middle of its back, nor a Blenheim with a black ear! Occasionally one hears of a few black hairs appearing on a Blenheim. Recently I have heard of a Blenheim with one black leg! Oh dear! This is an extremely rare occurrence, but if either parent consistently has puppies with such unusual markings it is questionable if one should continue with them in a breeding programme.

Besides the coat colour the colour of the eyes and noses are thought to be passed by complicated modifying genes.

EYES: The colour of the iris gives the dog the colour of his eyes. The true colour of the iris of the Cavalier is *very dark* brown or black in all coat colours. Rubies and Blenheims cannot be excused lighter eyes with the explanation 'they blend with the coat'. Mrs Pitt wrote in 1953 'The darkest of large eyes and the dense black pigment are two important features. These are essential to the first class Cavalier and are easily lost.'

Light eyes are when the iris is light brown going through a mid brown to a bright yellow in extreme cases. It is thought, though not fully established, that a modifying gene for eye colour is a recessive. A puzzling phenomenon has been reported (not only in Cavaliers) of dogs who have had the darkest eyes as puppies, but by the time they are two years old have developed light eyes.

NOSES: Pale noses spoil the characteristic expression of the Cavalier. Breeding black-nosed Blenheims to black-nosed Blenheims for many generations should diminish the number of pink noses. Before introducing another colour to the line make sure the nose colour is good behind the new dog or you may lose the good colour you have established by introducing a recessive for pink noses.

Some pink noses are caused by hormone changes. A bitch coming into season and who is in season often has an off-coloured nose. Young bitches often have black ones, but after their first season their noses remain 'off'. Bitches with pink noses in ordinary times usually have the beautiful jet black nose of Ann's Son, when feeding puppies.

Although light eyes and pink noses are not wanted in the perfect Cavalier, the great worry is when a recessive gene causes some physical or mental abnormality such as patella luxation, hip dysplasia, fits and eye problems which affect the dog's health, causes untold misery to owners and anguish to the breeder.

Unfortunately these wretched abnormalities are often inherited by the action of several genes and are called polygenic. These are much more difficult to eradicate than the simple Mendel mode of inheritance, because so many factors are involved. The council of perfection would be not to breed from the parents, grandparents and litter mates of affected Cavaliers.

Arranging a mating

Having chosen the dog who appears to be the perfect mate for your bitch in colour, pedigree, looks and of course the most important of all, with the true Cavalier temperament, contact his owner to make sure he is at public stud and under what conditions his owner will accept your bitch.

Some owners ask for a veterinary certificate to say the bitch is free from any vaginal infection.

Inquire what the dog's stud fee is. If there is a time lapse between your first inquiry and when you make your appointment for your bitch to be mated, check again. The dog may have become a champion, sired several top winners and be in great demand. If this is so, the owner may well have raised his fee. It can be very embarrassing if when the mating is over you are expected to pay a higher fee than you bargained for!

Timing your litter is very important. Cavalier bitches can be bred from at the second season. Before you get too deeply committed it is worthwhile consulting your diary. I prefer spring or early summer for the birth of a litter for the puppies then have the summer to grow. They can be out in the fresh air and sun to romp and play, and even sleep during the day. Puppies are easier to house train when you can just pop them out in the sun rather than the snow! Heating costs are less and after all spring is the natural time of the year for the young to be born – baby birds, lambs, rabbits and deer all testify to that!

Having puppies in the spring is not the ideal time for selling them. Sensibly, new owners do not want to take a new puppy, have him at home for four or five weeks and then to kennel him while they are on holiday.

Ch. Salador Crystal Gayle born 4.2.78. Older full sister to Ch. Salador Celtic Prince, owned and bred by Miss Sheila Smith.

Although it is usual for the bitch to travel to the dog, sometimes stud dog owners will take their dog to the bitch. If the bitch is a bad traveller this could be a great help. In these circumstances it would only be fair for the owner of the bitch to pay the stud dog owner's expenses.

The average bitch is usually mated on the eleventh or twelfth day of her season, but bitches are individuals and do not all conform to hard and fast rules. One hears of bitches being mated on the third day of their season and having litters of lovely puppies, while it is quite well known that a bitch can be returned to mixed company after the three weeks separation for her season, to have a clandestine meeting with a male and produce puppies which must have been conceived on the twenty-second or twenty-third day after the beginning of her season.

Remember to segregate in-season bitches from all male dogs. One has heard stories of naïve owners who are terribly upset when they find their bitches pregnant. They declare they could never have been mated, but were only with their father or brother all through the season. I am afraid that dogs, not even Cavaliers, obey the laws of marriage as prescribed in the Book of Common Prayer! To a male dog any in-season bitch is his whatever their relationship, or even breed.

A bitch is ready to be mated when the ovum or eggs are released from the ovaries and are ready to be fertilised by the male sperm. If the bitch is mated too early she may have a small litter or no puppies at all because the ovum have not been released. If she is mated too late in the season the ovum may have died off and passed out of her body unfertilised. Again a very small litter or no puppies may be the result.

Getting the correct day is the problem. Most bitches do conform to the eleventh or twelfth day rule. I find the best guide is the bitch's behaviour. If you have more than one bitch, it is easier because the bitch in season will 'flirt' with the others. For a few days it will be mild, but as she reaches the optimum day she will be really throwing herself at the other bitches and asking them to mount her. If she is your only bitch, tickle the base of her tail and if she gives it a sideways swish you know she is probably ready.

A good guide to when the bitch is ready is when the heavy dark red blood discharge has ceased and the colour is pale and the vulva is soft. Some beginners wait until the colour has stoppped altogether and then find they have left it too late and the bitch is over her season by the time she meets the dog.

For a maiden bitch arrange to have her mated on the eleventh or twelfth day. Usually this is the right day, but if she fails to have a litter reconsider another day for the next attempt at the next season. If she seemed to show colour for a day or two after the eleventh or twelfth day, next time take her later in the season.

Make sure you start counting from day one, when the vulva is swollen and there is blood. If you are not quite sure squeeze the vulva and swab it with cotton wool. If it is a dark red blood discharge, your bitch is in season. If browny keep a careful watch and count day one from when the discharge turns red. The bitch will give you a clue by sudden vigorous cleansing of her vulva. Blenheims and tricolours are easier to spot than the whole colours. If you are going to breed from your bitch do inspect her daily.

There is nothing more frustrating for a stud dog owner to hear a prospective client say when telephoning to make an appointment for the mating 'Well I think she may have come in on Friday! I looked at her Tuesday and she wasn't then'. The bitch could have been in for several days before the owner noticed, and then it is difficult to judge the correct day. Very rarely bitches have a colourless season. Their vulva is very swollen and they have a clear discharge. They can have a perfectly normal litter from such a season. Bitches do vary in the amount of swelling. Some are very large and hard. It looks very uncomfortable. In these cases it is better to wait until it is slightly less swollen and softer. Some, mostly whole colours, remain very small and it is difficult to note that they are in season.

I am afraid we have tried to make our bitches adapt to the hurly burly of modern times. It is amusing how many bitches are just ready for mating at the week-end. Sunday morning at 11 o'clock is a very popular time. If there is an important show in the area of the stud dog's home, it is amazing how many bitches are 'just ready' on the day of show so that her owner doesn't have to make two journeys. Of course, it may be the correct day, but I do suspect many bitches are mated too early or too late to fit in with the family arrangements.

Before the war when cars were not such a way of life and we were served by an efficient railway to all parts of the country, bitches were frequently sent to the dog by train, in travelling boxes of course, very early in their season, under the care of the guard. The bitch stayed, had one or two matings and returned home by the same method at the end of the season. This resulted in bitches producing good litters of several puppies. This was partly due to the mating taking place at the correct time and without hurly burly. With the present-day rail service, the practice is not practical and in fact it would be foolhardy to send your bitch unaccompanied.

These days the bitch is taken on the day the owner thinks is correct and sometimes the poor bitch is almost raped with the aid of her owner and the stud dog's owner. This is quite cruel. It is far better to go early in the season and if the bitch is not willing, either leave her with the stud dog owner, or make the journey again 48 hours afterwards. If the stud dog owner has no accommodation for visiting bitches, they often have an arrangement with a local boarding kennel who takes bitches in season and arrange for the mating when she is ready. Of course it is more satisfactory if the mating can be accomplished with the owner present both for the bitch and her owner but it is a good compromise if it is difficult to visit on the correct day.

If the bitch has missed at the previous season, arrange to have two matings at the next season with 48 hours between each attempt.

The vet can help by taking vaginal swabs and examining them under a microscope for the change in cell structure which takes place at the optimum time for mating. This is an expensive procedure both in time and money as it means several trips to the vet for three or four days. By the time the cell structure tells you your bitch is ready, the stud dog of your choice may well be booked to another bitch!

Australian Ch. Chandlers King Midas. Born 9.75 by Ch. Chandlers Phalaris ex Chandlers Regina. Bred by Mrs V. Preece and exported to Mr Denis Montford, Australia. There he won many major awards and became a very influential stud dog.

The mating

As soon as your bitch is in season, ring the stud dog owner and arrange the date. Do be punctual. It is very annoying for the owner of the stud dog if the bitch is due at 11 am and arrives at 2.30 pm. Of course you may be delayed by traffic or by the car breaking down, but it is only common courtesy to find a telephone as soon as you realise you are not going to be on time, and explain the situation.

When you finally arrive, do remember the Dog Owner's Code. Do not walk your bitch up and down outside the stud dog owner's premises to relieve herself. It is anti-social and could attract all the uninoculated canine Romeos in the area to the premises. If she has puppies and young stock the stud dog owner certainly does not want roamers spreading disease. When you telephone for your apointment ask if the owner minds your bitch spending pennies on her premises, or could she suggest a nearby piece of ground where you could walk your bitch without causing any nuisance. This will make the bitch comfortable for when she meets the dog.

It would be ideal if one could put the dog and bitch together in an enclosed paddock and allow them to get on with it in their own way and time. Unfortunately we do not live in an 'ideal world', and so we have to 'help' nature along. In the wild the dog would not have the heavy feathering to impede him. He would have several bitches, all well known to him, in his pack. There would possibly be several in season at once, so he would only choose the ones who were absolutely ready and because he was the stud dog of the pack he would be extremely forceful.

Here we have artificial situation. A strange dog and bitch are introduced to each other for the first time and expected to mate immediately. It must be especially bewildering and frightening for a maiden bitch who is on foreign territory to be pounced upon by an enthusiastic male dog. Stud dog owners should know how to control their dogs. If he is so keen that he is likely to frighten the bitch, he should be kept on the lead, allowed to whisper 'sweet nothings' in her ear and then to play before serious business begins. Once the bitch is relaxed, playing with the dog and twitching her tail to one side, you know you are there in the correct time of her season. An extra few minutes spent in the preliminaries are well worthwhile. Do allow plenty of time for the mating. Do not be looking at your watch and impatient to be off.

Because crawling around the floor with the couple is such a back breaking business, many breeders with small breeds of dogs use a table. We use the top of our chest deep freeze with a non slip mat on top. It is exactly the correct height and area, 34in high × 25in deep × 52in long (864mm × 635mm × 1.32m) and extremely steady. I had to be very firm with a salesman who was trying to persuade me to buy an upright model when we had to replace our old freezer! He was extolling all the virtues of the upright variety and all the disadvantages of the chest variety. I didn't tell him why the chest was *so* ideal for *my* purpose! If the bitch is ready she doesn't mind being on top of the table (or freezer) but if she becomes apprehensive and uncooperative, it would be better to revert to the floor.

The bitch's owner should gently hold the bitch's head and speak quietly to her. The dog will mount her rear. If she is ready she will twitch her tail sideways and lift her vulva to make it easy for the dog to enter. If they are both heavy coated the stud dog owner may have to hold the feathering out of the way and guide the dog. A good stud dog will allow his owner to do this. With a maiden bitch, he may have several attempts before he succeeds in penetrating. When he finally gets there, the bitch may shoot forward and unseat the dog. The bitch's owner must prevent this and hold the bitch steady. The stud dog owner should warn novice bitch owners that Cavaliers can be very vocal during the mating. If this does happen reassure the owner all is well. It can be very frightening to hear your bitch screaming.

When the dog is well in the bitch, his penis will swell until he is firmly tied to the bitch. It is as well to hold him in that position for a minute or two until he is really extended. He will want to dismount and turn so that the dog and bitch are joined, but standing back to back. This is known as the tie. The purpose of the tie is not fully understood, but it is a commonly held theory that it is a legacy from the wild dog days when the pair would be in danger of attack from behind if the dog was mounted over the bitch. By adopting this posture they could see danger from all angles and defend themselves. It is a curious phenomenon and every stud dog owner is relieved when it takes place, even though it is the strength of the bitch's vaginal muscles which control the duration of the tie. They can remain in this attitude for several minutes up to over an hour. The bitch sometimes becomes restless and tries to pull away. She should be gently restrained as she could injure the dog if she is too forceful. Some bitch owners grasp the bitch violently around the loin to prevent her moving. I have heard that this could restrict the flow of semen, but can find no scientific evidence for this! However, it is as well to be careful. Some stud dog owners hold their dogs to 'Attention', during the tie. However it is not really necessary because as long as both the dog and the bitch are comfortable they will come to no harm. If my stud dog wants to sit or even lie down, I let him. Keep a watch for them parting. The dog will usually tell you, because he will step away from the bitch, sit down and begin to clean himself and make himself tidy. Bitches do have puppies without a tie. The semen bearing the sperm is ejaculated during the first few seconds of the male thrusting, but stud dog owners are not entirely happy unless there is a tie. Some dogs are anxious to turn before they are fully extended, but experienced handlers are ready for this and hold him on until it is safe to do so.

The bitch may growl and be very unpleasant to the dog if she is frightened and not ready for mating. Owners are often really horrified if their sweet natured little bitch suddenly shows an uncharacteristic side to her. Do not be alarmed! Mating is getting down to basics, and this is her basic instinct to defend herself against the attentions of the aggressive male. If she is persistently against the dog, separate them, have a cup of coffee, and then try again. If no progress is made and she continues to object you probably have not found the right day. It would be better for all concerned to call it all off and try in 48 hours' time. If the bitch still objects she is very likely over the peak of her season.

Some bitches have a vagina stricture, which may cause the dog trouble. He may be able to break a slight one, but a strong one should be dealt with by a veterinary surgeon. Some dog owners smear the vulva and vagina with vaseline on their finger. This could be a dangerous practice because unless a sterile finger stall and sterile vaseline is used, germs could be introduced which could prevent pregnancy or cause sickly puppies.

There are many old wives' tales concerning mating which have no scientific backing, but are rather fun. Here are a few:

If a bitch licks her lips during the tie she will have puppies!

If the pair face east during the penetrating period the bitch will have more bitch puppies.

If you tip the bitch on to her right side after the tie is over, you will get bitches because right side is the strong side and if the bitch is lying on that side the sperm cannot reach there!

By the same theory if you lay the bitch on her left side you will get dogs, because the weaker (?) sperm making bitch puppies cannot get there!

If you tip the bitch up on to her front feet after they separate you will shake the sperm into the correct place.

If you allow your bitch to spend a penny a couple of hours after the mating, you will wash out the sperm.

Nonsense, of course!

After the mating is over let the bitch rest quietly. If she is used to the car and it is not too hot that will be an ideal place for her to settle and have a nap. Remember she can still be mated by another dog and have puppies by both him and the stud dog of your choice. Take care that she is kept apart from *all* other male dogs until her season is well over.

With the bitch resting quietly there are the formalities to be completed. The bitch's owner pays the stud fee and receives from the stud dog owner, a copy of the dog's pedigree and a receipt with conditions for repeat service if the bitch should miss in this case. Some stud dog owners will allow another bitch to be brought to one of her dogs, but some will only allow the same bitch to the same dog. The owner of the stud dog will also give you a signed copy of the Kennel Club Form 1 known as 'the blue form'. The dog's owner has to sign that the bitch has been mated on such a day by the dog named. It is supposed to help against fraudulent pedigrees. However I have never heard of the Kennel Club checking with the stud dog owner that such a mating had taken place. The bitch's details are usually left for the bitch's owner to fill in. It does seem rather pointless.

With the first stage towards the production of that carefully thought out litter completed, the bitch owner will spend an anxious time until it is confirmed that she is in whelp. This will be dealt with in the chapter on bitches.

8 The Bitch

ONE of the first questions asked by a new owner of a bitch is 'when will she come into season?' This is an impossible question to answer for all bitches are individuals. A young bitch can have her first season any time from six months of age up to fourteen or fifteen months. There is some suggestion that the increase in daylight intensity helps to bring bitches in. Whether this is true or not, spring seems to be a busy time for stud dogs. If you have more than one bitch, they often come in season together or follow each other in. The interval between seasons is reckoned to be six months, but Cavaliers can go from five to twelve months between without any ill effects. If the seasons are more frequent than five months and are abnormal in the amount of discharge, one should seek veterinary advice.

Old bitches seem to continue with seasons to a very great age. An old fourteen-year old of mine has been frisky with a full three week season. If old bitches show any abnormal discharge or seem to be drinking large quantities of water, a visit to the vet is indicated.

The usual pattern for the season is the swelling of the vulva and a brownish discharge. This is followed by a heavy red discharge which lasts for ten days. Count day one from the day this type of discharge begins. About the eleventh day the discharge thins and the bitch is considered ready for mating during the next few days. By twenty-one days the dicharge has usually stopped and the vulva returned to normal. This is the general routine for the average bitch, but some have very short seasons and need to be mated on the fourth or fifth day while others need to be mated on the sixteenth and seventeenth day.

Even if the bitch hasn't been mated sometimes she will behave as if she was. She could be having a phantom or pseudo pregnancy as described in Chapter 7. About three months after her season, the bitch will lose her coat and not appear at her best. Usually she will grow it again and just before her next season will be in full coat. Coat growth is closely allied to the reproduction cycle. Bitches who are spayed often have very heavy coats. Bitches who have short cycles of five to six months never grow the really glamorous coats which bitches who go nine to ten months between seasons do.

It was stated in the Breeding Chapter that much careful thought should go into the matter if you are contemplating breeding from your bitch. A bitch not used for breeding needs to lead a normal healthy life. She will need plenty of exercise and a good balanced maintenance diet to keep her trim. Pet bitches sometimes become very content and lazy and sometimes put on weight. This is neither good for their health nor their beauty, so keep a careful watch and adjust their diet if necessary.

The question of spaying a pet bitch is a problem which needs much thought. Spaying is a hysterectomy, which is a surgical operation to remove the uterus and usually the ovaries. If it is necessary to perform the operation in order to save the bitch's life then of course it is essential. If the operation is being contemplated for the convenience of the owner so that they do not have to bother about seasons, that is another matter. Many animal societies advocate that all pet bitches are spayed. With the vast numbers of stray and unwanted puppies and dogs they have to deal with, one can understand their attitude. Surely no Cavalier owner would ever allow their bitch to stray whether in season or not, and so the problem of unwanted mongrel litters does not arise. When the bitch is in season there are simple precautions that can be taken to dissuade unwanted stray males coming near your home.

Never take an 'in season' bitch for a walk by walking out of the garden gate and along the pavement and so leaving an interesting scent trail for stray dogs to follow back to the house. If you have a garden which is dog proof, which you should have, there is really no need for an 'in season' bitch to be taken out for exercise. Games with a ball in the garden would be sufficient for three weeks. Do not leave her unattended in the garden if there is a possibility of dogs getting in. If you feel you must take her out, carry her to the car and take her to the exercise ground. That way no trail is left.

There are many preparations sold to discourage males by disguising the scent of the 'in season' bitch. Sprays and aerosol deodorant may help. I had a stud dog who always pricked up his ears and sniffed the air expectantly when he smelt the old fashioned tell tale citronella meant to disguise the 'in season' smell, but told him there was an interesting lady about! Modern products are more scientific than the camouflage smells, and do help.

Some people find chlorophyll tablets given in time and in sufficient quantities helpful, although the veterinary profession rather scorn them.

If you feel it is necessary to spay your bitch, consider these points:

1   Never spay a bitch before her first season. If you do, she could well suffer from vulva dermatitis because her vulva remains immature. This is difficult to treat.
2   Some spayed bitches suffer from urine incontinence, especially if they are spayed too young.
3   Urine scalding can result from spaying a bitch too early.

4 Some spayed bitches grow enormous coats not only in thickness, but also in length.
5 Many spayed bitches lose their personality and become stodgy. If spayed too young they are often dull and lethargic, both with humans and other dogs.
6 Very often spayed bitches put on weight, so their dietary needs must be carefully controlled. It is sad to see a spayed Cavalier bitch grossly overweight with an unkempt haystack of a coat.

Contraceptive preparations are available from veterinary surgeons. They are hormone preparations and come in two forms, tablets and subcutaneous injections. They can be used in three ways:

1 To stop a season which has just started. In this case keep your bitch away from all male dogs for a week after administering the dose so that the hormones have time to work.
2 To prevent the season starting, in which case the dose should be given at least a week and preferably two weeks before the bitch is due.
3 The permanent postponement of the season in which the bitch will need a course of hormone preparation. Discuss the problem with your vet especially if you are planning to breed from your bitch at the next season.

Thought should be given if you are contemplating giving a young bitch a contraceptive dose to suppress her first season.

These preparations are made from synthetic hormones and should be used with great care. If you are using the tablet form do follow the instructions carefully. Do not increase the dose unless the vet gives permission. You could do great harm.

Incidentally these preparations have proved very useful in the treatment of false pregnancy and some mammary tumours in bitches, and also over-sexiness in male dogs. Of course they should only be administered under strict veterinary supervision.

If you want your Cavalier solely as a loving companion, and you really do think the problem of the season will be a worry, consider having a male. They are every bit as affectionate and companionable as the majority of bitches.

Difficulties do arise if you want to keep dogs and bitches together in the same house unless you have plenty of room to segregate them when the bitch is in season. A lot depends on the dog. He may be very placid and seem to take little or no interest in bitches even at the height of their season. Never take a risk and leave them unchaperoned, even if he does seem disinterested, unless you want a litter.

Some dogs become very excited and worry about bitches in season.

They often go off their food, lose condition and howl! It is far better to send one or the other to kennels. It is expensive every six months, but it is kinder to the dog and apparently bitches become used to kennels at such times. If you have plenty of room and the bitches can be quite separate from the males and have separate exercising grounds, then dogs and bitches can be accommodated on the same premises. Do not bring the bitch back into mixed company too soon. Litters can be conceived on the twenty-third and twenty-fourth days of the season. Give the bitch a good bath and spray her with a good doggy deodorant so that there are no lingering smells on her coat to excite the dog. Some people manage in small premises, but I haven't been very successful. By the end of the three weeks I have had a thin scraggy dog, a frustrated bitch, a chewed door frame where the bitch tried to bite her way out, a household who were thoroughly tired of making sure the two didn't meet, and the miserable complaints of all!

If your bitch should get mated to an undesirable dog, there are three courses open to you:

1   Take the bitch to the veterinary surgeon within twenty-four hours of the mating for an injection to prevent pregnancy. The bitch will continue in season for a further three weeks after such an injection.
2   Allow the bitch to have the unwanted litter. When the puppies are born steel yourself to cull the litter and just keep two for the bitch's sake.
3   Have the bitch spayed before the pregnancy is too far advanced.

The age at which you breed from your bitch for the first time depends on the timing of her seasons and the maturity of the bitch.

If she comes in season before she is eleven months old, then her second season would be the earliest time. If she comes into season for the first time after eleven months, then she *could* be bred from at that season, but it would be preferable to wait until the next time. Any time up to three years of age is in order for a first litter, but after her third birthday I would consult a vet before breeding from a bitch for the first time.

A bitch can have a litter every other season quite happily, provided she whelps normally and there are no complications. Only in exceptional circumstances should a bitch have litters at two consecutive seasons, and then she should have a rest of three seasons afterwards before having the next litter. A bitch who goes twelve months between seasons could be mated each time, provided she is in tip top condition and has strong healthy puppies.

Six and a half years to seven years is really the age for a last litter from a Cavalier bitch. They usually do their puppies very well. Breeding from them after the seventh birthday could be a strain on their reserves. Even at

Ch. Kindrum Rose Red, ruby bitch born 30.10.78 by Kindrum Jiminy Cricket ex Kindrum Victoria Plum. Owned by Mr G. Porter and bred by Mrs P.E. Thornhill.

six and a half, I would have the vet check her over to make sure her heart was in good order.

All bitch owners, both novice and experienced, are anxious to know if their bitches are in whelp. Even after the most successful mating, there is no guarantee that the bitch will have puppies. The gestation period for a bitch is reckoned as sixty-three days, but puppies can be born after fifty-six days and will survive if adequately cared for. Some can be born as late as seventy days. If your bitch is late, do check your diary and dates. A bitch who came to my dog was due for a caesarian if no puppies had arrived by the next morning. I had an extra check with my stud receipt book and found the owner was a week out. This was easily done, as the New Year calendars came into use between the mating and expected arrival of the litter! The bitch had six puppies naturally on the sixty-second day and there was a very red-faced owner who was an extremely experienced breeder in another breed.

It is not advisable for the inexperienced to prod and poke a bitch to see if she is in whelp. If you must know at the earliest possible moment consult your vet. They all have their pet days for diagnosis, usually between the twenty-sixth and thirtieth days. From twenty-one to thirty-one days the foetuses are strung out rather like a string of beads in the uterus and can be felt rather like peas. After that time the horn becomes uniform in shape and the individual pea-like embryos are difficult to feel.

Pregnancy testing with urine is not reliable in the bitch and x-rays should not be used unless the vet suspects complications, and are not much use before the fiftieth day.

The bitch's 'undercarriage' is quite a good indicator. By the beginning of the fourth week the nipples begin to stand away from the body and become pink – the mammary glands themselves begin to develop, but sometimes a phantom pregnancy can cause this. Some bitches scratch their undercarriage with a back foot in a very undignified way, when changes begin to take place about the thirtieth day.

Most bitches have a slight sticky colourless discharge from about the thirty-second day. Providing it is not green or blood stained this is an encouraging sign. If the discharge is excessive or coloured in any way, check with the vet.

Slight changes in behaviour can be a good indicator. Greedy bitches often 'go off' their food at about four and a half weeks and owners become quite worried if it persists for more than a few days. However, the puppies do not seem to suffer even if their mum seems to have eaten far less during pregnancy than their owner would have wished! A word of warning! A bitch of mine who was mated several times, never became pregnant. On the last occasion on the thirty-fourth day after mating, she stopped eating and looked rather miserable. I was delighted because I felt at last she was in whelp. Imagine my horror the next morning when I could see she was really very ill. Thanks to the prompt action of my veterinary surgeon, she was successfully operated on for a very acute pyometra, and lived to tell the tale – but alas no puppies!

Weighing a bitch each week can give an indication if she is in whelp. This is not very reliable because she may be having extra food or forming fluid if she is having a phantom pregnancy. Anyway a Cavalier bitch carrying four or five puppies would only put on ½oz (14g) in puppy weight in the first four weeks.

Many bitches become extra affectionate and have an even more sentimental expression during pregnancy. She must not be molly coddled, but given a normal healthy life with plenty of excercise until she becomes heavy. Then it is advisable to stop her jumping up or rushing through door-ways with the mob. During the last few days you can see the puppies move and you can feel them if you place your hand on her flank.

The danger with many novice breeders is to overfeed their pregnant bitches so that they become fat and not in fit condition with good muscle tone at the time of whelping. They need no extras for the first four weeks, but from the fifth week the amount of food can be gradually increased. If you are feeding a complete feed make sure you are using the grade intended for the pregnant bitch. If you are using meat and biscuit increase the meat. Scrambled egg and fish are useful extras. Make sure your bitch is receiving her vitamin and mineral supplements. Use them carefully and to

Ch. Millstone Folly of Magjen. Blenheim bitch born 14.2.78 by Dunhelm The Admiral ex Millstone Melba, owned by Mrs & Miss Stroud, bred by Miss S. Mills.

the manufacturer's instructions. Cavaliers need easily assimilated calcium and during the last weeks of pregnancy a colloidal form of calcium with phosphorus and vitamin D should be given. This product is available from the vet and he will recommend the dosage.

By six weeks of pregnancy the bitch should be receiving two smaller meals a day rather than one large one. If she will take milk an extra drink of this is beneficial as it is a good source of calcium. If the lactose causes loose motions, try goat's milk. Meat has no calcium!

During the last few days of pregnancy, the bitch may well become very finicky! She may refuse all food for thirty-six hours before whelping. Other bitches have been known to eat a hearty meal an hour before producing their puppies. Because of the pressure on the bladder if there is a large litter in the uterus, bitches are often unable to get through the night without urinating. Very fastidious bitches will get their owners up once or twice a night during the last ten days. Others just cannot wait and it is as well to provide newspaper on the floor. When the puppies are delivered, the pressure relieved, the bitch will be house clean again.

When the puppies have arrived is the time to step up the feeding. A strong healthy puppy will double its weight in a week. If there are five or six puppies in the litter, the bitch has to produce vast quantities of first-class milk to maintain this growth. If she is not adequately fed, the milk supply will diminish, the puppies' growth will be retarded, the bitch's condition will deteriorate and she could even develop eclampsia and die. (Eclampsia is dealt with in the chapter on diet.)

The bitch's food should be divided into three meals daily. If feeding the 'complete food' type, make sure you are using the 'lactating bitch' grade. If it is the dry porridge type, mix with milk – preferably goat's milk to lessen the risk of diarrhoea. Feed some good quality protein, milk, meat, fish, chicken or egg. Some advocate leaving a bowl of expanded pellet type food for the bitch to feed *ad lib*. With the biscuit and meat diet, step up the meat, egg custard and milk content. Always leave an adequate supply of fresh drinking water which must be available at all times. Bitches feeding puppies drink prodigious amounts, especially if feeding large litters.

A bitch with a small litter, of course, will not need such generous amounts. Make sure she has sufficient to meet her needs and those of her puppies. Excess food will cause a weight problem later.

As you wean the puppies, gradually begin to decrease the amount of food the bitch is having. One really has to be guided by the condition of the bitch in this matter. Some look dreadful after feeding their litter, thin, scraggy and their coats are very sparse and lack lustre. Continue to feed a good quality protein diet with a balanced vitamin and mineral supplement until she regains condition. Often bitches do not lose weight and indeed some even put on weight and need careful dieting to regain their figures.

Coats suffer from a bitch having a litter, but again they vary from bitch to bitch. Occasionally one sees in the show ring a well coated bitch who had a litter ten or eleven weeks previously. Her moult is still to come. Usually bitches begin to lose their coats when the puppies are four to five weeks old, and they have a complete moult. One can see the skin through the sparse hairs. Tails are the last to moult and the last to regain their beauty. Be patient and that 'rats tail' will get back to its original glory. A little polyunsaturated margarine on the food will help.

Preparations for whelping

Before you mated your bitch you should have thought carefully where you would like the puppies to be born. A lot depends on the temperament of your bitch. For the first litter it is advisable to find a quiet, adequately lit and heated place and one with which the bitch is familiar. If it is to be an outhouse, it is unkind to put a bitch out there in an unaccustomed place just before she is due to whelp. If it has to be an outhouse, make sure it is dry, draughtproof, has electricity and that there is plenty of room to move around the box. A box-room or a quiet corner of a little used room are ideal provided the bitch has been allowed to spend time there getting used to it before whelping. Carpets and furniture should be moved or covered up because whelping can be a messy affair. The feathering on a bitch's tail can become very mucky. When getting in and out of the box and wagging her tail the bitch can unwittingly make a horrid mess on furniture, carpets and even walls.

If she is your only dog and you are a small quiet family, a warm spot in the kitchen will do. If you have more than one dog and have a busy family, kitchens are noisy, bustly places which could be very distracting to a bitch.

Natural instincts die hard and bitches will often try to dig a nest under hedging, sheds, and bushes to provide a natural home for their puppies. Our cypress hedge has a mass of holes dug under it where generations of Cavaliers have dug both for their real litters and for the imaginary ones when they have had phantom pregnancies. I blame their ancestor Rangers Nicky Picky who dug a hole and had several puppies in it without her owner knowing where she was!

Some bitches have been known to hold up whelping if they are put into unfamiliar surroundings. They may have selected a place which *they* decide is suitable. Providing it is not out of the question, through danger, lighting or cold, it may be as well to humour the bitch and to allow her to have her puppies where she thinks. When they have all arrived move them all into your chosen place. She is usually too busy feeding, washing and admiring the puppies to worry about the move. However, she may suddenly think some are missing and rush back to where she whelped to make sure. If you have to move her and the box do clear up very thoroughly, get rid of any dirty newspaper, or synthetic fur bedding. Disinfect well so that no smell of the puppies remains.

Some breeders have the litters in their bedrooms and move them to more suitable quarters when the puppies are about three to four weeks old. Again remove all evidence from the original area, because bitches often need a lot of convincing that they have not left a puppy behind. She will return many times to make sure there isn't a spare puppy under the bed!

The outlay for the first litter is often expensive but if the equipment is well looked after it will last for generations of puppies. The most important thing is a whelping box. One can buy purpose-built models or the family handyman could quite easily make one.

WHELPING BOX: The purpose of the whelping box is to provide the bitch with a closed-in bed where she is cosy and warm and where the puppies are safe. If you are only having the occasional litter, it is a good idea to have a box which can be easily dismantled and packed away flat. When it is wanted again, it can be re-assembled and bolted together.

Make sure the box is big enough for the bitch to lie out flat, and also room for the puppies to grow. About 3 to 4in (76 to 100mm) from the base, there should be a shelf to make a crash barrier. Puppies often crawl behind their mother's backs. The crash barrier leaves space for the puppy between the shelf and the floor and saves it from being crushed if the mother should lean back on it.

Make sure the barrier is of solid construction. On a purpose-built box ½in (13mm) iron dowelling was fitted. This certainly prevented the mother from crushing the puppy. However, the puppy became wedged between the dowelling and the back of the box. It was only the distress calls of the puppy that alerted his owner to his dangerous predicament. The dowelling was removed and a wooden shelf without a space between it and the box fitted, so preventing further troubles.

I prefer a whelping box with a removable lid. When wanting to attend to the bitch it can be lifted up and you have easy access. When in place it provides a cosy warm bed, because most of the heat from the bitch and her puppies is kept in the box.

A high-sided box without a lid is useful if you are using an infra-red lamp to provide gentle warmth. Many breeders of all breeds swear by them, but I have had a Cavalier bitch remove her puppies from the box because she didn't like the infra-red heat. Also cold air is drawn to the lamp causing cool draughts above the litter. I use an electrically heated metal pad with a towelling cover. It is very safe, well insulated, gives off a gentle heat and is very economical to run. It occupies about one third of the floor area of the whelping box, so that the puppies can migrate to it if they are cold and away from it when they are too warm. It is convenient to have a front flap which can be lowered. When the puppies begin to get out the box, this makes an easy ramp for them to climb back into the box.

There are sophisticated boxes with cavity walls and bases which are lined with heavy foil or even fibre glass between the two walls for insulation. If your bitch is to be in a cold outhouse, this may be necessary.

Beside being the correct size, a whelping box must be easily cleaned. Wood can be scrubbed with soap, water and household bleach. Fibre glass is also easy to keep clean. When the whelping box is finished with, scrub the box very thoroughly and then leave it out in the air for several weeks. Sun, rain and even frost are first class disinfectants. If the box is the dismantling type turn the parts regularly. After a few weeks in the open, the box can be scrubbed again, thoroughly dried and stored until wanted for the next litter. The base of the box can be covered with modern vinyl floor covering which can be removed. This will stop urine soaking into the wood.

One of the better inventions of the late 1970s for dogs and their owners is the synthetic sheepskin type bedding made for veterinary use. This has a thick pile about 1in (25mm) deep embedded in a firm backing. If placed on newspaper moisture soaks through the fibres leaving the bed dry and the newspaper quite damp. The bedding can be easily washed in the washing machine and then tumble dried. When new they are white and pristine, but they do become rather shaggy after hundreds of washes. I have pieces which I have used for the last five years, first for whelping and now for general use when I purchased new ones for puppies.

Ruby bitch with three ruby puppies and one black and tan puppy. As ruby is recessive to black and tan, the ruby mother can only give ruby genes, therefore the father of this litter must have been a black and tan carrying recessive ruby genes. His recessive ruby genes combined with the mother's ruby genes to produce the ruby puppies. His black and tan gene combined with the mother's ruby gene to produce the black and tan puppy. This black and tan puppy would carry a recessive ruby gene, and be capable of having black and tan and ruby puppies. Note the safety barrier around the box and the synthetic 'sheep skin' bedding.

To summarise:

EXPENSIVE EQUIPMENT WHICH CAN BE RE-USED:

1   Whelping box.
2   Heating pad – make sure it is a veterinary type.
3   Three pieces of synthetic sheepskin veterinary bedding.

OTHER ESSENTIALS:

1   Masses of clean newspaper.
2   Plenty of clean towels.
3   Cardboard box with warm hot water bottle and soft bedding – old clean woolly jumper is ideal.
4   A packet of disinfectant powder made for washing babies' nappies. This is ideal for puppy bedding. Follow the manufacturer's instructions.
5   A large plastic bucket to soak the bedding in the nappy disinfectant.
6   Scales and notebook – and pen!
7   Honey, glucose and colloidal calcium for the bitch.

OTHER EMERGENCY ARTICLES: We hope these will not be necessary, but it is as well to be prepared in the belief that if one is ready, it will not be required.

1   Premature baby feeder.
2   Specially formulated substitute bitch's milk powder.
3   A steady table with a good light and washing facilities if you need the vet.

Timetable for a Brood Bitch

1   *Anoestrus* a period of no reproductive activity.

2   *Pro Oestrus* the first part of the season, a period of 10 to 12 days when a dark red discharge can be seen. The bitch is not ready for mating.

Timetable for Brood Bitch's Owner

1   Bitch's owner should make a provisional booking with stud dog owner.
2   Check with vet the latest thought on vaccination for parvo virus and other diseases. Have the bitch vaccinated if necessary.
3   If the bitch has been regularly wormed as a puppy, there will be no worms in her intestine. The worm larvae are embedded in tissue, parts where no worm mixture can reach, so there is no need to worm her.
4   Make sure she is free from external parasites, as there is some thought that the use of insecticides during pregnancy could be detrimental to the puppies.
5   Make sure the bitch is having a well balanced diet, that she is having plenty of exercise, and that she is not carrying any excess weight.

1   On first day of season confirm booking with stud dog owner.
2   If a veterinary certificate that the bitch is free from vaginal bacterial infection is required, have swab taken immediately colour is seen.
3   Segregate the bitch from male dogs.

3   *Oestrus* The second part of the season. The crucial time when the bitch ovulates. The discharge is less bloody, the vulva soft and she will normally be willing to be mated from the eleventh to fourteenth day.

4   *Meto Oestrus* The period when the bitch is pregnant if mated or imagines she is if she is having a false or phantom pregnancy.

1   Watch the bitch carefully. If she is flirting with other bitches, twisting her tail and inviting them to mount her, she is ready for mating.

2   Still keep her away from male dogs until season is well over.

Timetable for Pregnant Bitch

Sixteenth to eighteenth day the fertilised egg becomes implanted in the uterus. **Twenty-first to thirty-first day**, foetuses are separate shapes within the uterine horns rather like a string of beads. Each embryo can be separately defined.
Twenty-eighth day nipples begin to stand away from the tummy and look pink.
Thirtieth day onward. Bitches often scratch their undercarriage with back foot.
Thirty-second day. A slight sticky colourless discharge is seen from the vulva. If coloured or excessive consult the vet. Spaces between the foetuses fill with fluid, making the horns a uniform shape and so difficult to feel individual embryos.
Thirty-fifth day. Changes often occur in feeding habits. Greedy bitches 'go off' food. Fussy feeders develop their appetite. Slight rounding immediately behind ribs.

Timetable for Pregnant Bitch's Owner

Feed normal amounts of well balanced diet, give plenty of exercise. Twenty-first to thirty-first day, if you are very anxious to know if she is in whelp, this is the time the vet can feel the pea-size foetuses. Do not poke or prod yourself.
If the vet confirms pregnancy, order the whelping box, veterinary bedding and heating pad.
Leave plenty of time for delivery. Also make enquiries and purchase a premature baby feeder and bitch's milk substitute.

Do not subject the bitch to any stress from this time on. Plenty of exercise, but not for too long periods at a time. If she gets wet make sure she is dried quickly. Avoid boisterous games with rough companions. However, do not molly coddle her.

Forty-second day. It is now obvious that the bitch is in whelp even if she only has a small litter. There is a sudden change in her shape. The uterine horns fold over and cause a drop in the outline of the abdomen. Added to this the mammary glands and nipples are developing.

Gradually increase the protein in her diet, extra eggs, meat, cheese and milk. As she becomes heavy divide her meals into two or three smaller meals.

Forty-ninth day. The puppies can cause pressure on the bladder and the bitch may need to urinate more frequently.

Don't scold her if she cannot last the night. Provide a thick layer of news-paper which she can use if necessary.

Fiftieth day. The skeletal bone is laid down and the puppies can be felt as rounded shapes.

Introduce her to the whelping box in the whelping area. Take your knitting and library book. Have a quiet half-an-hour getting on with your task while she gets used to the box – good for both of you!

Fifty-second day. Puppies can be felt moving.

Allow the bitch to decide how much exercise she needs.

Fifty-sixth day. Puppies can be seen moving. The uterus and the contents drop even further leaving the spine and flanks looking gaunt.

Have whelping quarters completely ready. Do not forget the drinking water.

From fifty-sixth day onward keep a careful watch on your bitch. The puppies could arrive any time now!

The whelping

There are many excellent specialist books written on whelping so I only propose to give an outline of what to expect in a whelping. It is as well to have a knowledgeable friend who will be willing to sit with you through your first whelping or at least to be at the other end of the telephone. Your vet should know the dates you expect your litter and some ask you to let them know when the bitch begins bed making.

Bitches usually give adequate warning that they are going to whelp, but again there are individuals who produce a litter without any warning. Many experienced breeders have been very surprised to find the bitch, who ate a hearty supper the night before, smugly nursing a litter, all dry and tidy, the next morning. Although this can happen, one usually has ample warning.

Keep an unobtrusive watch on your bitch especially if she is digging holes under the hedge or garden shed. Wash her undercarriage with a mild disinfectant, rinsing it well so that the puppies are not discouraged from sucking by the disagreeable taste of disinfectant and soap! If the bitch has quantities of feathering, it could help to thin them out. Don't worry! She would lose them naturally by the time the puppies are three months old. It does save a lot of time in cleaning up the bitch and does help to keep the bed dry.

As a rule the bitch wants solitude when she begins to whelp. She may well appreciate the discreet presence of her owner to reassure her, and the presence of a knowledgeable friend to reassure her owner, but the rest of the family should be barred from the whelping room. Do not sit in front of the box staring at her, but watch discreetly while reading or catching up with your correspondence!

FIRST STAGES OF LABOUR:

1   A few days before the bitch's temperature, usually 101.5°F begins to drop and can go as low as 98°F.
2   Thirty-six hours beforehand she may go off her food.
3   She will urinate often and frequently pass small quantities of faeces. Watch her as she goes out to relieve herself as very occasionally puppies can slip out while she is straining for a bowel action.
4   She makes her nest by digging and tearing up the newspaper and bedding in her box. Give her plenty of newspaper to work on.
5   She will pant and tremble as the birth becomes more imminent.
6   Her milk will often drip from her nipples.
7   This stage can last from 12 to 24 hours, often longer with a first litter. After 24 hours with no result, it might be as well to advise the vet.

SECOND STAGE OF LABOUR: This is when the bitch begins to strain to expel the puppies. This usually follows a period of very vigorous digging and then a minute or two of quietness. The bitch may be on her side, on her front legs or squat as if passing a motion. The puppy comes down the uterine horns and places itself to come through the cervix. It is a rather tight fit! The ideal position is for a puppy to engage its head resting on the front paws and to emerge in a nose first position. Forty per cent of all puppies are born hindquarters first. This is usually satisfactory, provided the head is released quickly so that the puppy can breathe. Trouble comes when the puppy tries to come broadside on, or one leg is engaged and the head deflected. This is when veterinary help is required unless the breeder is very experienced and has been trained how to turn the puppy. It is essential to watch the birth carefully throughout stage two labour. If purposeful straining continues for more than an hour without any puppies appearing, or if the bitch just gives up after straining hard, and appears to go back to stage one, it is as well to inform the vet. Usually one just gets through on the phone when the bitch gives an almighty push and yell and

the puppy arrives. The action which will tell you the birth is really imminent is the arching of the back, lifting of the tail, a bulge in the vulva and the bursting of the water bag.

THIRD STAGE OF LABOUR: This is the actual birth. Each puppy comes in its own bag. Sometimes these bags are broken during the journey of the puppy down the birth passages. Usually they are intact and as soon as the puppy's head appears, the bitch will break the sac and wash the puppy's face to clear the mouth and nose to free the air passage so that the puppy can breathe. With the first litters, a bitch may be very puzzled and lie there giving the puppy in its bag a very quizzical look. Then the owner should break the sac and clear the air passages. The rest of the puppy may not be born. Don't worry as long as the head is free and the puppy can breathe. After a little rest, the bitch will push again and the rest of the puppy will appear attached by the umbilical cord to the placenta or after birth. The placenta may come away with the puppy or it may not. Watch to see if it is expelled by the time the whelping is over, because if it is left behind it could cause trouble.

First-time mothers may not realise they have to break the cord, so the owner may have to break it herself. It is best to tear it with finger nails or cut with blunt scissors as this crushes the blood vessel and prevents bleeding. Sharp scissors cut in such a way that the cord could bleed. A linen thread tied as a tourniquet about an inch from the puppy will stop this, but you do need someone to hold the wriggly puppy while you tie it.

Some bitches will not leave the cord alone. Watch carefully she does not nibble it too close to the body to make it bleed. Usually by the time two or three puppies arrive she has to divide her attention and they are safe. In the wild, the placenta provided the bitch with a nutritious meal, so that she did not have to leave the nest and puppies to forage for herself. However, with the modern bitch, eating more than one or two can cause diarrhoea. Experienced bitches will quickly gobble them down before her owner can intervene.

The interval between the arrival of each puppy varies. Some bitches will settle down and have a nap between each puppy. If, however, the gap is more than three hours, veterinary advice should be sought. If the bitch is not distressed usually all is well. The average time between each puppy is 10 to 60 minutes. Between the birth of each puppy, bitches can be offered a little warm milk with honey or glucose added, plus a teaspoonful of colloidal calcium. If it makes her sick, of course don't try again, but wait until the whelping is over. When the next puppy seems imminent, remove those born and put them into the box with the warm hot water bottle and warm woolly. The bitch may be energetically bed making and kick the puppy inadvertently, and the fluid from the next puppy may make those who have arrived very wet and chilled.

If a puppy does not breathe, clear the airway of fluid. Hold him down, shake him, rub him vigorously with a rough towel. One cannot say how long one should carry on this resuscitation treatment. If the puppy does not begin breathing fairly quickly, its brain could be damaged because of the lack of oxygen and you may have an invalid puppy.

Even if the puppies are breathing and crying lustily, it is a good idea to rub them dry with a rough towel. This stimulates the blood system, besides drying off the puppy quickly. This will prevent too much heat loss. New born puppies need steady warmth to overcome hypothermia. Puppies in an enclosed box with veterinary bedding and a heated pad, snuggle up to their mother to feed and are usually warm enough. They will be relaxed, feeding well and looking sleek. Chilled puppies are whiney, and squirm around the box. Although they feed, it is not very vigorous sucking. If puppies show these symptoms do check they are warm enough. It is thought, because puppies are reliant on the ambient temperature to prevent hypothermia, cold is one of the main causes of puppy deaths.

When all the litter has arrived, the bitch settles down and wants to rest. Take her out to relieve herself. Watch her just in case there is another puppy all ready to slip out! While she is out, get someone to remove all the soiled newspaper and bedding, and replace it with a clean piece of veterinary bedding and settle the puppies on it. Steady the bitch when she rushes back, as sometimes they leap in and jump on the puppies and could cause damage.

Most Cavalier bitches whelp normally, without any help from owners, knowledgeable friends or vet. However, if you are worried, do get help.

If the vet should advise a Caesarian section operation do not be too dismayed. With modern anaesthetics and up-to-date surgical procedures, it is a very safe operation for bitch and puppies, providing it is performed before the bitch has become exhausted.

There is no more pleasing sight for a breeder than that of a bitch feeding a litter of contented, round, sleek puppies, but one must be vigilant.

Puppies should be inspected for any abnormalities such as hare lip, cleft palate and deformed limbs. Keep a check that each puppy is gaining weight. If a little one is being pushed out, put him on the choicest nipple. Check the mammary glands to make sure the bitch is not developing mastitis. This is when one or more of the mammary glands becomes hard, red to purple in colour and swollen. This usually happens in the back two as the puppies very rarely feed from these. A hot towel wrung out as dry as possible often eases this. If it persists antibiotics may be prescribed. Some vets are rather loathe to give nursing bitches antibiotics as the puppies, receiving small quantities through their mother's milk, could build up an immunity against such drugs.

There is sure to be some vaginal discharge, but if after three or four days this becomes excessive, black and tarry, the bitch runs a temperature, has a real thirst and becomes disinterested in her puppies and food, seek veterinary help, as she may be developing metritis, possibly due to an after birth or even a dead puppy being left behind in the uterus.

Eclampsia has been dealt with in the chapter on diet. Do watch out for it, as it is very alarming and needs urgent attention. Cavaliers are very generous mothers and with several puppies doubling their weight in a week, it is no wonder it is a strain on the bitch's calcium resources.

On the third or fourth day the dew claws can be removed, but there is some modern veterinary thought against this. Cavaliers can have back dew claws and they should be removed. If you must have the tails docked this is the time. If you are a novice do not attempt this operation yourself. Get an experienced breeder, or better still a veterinary surgeon to do the operation.

ORPHAN PUPPIES: If, unfortunately, the bitch is unable to look after the puppies there are two main alternatives. The ideal would be to find a foster

Ruby Cavalier bitch – with her one and only black and tan puppy and two orphan pekinese puppies, whom she adopted at 24 hours of age and reared as her own.

mother. A Cavalier of mine had one puppy. When he was 48 hours old we were asked if we could foster two orphan pekingese who were 24 hours old. They arrived on a dreadful wet winter's night in a shoe box. The Cavalier bitch was taken out and the Pekes were rubbed very thoroughly with soiled bedding and with the sole Cavalier puppy. We all kept our fingers crossed when the bitch returned to the whelping box. She looked very puzzled as if to say 'I didn't think they were there when I went out. Oh well, I suppose they are allowed.' With that she got into the box, gave them a good sniff, settled down with them, licked them and allowed them to feed. All in the space of two or three minutes she was settled with them and brought them up as her own.

The foster mother's puppies should be about the same age as the orphans. Only in extreme cases should day-old puppies be given to a bitch at the end of her lactation. Often a bitch with a phantom pregnancy will produce milk and look after an orphan litter, but there may be a need to feed artificially, for a day or so, until her milk is flowing adequately. Make sure this type of foster mother receives substantial diet with vitamin and mineral supplements because feeding an orphan litter will be as big a strain on her as if it was her own.

It is not often that a suitable bitch is available when there are puppies needing a foster mother; so the owner will have to set about the daunting task of hand rearing. You are taking over the role of mother and must provide as nearly as possible a natural environment. The physical and psychological needs of the litter must be met. The first essentials are patience and thoroughness as it is a time consuming business, but very rewarding when at the end you have a strong healthy litter saved by your efforts.

Puppies can only take the ambient temperature as their own, and with no mother to cuddle up to, they are more susceptible to cold. Keep them very warm in an enclosed box with veterinary bedding and part of the floor heated with a purpose-built electric pad. The temperature should be 85° – 90°F. Make sure the puppies can move away from the heated pad if they so wish. Overhead infra-red type heating should be avoided with orphan puppies because contact heat is more natural and without the constant licking of the puppies by the mother they could become too dry. Watch out that they do not suck each other's extremities causing soreness. If they do, put barriers to keep them separate. Keep the bedding scrupulously clean, changing it as soon as it is soiled.

For the first week, orphan new born puppies will need feeding every two hours day and night with milk reconstituted from a good quality bitches' milk powder. Calf rearing and dried milk for human babies are dangerous for orphan puppies, so stick to the purpose-made products. These are carefully formulated to have the essentials including minerals and vitamins in the correct proportions. Do follow the manufacturer's instructions carefully. Making it up too concentrated or too weak could cause problems with delicate digestive systems. A premature baby feeder is the best thing to use. An eye dropper does not allow the puppy to suck at a controlled rate and often harm is caused by milk getting into the lungs. Sterilise the bottle, teats and mixing vessels as you would equipment for a human baby.

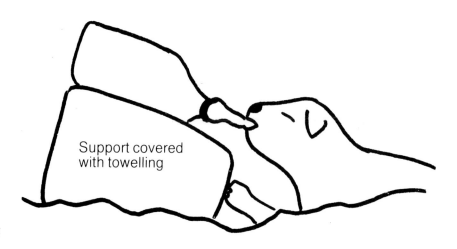

Fig. 6. Stand for feeding
orphan puppies

After the first week, if all is well, the feeds can be cut down to every three hours, and after 12 days leave out the 3 am feed. Increase the amount the puppies take at each feed. If they seem to lose condition, go back to the old regime for a few more days. Between two and three weeks see if they will lap. Bottle fed puppies seem to lap more easily than naturally fed ones. Natural bitch's mik contains colostrum for the first few days. Colostrum passes antibodies to the puppies which combat canine infections. Artificially fed puppies do not receive this colostrum so they are at risk from canine infections. Consult your vet about very early vaccination. Some serums can be given at three weeks. Take every precaution to protect your litter, and although you are very anxious to show off the litter on which you have worked so hard, do not allow visitors until the puppies are protected, even if it may retard their socialisation. If they must be seen, make the visitors remove their shoes or put their feet in plastic bags, as shoes are a bad source of infection and hand reared puppies are very vulnerable.

Bitches stimulate the puppy's bodily functions by massaging their abdomens with their tongues, often quite roughly. You must imitate this action by gently, but vigorously massaging the ano-genital area with warm cotton wool after every feed. Also wipe their eyes and the corners of their mouths.

Puppies pummel the bitch's mammary glands with their front legs, so do not hold the legs so they cannot kick while feeding. A bottle fitted into a towel covering stand (see illustration) will give the puppy something to kick against and may stimulate this action.

Weigh the puppies daily and if they are not gaining weight steadily consult the vet and also if they have diarrhoea or are constipated.

Hand rearing a litter is a rare occurrence in Cavaliers and we hope never necessary, but it is as well to be prepared. Sometimes a bitch has a large litter and needs help. It is greedy to leave a bitch with nine or ten puppies to rear without help. They may not grow as you would wish and would be a great strain on the bitch. You could cull the weakest puppy or the less well marked, or you can help the mother.

There are two schools of thought:

1   Give all the puppies a bottle feed night and morning.
2   Take two or three puppies away after they have had their colostrum, solely bottle feed them but return them to the mother for her to administer the ablutions!

THE HEALTHY PUPPY: Normal healthy puppies have a contented air. They are fat, sleek, with shiny coats. Black and tans and tricolours look as if they are in satin nighties! They are quiet and although strong in their movements not over active. A litter with a scrawny look who are noisy and squirming around the box give cause for concern. Make sure they are warm enough and that the bitch has sufficient milk and is allowing the puppies to feed.

Eyes open from 12 to 15 days and focus from 21 to 28 days. Ears pen at about 14 days and teeth appear at about 28 days. Noses are born pink and begin to go black almost at once. Puppies' nails are very sharp and need cutting at about 10 days to prevent the mammary glands becoming sore. It is easy to see where to cut even on black and tans at this age, as the tips of very young puppies' nails are white. When the weather is very cold the bitch's undercarriage sometimes becomes chapped. They go out into the very cold air with it damp and it soon becomes sore. This may make the bitch reluctant to let the puppies feed.

Puppies should be given their first worm dose at three weeks. (Worms and treatment are dealt with under ailments.)

WEANING: One can give guidelines on weaning, but each litter is different and weaning must be adapted accordingly. Providing the bitch is fit, enjoying her puppies and they are doing well I am never in a hurry to begin weaning. I thoroughly condemn the practice of weaning the puppies early so that the bitch can get back into the show ring – a very selfish practice.

Some breeders first introduce puppies to a milky meal made with the same reconstituted milk used for orphan puppies or goat's milk fortified with a baby cereal, or if this causes loose motions, use wholemeal bread or even well soaked wholemeal puppy meal. Dip your finger into the gruel and put it in the puppies' mouths. When they get the taste put their noses into the dish. Supervise very carefully as the greedy ones will take too much and the less interested not enough. My puppies seem to think this type of meal is meant for walking in. They get in a sticky mess, but spend time cleaning each other!

I prefer the first solid meal to be a little scraped meat. A piece of raw stewing beef scraped with a sharp knife or well processed in a food processor provides a pulp easily digested by puppies. Butcher's mince for human consumption and pet quality mince are not good enough for puppies at this stage. A good quality tinned puppy food could be used. Offer them a tiny ball of this, about the size of a pea. Patience is needed at this time. Some will take it immediately. Others will keep it in their mouths for a minute or two and then spit it out. You need to make sure each puppy gets his fair share. Put the mother out while you begin to wean the puppies as she often does not see why you should usurp her privileges. One lick of her tongue and all your carefully prepared meat balls disappear.

Puppies should be allowed to feed from their mums as well as taking food from their owner. Weaning should be a very gradual process. Do not introduce too many different types of food too quickly as this could cause tummy upsets. Cleanliness is essential in preparation of puppies' food. Dishes should be removed quickly so as not to attract flies and wasps. Usually when the bitch is returned to the litter she will wash up the dishes and the puppies!

In the wild, bitches would regurgitate their food for the puppies. This instinct dies hard and bitches will still bring up their dinner for the litter. If the bitch is very thin and the puppies fat and not wanting your weaning food, do watch carefully in case the bitch is weaning them her way. If so, keep her away from the puppies for at least two hours after she has been fed.

By five weeks the puppies have their teeth and bitches may find it uncomfortable to feed them. The puppies will then be more willing to take the food you offer. The main protein meals should be fed individually. The milky meals can be fed in communal dishes, but under supervision. Feed puppies little and often. After their meal they should have a nicely rounded tummy, not hard or bloated. At 6½ weeks they are independent of their mother for food.

DIET AT EIGHT WEEKS:

Breakfast: ½ Weetabix, or ½ Shredded Wheat, or Farlene, or Farley's Rusk plus S.A. 37 Vitamin Supplement available from the vet or Boots. Puppies are very small and only eat a small amount. They often wean themselves away from milky meals. As long as they are lively and growing, do not worry!

Midday: Finely chopped raw meat or cooked boned fish, about 2oz (57g) gradually increasing until at 4 months the puppy is having 4oz (114g). A good quality tinned puppy food is very acceptable – mix the meat with a good wholemeal puppy meal such as Lowes Wholemealk (available from Boots).

Tea: As for midday. Egg custard without sugar could be given some days.

Supper: Until 3 months as for breakfast. After that baked brown bread or small biscuits.

Continue as above until 6 months, then gradually merge midday and tea meals and after 9 months gradually discard breakfast.

Some people separate their bitches completely from the puppies. I give them a bed away from the puppies but access to them if she so desires. I am sure both puppies and bitches get a lot of pleasure from playing together. It is nature's way to develop strengthening muscles and developing social habits.

From four weeks puppies should be introduced to household noises, to be handled gently by other people, and meet your other dogs provided your dogs have not been to shows or mixing with uninoculated animals. This is the age when they are learning how to socialise. It is a difficult time because the maternal immunity to infectious diseases given in the antibodies present in the colostrum, could be waning. For the puppies to become well balanced family dogs it is essential for them to meet people and dogs at this age! If the mother is a shy nervous bitch there might be a case to take her away from the puppies at four weeks because at that age she can pass on to her puppies her fears and phobias.

There has been discussion at what age puppies should leave home. Some advocate as early as six weeks, others not until the puppies are fully innoculated at fourteen weeks. A lot depends on the home to which the puppy is going and the home you can provide until he does go. Before eight weeks seems very young to me, but some experts say they adapt to domesticated life much quicker at that age and that they are easier to house train.

When the time comes for the puppies to leave I think it kinder to the bitch not to let all the puppies go on the same day. Spread their departure over a few days. You have a responsibility to your puppies and if you are at all doubtful about the type of home a prospective buyer can offer, *don't* sell them a puppy. One has disappointments even from people whom you thought would be ideal, so don't take chances.

Point out the bad as well as the good points in the puppy, especially if he is over or undershot, or if he has an umbilical hernia or inguinal hernia. Warn prospective owners that some vets can be alarmist over these conditions. Do not persuade a client to buy a puppy if they are reluctant. You were instrumental in the puppies being born and you are responsible to see they get the most loving and sensible home.

Suggest your client has the puppy vetted within 24 hours of leaving home. If the vet finds a defect have the puppy back and return the purchase price. This is far more satisfactory than leaving it until the puppy has been gone for four or five weeks and then receiving a complaint. There are several schemes by which breeders can insure puppies for their first few weeks in their new homes. It may be useful to look into these. Do not claim more for the puppy than is apparent. For example, never claim a puppy will make a show dog. All you can say is that he is promising as a potential show puppy. Never say a puppy will definitely be a certain size when adult. They do vary so.

Send the puppy off with a pedigree, and a receipt with conditions of sale, eg you are to be offered the puppy back if they are unable to keep him. If you sent off the Kennel Club Registrations when the litter was about three weeks old, you should have had the Registration Certificates back by the time the puppies are ready to leave. It certainly adds to the importance of the occasion if you have 'official looking' documents.

Explain your diet sheet and your list of 'useful hints'. Supply a tuck box with a few days' food so there is no abrupt change in the type of food offered.

A FEW 'USEFUL HINTS':

1 Always put your puppy outside immediately after meals and immediately on waking. As soon as he performs praise him. If he transgresses put him out at once even if it does seem too late.
2 Never give a puppy bones other than beef marrow bones.
3 See that your puppy has plenty of fresh clean drinking water available.
4 Train your puppy to walk to heel on the lead without pulling as this may spoil his movement, besides being a nuisance to you. A well-trained obedient dog will bring you great joy, but a badly trained and disobedient dog will be a trouble to you and possibly to others.
5 A puppy can play only for short periods and then he must have long periods of sleep if he is to grow strong and healthy. He will miss his family for the first few nights, so be patient with him if he is lonely. A cuddly toy or old slipper will often comfort a lonely pup.
6 It is not necessary to bath Cavaliers often. A daily brush and comb

keeps the coat in good order, with an occasional dry foam shampoo for white shirt fronts.

7 Never let your Cavalier off the lead in the road.

8 If, in spite of all your care, your puppy should be off colour at any time do not 'trust to luck' but consult a qualified vet.

9 Although your puppy will have been wormed it is advisable to ask the vet's advice about further worming when he is inoculated.

10 Never take your puppy out into the roads or where he can come in contact with other dogs until he has been inoculated by a qualifed vet. See your vet about the best time and method, as research is still going on.

If you are a conscientious breeder it should not be the end of the matter when you wave 'goodbye' as the car carrying your puppy speeds away. You should keep in touch, and give advice if needed. See the puppy from time to time so you can see how successful your breeding plan has been. This will give you a guide when planning further litters. Some will disappoint, some will pleasantly surprise you, but that is the challenge of breeding.

TIMETABLE FOR REARING PUPPIES:

	Normal Litter	Hand Reared Litter	Care of bitch
Day 1	Examine puppies for defects and weigh them		
	Keep very warm.	Keep extra warm. Feed every two hours.	Light diet. Plenty of fresh drinking water.
	Make sure all puppies are feeding as colostrum in first milk is important.	Massage abdomens to stimulate bodily functions.	Insist she goes out to relieve herself. Control return to box.
Day 2	Continue to watch carefully.		Examine mammary glands and note type of discharge from vulva. Begin to increase food with milk, eggs, meat, cheese and fish. If tummy loose
Day 4	Have dew claws removed.		substitute goat's milk or bitches' powdered milk. Divide food into four meals. Remember calcium.
Day 8	Birth weight should be doubled. Reduce heat slightly.	Feed three hourly.	
Day 10	Cut puppies' nails.		Examine mammary glands for soreness.

Day 12–15	Eyes open. Leave out 3 am feed.	
Day 13–17	Ears open.	Watch out for eclampsia.
Day 21	Puppies sit up and focus. Encourage to lap from saucer. Continue with bottle.	Register puppies with Kennel Club.

WORM

Examine nails and cut again if necessary.

Day 28	Offer small quantities of scraped meat.	
	If lapping well gradually discard bottles. Discuss with vet vaccination with serum.	Watch for regurgitation. Bitch leaves puppies for longer periods.
	Teeth appear.	
	Begin socialising.	
	Begin milky and cereal feeds.	Gradually decrease food intake as puppies are weaned. Keep up calcium.
Day 35	Puppies can go out in garden if it is warm and dry. Watch they do not get chilled when sun goes in or too hot if the shade moves. Gradually introduce other foods, eg egg custard, fish and chicken.	Begin writing Pedigrees for clients. Advertise puppies in respectable paper if necessary.

WORM AGAIN

Day 42	Puppies having four solid meals a day, plenty of play, socialising and sleep. Discuss vaccination procedure.	When no longer feeding or clearing up puppies, worm her and give a good bath.
Day 49	WORM AGAIN	
Day 56	Ready to go to their new homes.	

9 Showing

WHEN buying your first Cavalier, the chances are you are wanting him as a pet. If he grows into a handsome dog and conforms to the Breed Standard you may find his breeder or your 'knowledgeable friend' may suggest you show him. This can grow into a fascinating hobby and to many dedicated exhibitors it becomes a way of life. One meets people from all walks of life, with one common interest – the Cavalier. Life-long friendships have been made at dog shows and when help is needed they rally round and help their fellow exhibitors with their dogs and even with family and domestic problems.

If you are thinking of showing there are two virtues you must possess. One is a sense of humour and the other a sporting nature. Anyone can be pleasant and friendly when all is going well and when one's dog is winning his class. The testing time comes when you and your friends are disappointed because an 'inferior' dog has beaten your dog. Remember Winston Churchill's words 'humour in defeat', and the words from the old school hymn:

> 'Help us too, in sport or game
> Gallantly to play our part
> Win or lose, to keep the same
> Dauntless spirit and brave heart.'

You must learn to lose before you can really win. It is a hard lesson, especially when you have had a long tiring day and have an exhausting journey home, when dogs placed above yours did not conform to the standard as well as yours. Remember the interpretation of the standard is a personal opinion, the judge's interpretation may differ from yours. In time, and with experience, you know which judges think your exhibit's virtues are the ones he admires and so worthy of an award and which judges do not value such virtues very highly and so leave them out.

If you think you have these qualities, how do you set about showing? Usually your 'knowledgeable friends' would invite you to go with them to a show as a spectator. Failing that, the best way is to contact a breed club and go along to one of their events to watch. Although there are regional breed clubs covering most parts of the country it may be more convenient for you to contact the local Canine Society. They would most likely schedule classes for Cavaliers at their open shows. Go along, watch and chat to the exhibitors, Cavalier people enjoy nothing more than talking about their lovely breed.

The most beautiful dog is not likely to win unless he displays his beauty to the best advantage, so before entering the ring take him along to the local Canine Society's ring craft classes. Here you will learn the best way to make the most of his good points and in some cases how to hide his bad ones! He will get used to the noise and bustle of having lots of dogs around him. He will absorb the atmosphere so that when he does get to a show he will be 'at home'.

All dog shows are licensed by the Kennel Club – the ruling body of pedigree dogs. No dog can be shown unless he is registered at the Kennel Club, so make sure he is and that he has been transferred from his breeder into your name. The only exception to this rule is for Exemption shows.

Exemption shows are fun! They are usually associated with a fête, flower show or festival, and therefore there are many other things to do besides show your dog. You can enter on the showground on arrival, so there is no need to make up your mind beforehand what classes to enter or even whether to go or not. Entry fees are usually pretty small, and profits go to charity, often some worthy local good cause, so you are helping to do good with your money, which should make the matter more attractive.

Exemption shows are also good places to bring your young unshown puppies, or other inexperienced dogs, to give them the flavour of the ring, and get used to having lots of other dogs around them. Though you may be the most respected dog owner in the neighbourhood don't expect to win at these functions, as such classes as 'Any Variety Toy' may well have forty entries on a fine late summer afternoon, and the judge may be an Old English Specialist, or local gundog trainer who may not be too well up in Cavaliers. He will, rightly perhaps, give his cards to a good one of a breed he really knows something about.

Kennel Club regulated shows come in four classifications. To enter any of these, you must obtain a schedule and entry form from the society organising the show, fill in the form with the required details, sign the declaration that you will abide by the rules and regulations and send it back to the secretary with the appropriate fees before the closing date.

Make sure you enter your Cavalier in the correct class – read the schedule carefully.

No puppy under 6 months can be exhibited. There are classes restricted to age groups, for example:

Minor puppy	6 to 9 months
Puppy	6 to 12 months
Junior	6 to 18 months

At the bigger breed club shows classes are provided for the different colours. There are classes for which your dog is not eligible if he has won first prizes. A dog is eligible for all classes not restricted by age and colour if he has never won a first prize, but champions are only eligible for the open classes. Dogs entered in the incorrect class are disqualified, so be careful to record all your wins.

The Kennel Club has rules for conduct of exhibitors and for the preparation of the dogs for shows, so it is as well to get a copy. Kennel Club Shows are:

1   Sanction shows which are confined to members of the society running the show. Dogs who are multiple first prize winners at open and championship shows are debarred. Read the rules before you enter.
2   Limited shows again are confined to members but only C.C. winners and champions are banned.
3   Open shows are open to all, but in Cavaliers it is an unwritten law that Champions are not exhibited.
4   Championship shows are the most important shows and are open to all. The winning of a first prize in certain classes will qualify a dog to be shown at Crufts. The most coveted award is that of a Challenge Certificate – known as the C.C. or 'the ticket'. To win this a dog or bitch must be declared to be the best of its sex in the breed on that day. The judge signs a certificate which declares:

'I am clearly of the opinion that ......Name of Dog...................... owned by .... , is of such outstanding merit as to be worthy of the title of Champion.,
                              Signed ....
                                    Judge

To become a Champion a dog or bitch must win three such certificates under three different judges. No easy matter in a breed such as Cavaliers where the classes are so large and competition so keen. There is no time limit, except a dog or bitch must win at least one C.C. after his or her first birthday. To date the youngest Cavalier to become a Champion is Miss S. Smith's Ch. Salador Celtic Prince who became a champion at 12½ months. Once the awards have been confirmed by the Kennel Club a Champion can keep his title for ever.

Cavalier Breed Clubs run shows of all four categories. These are of course confined to Cavaliers only and are the highlights of the Cavalier calendar. The large multi-breed Societies hold Championship shows in various parts of the country. These are usually two or three day events, with most breeds scheduled, so make sure you go on the day the Toy group is exhibited if you wish to see Cavaliers! I do suggest, whichever type of show you visit, that you go as a spectator for the first time.

CRUFT'S DOG SHOW - February 6th & 7th 1970

Breed   CAVALIER KING CHARLES SPANIELS   Sex   BITCH

Kennel Club
Challenge Certificate

I am clearly of opinion that

Millstone Crispie Joy
(Name of Exhibit)

owned by   _Mrs I M Booth_
(Name of Owner)

is of such outstanding merit as to be worthy of the title of Champion.

(Signed)

_____ . (Judge)

The most coveted award – a Challenge Certificate, or C.C. Three of these awarded by three different judges qualify a dog to become a Champion.

Crufts is a show on its own. At one time it was another Championship Show, run at first by Charles Crufts. After his death it was taken over by the Kennel Club. A great mystique has been built up around the show. The number of entries became so unmanageable that the qualifier was introduced to keep down the numbers of exhibits. Crowds of spectators are enormous, with parties of dog enthusiasts from abroad swelling the numbers. The stalls and stands display an abundance of merchandise from diamond encrusted collars to nail clippers. Each year you will hear exhibitors and visitors declare 'Never Again!' but they are all back the next year, such is the draw of Crufts. Its popularity is helped by it being the only dog show to be reported on the television.

The highlight of the three day show is the Crufts Best in Show award on the last day. First all the best of breed winners are judged in their

The final line up at the Southern Cavalier King Charles Spaniel Club Ch. Show April 1983. Mrs M.M. Talbot judge of the dogs, Mr M. Quinney judge of the bitches, with Mrs P. Rooney and her Blenheim Highcurley Phyzz who won the dog c.c. and Mrs S.M. Allerton with her tricolour Deeriem Moonclova who won the bitch c.c. Highcurley Phyzz was declared Best in Show.

appropriate groups to find the best of that group. The group winners then compete for the overall winner – considered by some to be the premier award in the world for pedigree show dogs. In 1973 Ch. Alansmere Aquarius won this, while in 1963 Ch. Amelia of Laguna won the Toy group. Ch. Jia Laertes of Tonnew repeated this feat in 1981 – all three wins were a great thrill for all Cavalier lovers.

Some dogs are natural show dogs and display themselves to advantage with very little help from the owners. One can learn a great deal by watching the experts showing their dogs. Do not be flamboyant in your dress or behaviour. It is not a competition for the exhibitors, but for the exhibits. Make sure you wear suitable shoes so that your movement is effortless and does not detract from your dog. Make sure your dog is in spotless condition. Show preparation was discussed in the chapter on grooming. It is insulting to the judge to present him with a dirty unkempt animal to handle. Anyway the dog is not at his best unless he has had a bath and is well groomed.

Certainly do not overdo the training. One can easily lose the spontaneity and get a dull bored dog who even if his 319 bones are in the correct position and in the right proportion and his marking perfect will not win, unless he has a sparkle of enjoyment.

A happy picture of Ch. Alansmere Aquarius with Mr John Evans, after winning Best in Show Crufts 1972. Born 10.9.71 by Ch. Vairire Osiris by Ch. Alanmere McGoogans Maggie May owned and bred by Messrs. Hall and Evans.

Ch. Jia Laertes of Tonnew winning Toy Group, Crufts 1980. Born 27.9.76 by Breklaw Challenger ex Jia Lady Camilla bred by Mrs D. Archer, owned by Mr & Mrs R.C. Newton.

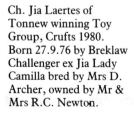

Two points can be practised from an early age so that they become second nature to him:

1   Stand him on the table, make a fuss of him, so that he becomes used to the table and does not just associate it with vets and inoculations!
2   Open his mouth to show his teeth. Many puppies are reluctant to allow this. Do not make an issue of the matter and have a struggle. Have a quick look every week, even with the aid of a finger dipped in honey.

When the great day for the first show arrives, allow plenty of time for the journey and parking. A puppy's whole show career could be ruined by arriving late and just rushing into the ring at the last minute. You will be flustered and your exhibit will not have had any time to compose himself. Your agitation will be transmitted down the lead and he will think 'Oh this is what happens on these occasions!' One hears of novice exhibitors saying 'I am so nervous'. Remember the judge is judging your dog and not you, and the ringsiders will be busy looking up in the catalogue your dog's breeding, not yours!!

'Today's novices will be tomorrow's experts', so the caring experts who remember their novice days will be only too pleased to help the beginners. In this way the wealth of knowledge learned often from the pioneers of the breed will be passed on so that the breed can progress. One should be wary

Mrs A. Hewitt Pitt with her Ch. Harmony of Ttiweh winning Best in Show at the South Eastern Toy Dog Society Show January 1951; judge Mr A.W. Fullwood. This was the first time a Cavalier went Best in Show.

of those who are still novices, or near novices, but think they are 'experts by lunch time the same day'! They think they know all the answers and can give misleading advice because they do not know the history behind their dogs. Above all avoid exhibitors who are over critical of the exhibits, especially ones which have been placed over theirs! Also most dangerous are those who spread rumours about undesirable traits in certain lines.

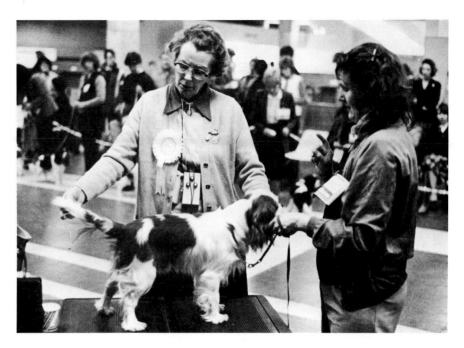

Judge Mrs M.M. Talbot studying the all over balance of Fontelania Tartan Lad, also among the prize winners, Southern Cavalier King Charles Spaniel Club Ch. Show April 1983.

The chances are that once you have begun showing you will want another Cavalier. You may want to breed your own or buy another. We have discussed that in previous chapters. Whichever way you add to your family do not accumulate too many of the same age. You will find their classes will clash and they all grow old together. If you decide to have more than two breeding bitches you will need a breeder's licence issued by the Environmental Health Department of your local authority. This should not be confused with the ordinary 37½p dog licence which every dog owner should have for every dog he owns. The breeder's licence has to be applied for with a fee varying from £5 to £30. Your premises are inspected by the Environmental Health Officer sometimes accompanied by a veterinary surgeon. If they consider your premises are suitable you will be issued with a licence entitling you to keep a specified number of bitches of breeding age.

Judge Mrs M.M. Talbot examining the shoulder placement of her eventual winner Highcurley Phyzz. (Featured earlier as a promising puppy and an elegant young adult.) Southern Cavalier King Charles Spaniel Club Ch. Show April 1983.

All successful exhibitors and breeders are soon faced with a problem. To have continued success in the ring there must be a steady stream of youngsters appearing. Common sense tells you that this will soon cause the problem of what to do with ones no longer young enough to win top honours – after all no lady of forty will win Miss World and it is not very likely that a bitch of six will win a C.C. although very occasionally an exceptional bitch will. A bitch of rising seven could have one last litter provided she is in good condition and the vet gives her a clean bill of health.

Stud dogs can go on siring puppies until they are quite elderly – but they should be restricted. Unless they have a lot to contribute to the breed, their services are not often called for. Sadly the up and coming youngsters usurp them.

Many breeders find homes for these middle aged dogs and bitches. They seem to settle and enjoy all the individual love and human company which cannot be given in their kennel home because of the numbers.

Some breeders keep all their old ones because they are members of the family and they cannot bear to part with them. Our kitchen is populated with five bitches over the age of nine years and up to fourteen. This means we cannot have any more youngsters for the time being. Although we do not want to lose any of our old friends, it is very limiting for showing and breeding. Having our old Cavaliers around us, enjoying their company, and their individual traits, gives us as much pleasure as the success in the ring.

I often wonder about the fate of bitches on puppy farms who have puppies every season to supply the multi-breed dealers. As the dealers are reported to put down unsold puppies once they are out of their pretty, cuddly, fluffy stage, and so less attractive to buyers, it does not need much imagination to guess what happens to their worn out mothers when they are no longer productive.

Another unfortunate consequence of good luck can be the novice whose first litter was a great success. The bitch has six or seven strong healthy puppies, who with the help of the stud dog owner and possibly with the help of the breeder of their bitch, were sold quickly and at a fair price. The novice made a monetary profit because there were no complications. She thinks 'this is easy money' and before long several bitches, a stud dog and even other breeds have been added to the establishment. The poor mums are turning out puppies every season. This is the unacceptable face of dog breeding.

There is nothing more despicable than an exhibitor 'taking it out' on her dog because he failed to win. I can truthfully say that in twenty-five years I only once saw a Cavalier owner behaving this way, but that was once too often. Mercifully such behaviour as bad sportsmanship, commercialism and bad temper is extremely rare. In the Cavalier world the majority of owners are genuinely interested in the breed and are kind and considerate. Long may that continue!

10 Ailments

SKIN ailments and external parasites have been dealt with in the chapter on coat care.

Internal Parasites

WORMS: At the mention of worms the anti-dog lobby throw their hands up in horror and spread alarmist stories. Worms are a nuisance to dogs and their owners and should be treated seriously. The chances of worm larvae causing blindness in human infants is about one in two million, but that one is one too many. Luckily modern drugs to destroy worms are very safe and cause very little discomfort to dogs or puppies and with careful management the worm problem could be greatly diminished. It could be practically eliminated if every dog, including strays, had systematic worming treatment. We are lucky that there are only two main types of worm in this country, but if your Cavalier comes in contact with dogs who have come from abroad, you may have other types to deal with.

The chief worm is the thread worm *Toxacara Canis*. To understand the treatment necessary to deworm a dog one should understand the life cycle of the parasite.

A bitch will probably have larvae of the *Toxacara Canis* encysted in her body tissues where they cannot be reached by deworming compounds. When she becomes pregnant the larvae migrate, enter the uterus and through the placenta infect the puppies. They hatch out in the puppies' intestines, so that by the time the puppies are 3 to 4 weeks old, they could be heavily infected, which can cause health problems. There are many safe preparations on the market to rid puppies of worms, but it is as well to get such preparations from the vet who can prescribe the correct dose for the size and age of the puppies. Give the first dose at 3 weeks. It may work quite quickly within 2 or 3 hours or take up to 24 hours. Be extremely careful in cleaning up all the faeces immediately the puppies pass them. Try not to let the bitch clear up as she could become re-infected. Take care to wash your hands very thoroughly each time you deal with the puppies.

Repeat the worming at 5 and 7 weeks of age. Suggest your client gets another worm dose from the vet when the puppy has its final inoculation, repeat the dose every two months until he is a year old. After that time they could be treated when they have their boosters.

Mature worms in the intestines shed eggs which pass out in the faeces. Rodents, lice and fleas become intermediate hosts. Dogs eat the host inlcuding the egg and so become re-infected. The larvae hatch out and then become encysted in the tissues to begin the cycle again.

If a child, playing on a worm-egg contaminated area, should swallow a *Toxacara Canis* egg, it is a one in two million chance that the larvae could migrate to the back of the eye and cause blindness. Therefore be fanatical about hygiene and most certainly do not allow your dogs to defaecate in children's play areas.

Tape worm is the other common worm in this country. These do not usually affect young puppies unless the sanitary arrangements are poor. Dogs are infected by eating fleas, lice, rabbit and sheep's droppings and rodents who are intermediate hosts. If a dog has small rice-like segments adhering to his tail or back feathering he probably has tape worm. The modern treatment for tape worm is safe, but make sure you get the correct dosage. The head of the tape worm is imbedded in the dog's intestines and if only the tail part is destroyed it will grow again.

If your dog is losing condition, it would be as well to take a faeces specimen to the vet for an examination under a microscope. This could determine whether your dog has tape worm or the less common hookworm or whipworm. Be thankful dogs in England are spared heart worm, which is very alarming and spread by mosquitos in the USA.

Infectious diseases

For many years the main diseases which were distemper (including hard pad), canine virus hepatitis, and two types of leptospirosis, have been successfully controlled by vaccination. Stray and roaming dogs which are not vaccinated keep pockets of the disease active, so make sure your dogs are fully protected and that their boosters are up to date. The timetable for the vaccination programme varies from manufacturer to manufacturer, but the usual pattern is the first injection at 6 to 7 weeks, the second after 12 weeks and then an annual booster. Check with the vet for the precise details.

If your dog should run a temperature, be listless and stop eating, get veterinary advice even if the vaccinations are up-to-date. Better be safe than sorry. Any of these diseases is serious and usually leaves permanent damage to organs. Owners should not try DIY treatments.

In 1978 veterinary surgeons, breeders, and owners were horrified by a highly infectious mystery disease which appeared all over the country and often proved fatal. Thanks to the work of Dr Irene McCandish, her research team at the Veterinary School, Glasgow, and to the drug houses, very effective vaccines were quickly manufactured to combat this virulent disease, now know as parvo virus. This shows how vigilant one must be as other nasty unknown diseases could appear at any time.

Kennel cough is an unpleasant infectious disease which dogs can pick up at shows and at boarding kennels. A vaccine has recently appeared and seems to be cutting down the incidence.

Thanks to a very strict quarantine policy we are rabies-free on these islands. It is the duty of every citizen to be vigilant against people trying to smuggle dogs and cats into this country and to report such suspected cases immediately to the authorities. One can understand people not wanting to be parted from their pets for 6 months, but by smuggling them in they could be endangering the lives of human beings, thousands of cats and dogs and much of the country's wild life.

Danger signals

Any of the following symptoms is a danger signal and should warn the owner all is not well. Take careful note of details because if you can give an accurate, detailed description of the condition which is worrying you, it will help the vet with his diagnosis:

> Lassitude
> Not eating
> Vomiting and diarrhoea, especially with blood
> Half closed eyes showing a red third eyelid
> Coughing
> Discharge from eyes, nose or mouth
> Tenderness in the abdomen causing the dog to lie flat on the floor
> Unconsciousness
> Excessive thirst
> Unpleasant smelling breath
> High or subnormal temperature (Normal 101.5°F taken through the rectum)
> Whimpering

First aid

A USEFUL FIRST AID BOX:
Disinfectant of Chloroxylenol Type Dettol
Antiseptic of Phenolic Type TCP
Thermometer with blunt end
Cotton wool
Crepe and cotton bandages of varying width
Scissors, safety pins, tweezers

Worm tablets
Ear and eye drops
Kaolin lotion or tablets
Antiseptic powder   } Purchased from the vet and kept
Insecticidal washes   for first aid use. Make sure these
Insecticidal sprays   medicants do not pass their 'date
Antihistamine cream   line', and so become less effective.

Do not keep antibiotic tablets 'in stock' unless directed to do so by the vet. Dosing with antibiotics which have not been specifically prescribed may cause an immunity to build up, and the antibiotics to lose their efficiency, with possible serious consequences later.

A few simple remedies for minor aches and pains

It cannot be stressed too strongly that if the condition you are treating does not respond to your treatment in a day or two *do* seek professional advice. Do use your common sense, and do not summon the vet every time your dog sneezes or has a hearty scratch. Dogs themselves are very good barometers of their state of health. They do not have mental hang ups about their physical condition. They usually feel either well or ill and the caring owner should know by his behaviour immediately the dog feels ill.

TUMMY UPSETS: Providing there is no blood in the motion or vomit, and the dog isn't running a temperature, give him a Kaolin mixture or tablet. Withhold food for 12 to 18 hours. Then give small meals of arrow-root made with water. Withhold milk and milky meals as this could aggravate the position. If the symptoms clear up and re-occur in a few days, seek advice. Dogs with tummy ache often crop grass and pass it out undigested, but it seems to help.

CUTS, SCRATCHES AND BRUISES: In the healthy dog these heal very quickly, but do watch he does not bite the wound and cause secondary infections. An antiseptic powder from the first aid box will help clear these quickly. Wounds in a dirty contaminated condition and those needing stitching should be treated by the vet.

EARS AND EYES: Ears and eyes are delicate organs and should be treated very carefully. Ear mites and canker are discussed in the chapter on coat condition. Eyes are sometimes injured in rough play. Bathe with lotion or apply eye ointment from the first aid box. If it does not clear up in a few hours seek help.

ACCIDENTS: Unfortunately in the best regulated circles, these happen. If the dog is seriously hurt get him to a vet's surgery as soon as possible.

There they have the equipment to help. If the vet comes to the accident it could delay the beginning of treatment. Keep the patient as still as possible, use a coat or blanket as a stretcher, rather than cuddling in your arms which could cause further injury. Support any fractured limbs. Use a pressure pad to stem bleeding or a tourniquet if it is very severe, but release it after 15 minutes so that blood can get to vital parts.

Even the most loving and gentle dog is frightened when hurt and injured and does not understand you are trying to help him, so beware and do not condemn if he tries to bite. Keep him warm and do not give any food, drink or stimulant. Even if a dog does not appear to be injured after an accident, it would be as well to have a check up.

INSECT STINGS AND BITES: In the summer Cavaliers are fascinated by flying insects and spend much time catching them. Unfortunately they get stung by wasps and bees. Remove the sting as soon as possible, apply an antiseptic analgesic lotion, a saline solution to dilute the poison, or use an antihistamine cream. Unless the swelling is excessive or the dog has difficulty in breathing, usually this home treatment is all that is required. Surprisingly dogs often seem to eat wasps and bees without any problem, but I do feel uneasy when this happens.

BITES FROM CATS AND DOGS: Even your perfectly mannered Cavalier can be attacked by ill tempered dogs and cats. Obvious wounds can be treated as you would cuts and bruises. The danger may be from deep puncture wounds, not very obvious at a casual inspection. Puncture wounds should be encouraged to bleed. If they become inflamed a course of antibiotics may be required to clear up the matter.

SNAKE BITES: In several parts of the country adders are to be found. These will bite a dog if trodden on! Veterinary help is required at once. In the meantime make the wound bleed and apply a tourniquet to prevent the venom circulating. If you know there is the possibility of snakes in your area, your vet will supply you with vitamin K tablets to carry with you for emergency treatment.

ANAL GLANDS: If your Cavalier vigorously bites and licks his anus or drags his bottom along the ground, he probably needs his anal glands emptying. Do not attempt this yourself unless you have been trained by a professional. Neglected and damaged anal glands can result in very painful anal abscesses. It is as well to have them checked when your dog has his boosters, but more frequently if he has a problem. In very chronic cases it may be necessary to remove the glands.

FITS: One associates fits with epilepsy, but there are many other causes such as distemper, acute pain, injury and poison. Allow the fit to take its course, but prevent the dog from injuring itself. Seek veterinary help.

POISONING: Cavaliers will often eat 'tasty' morsels they find. These could be lethal. Slug bait, Warfarin for killing rats, strychnine for foxes and even drugs for human use, are left where dogs could find them. Birds also scavenge and drop such bait in the garden which your Cavalier may pick up. A sudden collapse and vomiting are both alarm signals and veterinary help should be sought quickly. Take a sample of the suspected poison, or failing that a sample of the vomit for analysis so that the appropriate antidote can be given as quickly as possible.

ELECTRIC SHOCKS: Puppies can chew electric cables with disastrous results. Turn off the current first, then free air passages and apply artificial respiration. You may be lucky and save him, but it is doubtful. Take great care no cable is ever in a position that a dog can chew it.

BURNS AND SCALDS: Put cold water on the affected part to take out the heat. Do not apply any other lotions or powders, cover with a clean cloth and seek help if an extensive area is hurt. Small scalds and burns can be treated at home without vet assistance, but do watch out for secondary infections. Severe burns could cause shock, so make sure the patient is kept warm, his air passages are clear and do not give food, drink or stimulants.

If your dog should fall victim to any of these ills, do keep calm. Talk to him and reassure him. As with humans, when dogs grow older they develop lumps, creaky joints and heart problems. Modern veterinary care can help to relieve these conditions, but they should be taken seriously.

On re-reading this it sounds as if you will be spending a vast amount of time and a fortune at the vets. You would be very unlucky if your dog developed all these ailments!! When contemplating buying a puppy remember that there is no National Health Service for dogs, so that vet's bills must be considered. There are several insurance plans available which, for an annual premium, cover vet fees. Do read the small print, as some exclude whelping complications and dogs over a certain age from benefit.

In common with all types of dog, mongrel, crossbred or pedigree, Cavaliers are heir to worrying diseases or abnormalities which may be of a hereditary nature. Do not spread gossip about blood lines which may have been unfortunate enough to have cases of these distressing troubles. Show sympathy and support, especially if the owner is trying to eliminate the problem. However, be very careful not to introduce a suspect line into your own.

In the 50s and 60s slipping knee caps or *patela luxation* was quite common. While playing or exercising the knee cap in the stifle joint would dislocate, usually causing great pain. The dog could not put any weight on the affected leg until the patella was replaced. This is done by gently extending the leg and pushing the patella back into position. In mild cases the dog could right it itself with very little or no discomfort. This condition could be in one or both legs. Severe cases could be treated with an operation. Dogs with this complaint should not be bred from, neither should their parents even if they show no sign of the abnormality themselves. The condition is passed on by a recessive gene. This means both parents must be carriers. Siblings should be suspect until test mated. Thanks to conscientious breeders discarding suspect dogs and bitches from their breeding programmes the condition is rarely seen, but cases do occur from time to time so be vigilant.

Occasionally one hears of cases of hip dysplasia in Cavaliers. This is where the hip bones are 'ill fitting'. It is not a major problem in the breed, as it is in retrievers and some of the large working dogs. Much research has gone into the cause and the mode of inheritance of this complaint in many breeds. The British Veterinary Association in collaboration with the Kennel Club run screening tests in which animals are x-rayed by specialists and if clear given a certificate to say so or a breeder's letter in mild cases. If many cases do appear in Cavaliers, it may be as well to encourage breeders to have their dogs x-rayed.

From time to time one hears of epilepsy, unspecified fits, catching imaginary flies and 'scottie cramp' appearing in certain lines. Although work has been carried out by some veterinary teaching establishments into these conditions in all types of dogs, little work has been done into the particular problems of Cavaliers. If your dog does have a seizure get veterinary help. Modern drugs can control the symptoms, but no dog with fits should be bred from.

In 1978 it became apparant that juvenile cataract was appearing in the breed. Breed clubs quickly arranged testing sessions at breed shows by some of the country's leading canine eye specialists. A committee was formed to raise funds and to work with Dr Keith C. Barnett, M.A., PhD., B.Sc., M.R.C.V.S., of the Animal Health Trust Research Station at Kennett, Newmarket, to research the problem. An expert can diagnose the disease in puppies from eight weeks of age. Intermediate B.V.A./K.C. certificates stating the dog had been examined by one of a panel of experts and declared free from the disease can be given. This is valid for twelve months only. The permanent certificate is not issued until the dog is re-examined after reaching the age of five.

So that this problem can be quickly resolved, every dog or bitch should be examined by an eye specialist before it is bred from. Breed clubs, or your veterinary surgeon will help you in this matter. When the mode of inheritance is determined, it will be a great help to eradicate this worrying problem. Dr Barnett has been a great help to many other breeds with their eye problems, so Cavaliers could not be in better hands. The juvenile cataract fund should be supported by every Cavalier owner, even if only to say 'thank you' that your Cavalier is free.

Progressive retinal atrophy is another hereditary eye complaint which very occasionally appears in Cavaliers. While your Cavalier is being examined for a clear certificate for juvenile cataract, it is an easy matter for the expert to examine for P.R.A.

If everyone is aware of the perils of these problems, is vigilant and does not breed from suspected cases (except in exceptional circumstances under expert veterinary supervision for research purposes) the incidence will become less and less and our lovely breed freed from taint.

11 Random thoughts on living with Cavaliers

WE have dealt with care of the brood bitch, stud dog and the puppies, but the majority of Cavaliers are family pets. I was tempted to write 'just pets', but that sounds belittling to an important member of the family. In the chapter on acquiring a Cavalier it is emphasised that the puppy should be wanted by the family. We discussed his first few weeks in his new home. How do we proceed from there when he is no longer a sentimental bundle of fluff? All young puppies go through an awkward stage of growth when one despairs of them ever growing into the glamorous little dog you expected or hoped for when he was such a pretty baby puppy. With patience and loving care he will return to his former glory, but with an elegance more appealing than short term prettiness.

For young bones and muscles to grow and develop correctly they must be able to expand, contract and extend. All dogs young or old should be given the opportunity to romp and run. It is essential for their mental and physical development. This is why a flat without a garden is no place for a Cavalier. Obviously no dog should be exercised beyond its capability so that he becomes exhausted, but in some breeds one hears of dogs being restricted in their exercise to prevent or hide an abnormality. This is really criminal and I hope will never happen in Cavaliers.

In discussing the standard and feeding the watchword was 'balance'. Living with Cavaliers is also a matter of balance even if a little lop-sided. Cavaliers are not any happier if they are thoroughly spoiled, or allowed to behave in an irresponsible way. If they learn certain mild rules of discipline when young it becomes second nature them and certainly improves their image.

Do not be anthropomorphic about your Cavalier. Many Victorian ladies thought their lap dogs, including toy spaniels, were creatures with little humans trying to get out! One must not lose sight of the fact that even the best loved Cavalier is a dog and no worse for that!

Even with all the loving care, Cavaliers grow old. They need special care and attention, shorter walks, tempting meals, perhaps divided into two smaller ones and even slightly warmed. If they get wet they should be dried thoroughly. Elderly dogs sleep very soundly, possibly because they may be going deaf. It is often frightening when they do not wake up when you enter the room, as they did in their youth. Several times I have had to touch an elderly dog who was in a deep sleep to make sure she was alive. She would sit up with a sleepy expression as if to say 'Oh do let sleeping dogs lie!'

If they should die in their sleep after a long happy life, one cannot wish for a better end. It is a nasty shock for the owner, but you had no decisions to make about having them put down.

When the time comes and your veterinary surgeon advises you that it would be kinder to say a final farewell to your friend, you should take his advice. One painless injection into a vein and they really are 'put to sleep' in a matter of seconds. It is a service you can give to your pets which is denied your suffering relations. If you are with them to the end they know no fear. Unfortunately their lives are short compared with ours. Eleven is a good age for a Cavalier. After that they are on borrowed time, although a few live to be fourteen and even fifteen years of age.

There are many interesting side lines for Cavalier enthusiasts to follow. A ten generation pedigree is a fascinating thing to compile. One can quite quickly trace back to Ch. Daywell Roger, Ann's Son and the King Charles beyond that. Breeders, Kennel Club Stud Books, and Club *Year Books* provide a wealth of information. Breed historians are only too delighted to look up their records and supply you with missing names. (I find it a welcome change from crossword puzzles and much more rewarding!)

One can collect pictures, or at least reproductions, of toy spaniels through the ages. Don't forget if you are sending your Cavalier friend a

Various Victorian Staffordshire Spaniels. Bottom left a quill holder.

holiday postcard, one of a painting depicting a toy spaniel from the local art gallery or museum would be much more appreciated than one of the beach! During the 1890s and early 1900s, picture postcards were regularly sent to one's friends for ½d. These did not necessarily depict classical works of art, but photographs, drawings and caricatures of King Charles Spaniels of that day – some of the Cavalier type were often sent. The messages on the back are often amusing. The most poignant one I have seen was a picture of black and tan and Blenheim King Charles on the front, while the message read:

On Active Service   Tues. Oct. 2 1917
France.

Dear Little Ian,
   Hope you have been a very good boy and that you will like these doggies.

With love
from Daddy

I hope he made it.
   Collecting these postcards is an interesting hobby, but as with modern cards portraying Cavaliers, the models do not always conform to the breed standard!
   Staffordshire pottery spaniels of Victorian and Edwardian times are attractive but do beware of modern copies. Rather than the standard pair seen on the mantelpiece of Victorian cottages, look out for the delicate little models often used as quill holders. They are exquisite.
   Victorian mosaic brooches with a 'toy spaniel' as the motif can be found. They were most likely made in Italy in the mid 1800s. The tiny coloured tessalations were made of coral and set into a jet background. These are then framed in gold. They can be quite small – about ¾in (17mm) in diameter to quite large rectangles 2in (51mm) by 1½in (38mm). Blenheims are the most popular, but I do have a tricolour in a scenic background. I have never seen a black and tan or ruby on one of these brooches, but no doubt some were made. Victorian ladies whiled away the hours sewing needlework pictures, often portraying toy spaniels. The Best of Breed award from the West of England Ladies' Kennel Society (known as W.E.L.K.S.) Championship show is a delightful Victorian needlework picture depicting Queen Victoria's tricolour Dash on a royal blue background. I spent many hours copying it, but alas not on such fine linen as the Victorian lady used – and she had no electric light to help her. There is a beautiful copy of this picture worked on flannel in the Victoria and Albert Museum.

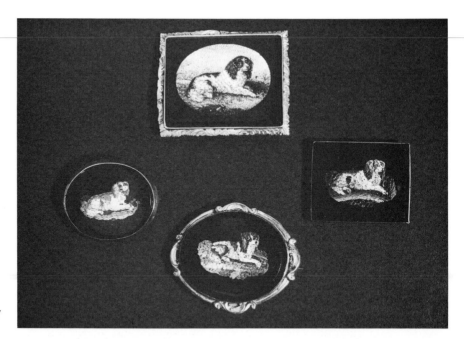

Victorian mosaic brooches showing toy spaniels.

Queen Victoria's Dash in a Victorian needlework picture.

A small picture called 'Jesus healing the blind man', worked on satin in 1830, shows a dear little toy spaniel complete with spot acting as a guide dog!

The Pares Wilson Needlework picture presented by Mrs Pares Wilson, later Lady Daniel, past president of the Cavalier King Charles Spaniel Club, for Best in Show at the Club's Championship show, is a large beautifully worked picture of a girl holding a tricolour in her arms.

Many modern needlepoint, or as it is usually known 'tapestry' pictures, portraying Cavaliers are available. These come in kits complete with a printed canvas and the wools needed to work the picture. One of the most original needlework pictures I have seen was beautifully worked by Mrs Dix. She had a coloured photograph of her ruby Benny transposed on to a canvas 20in × 16in (50cm × 40cm). This is carefully worked into a beautiful picture – no mean task with so many subtle shades of chestnut found in a ruby's coat – a lovely idea to work a picture of one of your own dogs.

Very few fun books with Cavaliers as their theme have been published. One is *Top Dog* supposedly written by a Cavalier C.M. McMuck, and published by Debretts Peerage Ltd. Another is a children's book *Gladwyn goes to Town* by Paul Callen, published by Hodder and Stoughton. It is really about a corgi, but he does meet several Cavaliers including one in Harrod's lift. The biographies of Gladys, Duchess of Marlborough, are extremely interesting and the part Blenheim Spaniels played in her life very revealing. The books are: *Gladys, Duchess of Marlborough* by Hugo Vickers, published by Weidenfeld and Nicholson, and *The Face on the Sphinx, a portrait of Gladys, Duchess of Marlborough* by Daphne Fielding, published by Hamish Hamilton.

Several of the Cavalier Clubs issue magazines in which members contribute articles, some of weighty matters, some of them light hearted, and some really sentimental, but all interesting to Cavalier lovers.

However many Cavaliers one has, they are all individuals, each with his own amusing and lovable character. It is interesting suddenly to notice habits and mannerisms appearing in a youngster which her great, great, great, great-grandmother displayed two or three decades ago!

Perhaps they are the same lovable characteristics that attracted the Tudor and Stuart Kings and Queens to the 'Spaniell gentle or comforter' and prompted Queen Victoria to write as an epitaph to her beloved tricolour Dash when he died on Christmas Eve 1840:

'Attachment without selfishness,
Playfulness without Malice,
and Fidelity without deceit.'
      – the true Cavalier.

Appendix

Cavalier clubs in Great Britain and Ireland

The Cavalier King Charles Spaniel Club
Mrs D.Maclaine, The Grove, Mundon, Maldon, Essex

Three Counties Pekingese and Cavalier Society
Miss S. Phelps, "Camargue", Hancocks Lane, Welland, Nr Malvern,
Worcs WR13 6LD

Scottish Cavalier King Charles Spaniel Club
Mrs Lindsay Gow, 9 Traquair Park West, Edinburgh EH12 7AN

Cavalier King Charles Spaniel Club of Ireland
Mrs Evelyn Hurley, 14 Grange Park View, Raheny, Dublin 5, Eire

West of England Cavalier King Charles Spaniel Club
Mr J. Evans, The Shieling, Gloucester Road, Standish, Glos GL10
3DN

Northern Cavalier King Charles Spaniel Society
Miss B.M. Henshaw, The Orchard, Wharf Lane, Sedgwick, Kendall,
Cumbria LA8 OJW

Midland Cavalier King Charles Spaniel Club
Mrs M. Rees, Little Oaks, 114 Hawkes Mill Lane, Coventry CV5
9FN

Eastern Counties Cavalier King Charles Spaniel Club
Mr E. Tweddel, 45 Parklands Avenue, Shipdham, Norfolk

Northern Ireland Cavalier King Charles Spaniel Club
Mrs B. Megarry, 21 Victoria Road, Ballyalbert, Co. Down

The South & West Wales Cavalier King Charles Spaniel Club
Mr A Close, 'Lamont', Claude Road West, Barry, S.Glam. CF6
8JG

Humberside Cavalier King Charles Spaniel Club
Mrs Lis. Farnill, 'Jayanna', Rise Lane, Catwick, Beverley, HU17 5PL

Index